# THE CIRCLE

## Ed Adams

a firstelement production

First published in Great Britain in 2020 by firstelement
Copyright © 2020 Ed Adams
Copyright © 2023 V2 Ed Adams
Directed by thesixtwenty

10 9 8 7 6 5 4 3 2

A CIP catalogue record for this book is available from the
British Library.

ISBN 13 : 978-1-9163383-6-4
Ebook ISBN : 978-1-9163383-7-1

Printed and bound in Great Britain by Ingram Spark

Ed Adams
an imprint of firstelement.co.uk
ed.adams@Ed-Adams.net
rashbre@mac.com

Mailing list: https://mailchi.mp/9f0b30712620/ed_adams

# The Circle

# Thanks

A big thank you for the tolerance and bemused support from all of those around me, especially Julie who has to make up the excuses. To the readers of my prior novels and to the requests for further frolics from Bigsy, Clare and Jake.

Sometimes one has to get out into the wild, and this trip around Route 66 and out into the deserts is a case in point.

Aficionados will realise that I didn't mention the Grand Canyon once, although I do still have the extensive video.

A big thank you for the tolerance and bemused support from all of those around me. To those who know when it is time to say, "step away from the keyboard!" and to those who don't.

To John, for hangin' in there.
To Caroline and Richard for patient cover reviews.
To Nick and Ned for their cover creation suggestions.
To thesixtwenty.co.uk for direction.
To the NaNoWriMo gang for the continued encouragement.

To those who provided inspiration at SPS London 2022 and 2023.
To the London hotel which gave me a wonderful free room.
To Topsham, for being lovely.
To the edge-walkers. They know who they are.
To Steve for musical suggestions to accompany writing.

And, to a few websites:

**Ed Adams Amazon Page:**
https://amzn.to/3NRPqXV

*Ed Adams Catalogues:*
https://ed-adams.net
https://ed-adams.mysites.io

*Rashbre blog:*
https://rashbre2.blogspot.com

Plus, the cast of amazing and varied readers whether human, twittery, smoky, artistic, cool kats, photographic, dramatic, musical, anagrammed, globalized, or maxed.

So, let's fly like eagles and let our spirits carry us into the wilds.

And thanks also to the cast of characters involved in producing this, whether real or imaginary

And of course, to you, dear reader, for at least 'giving it a go'.

# Ed Adams Novels

| **Triangle Trilogy** | | **About** | **Link** |
|---|---|---|---|
| T1 | The Triangle | Dirty money? Here's how to clean it. Money laundering | https://amzn.to/3c6zRMu |
| T2 | The Square | Weapons of Mass Destruction – don't let them get on your nerves. A viral nerve agent being shipped by terrorists and WMDs | https://amzn.to/3sEiKYx |
| T3 | The Circle | The desert is no place to get lost. In the Arizona deserts, with the Navajo; about missiles stolen from storage. | https://amzn.to/3qLavYZ |
| T4 | Cosy | Cosy Crime in Devon | https://amzn.to/3wQVNED |
| **Archangel Collection** | | | |
| A1 | Archangel | Sometimes I am necessary. Icelandic-born, Russian trained agent Christina Nott, learns her craft. | https://amzn.to/2Y9nB5K |
| A2 | Raven | An eye that sees all between darkness and light. Big business gone bad and being a freemason won't absolve you. | https://amzn.to/2MiGVe6 |
| A3 | Card Game | The power of Tarot whilst throwing oil on a troubled market | https://amzn.to/2Y8HLgs |
| A5 | Play On, Christina Nott | Money, Mayhem, Manipulation. Christina Nott, on Tour for the FSB | https://amzn.to/2MbkuHI |
| A6 | Corrupt | Parliamentary corruption. Trouble at the House | https://amzn.to/2M0HnOw |
| A7 | Sleaze | Autos, Politics, Gstaad | https://amzn.to/3sE3UDt |

| **Big Science** | | | |
|---|---|---|---|
| B1 | Coin | Get rich quick with Cybercash – just don't tell GCHQ | https://amzn.to/3o82wmS |
| B2 | An Unstable System | Creating the right kind of mind | https://amzn.to/2PRJciF |
| B3 | The Watcher | We don't need no personal saviours here. From the Big Bang to the almighty Whimper | https://amzn.to/3kTFWjg |
| B4 | Jump | Some kind of future. | https://amzn.to/3sCzK3h |
| B5 | Pulse | Sci-Fi dystopian blood management with nano-bots. Want more? Just stay away from the edge | https://amzn.to/3qQlBvL |
| B6 | Rage | A madman's war | https://amzn.to/3MEuKlL |

| **Blade's Edge Trilogy** | | | |
|---|---|---|---|
| E1 | Edge | World end climate collapse and sham discovered during magnetite mining from Jupiter's moon Ganymede. | https://amzn.to/2KDmYOW |
| E2 | Edge Blue | Endgame, for Earth – unless? | https://amzn.to/2Kyq9au |
| E3 | Edge Red | Museum Earth an artificially intelligent outcome – unless? | https://amzn.to/2KzJwjz |

**Master Collections**

| | | | |
|---|---|---|---|
| C1/T4 | The Ox Stunner | The Triangle Trilogy – thick enough to stun an ox Triangle, Circle, Square in one heavy book. all feature Jake, Bigsy, Clare, Chuck Manners | https://amzn.to/3sHxIgh |
| C2/A4 | Magazine Clip | First three Archangel novels | https://amzn.to/3pbBJYn |
| C3/A8 | Ignoble | Corrupt and Sleaze omnibus – double album | https://amzn.to/3sp6EUL |
| C4/B7 | The Dealer | Jump, Pulse and Rage Collection | https://amzn.to/3AlZmWg |
| C5/E4 | Edge of Forever | Edge Trilogy | https://amzn.to/3c57Ghj |

# Contents

# PART TWO     182

# Part One

# Starting Out

There's talk on the street
It's there to remind you
It doesn't really matter which side you're on
You're walking away
And they're talking behind you
They will never forget you 'til somebody new comes along

*Glenn Lewis Frey, Don Henley*

# *Arizona*

Bigsy was bent into an unusual shape. He draped over the front seat of a car at a diagonal angle to the dashboard. Everything looked blurry, and he knew the car was moving fast. Intense heat as his head angled back towards the sky.

He tried to remember how he got here. His head pain and lack of limb control made it challenging to focus on anything. He made out a driver shape and the bumpiness of the route. He heard a pulsing sound, like a deep bass note mixed with a metallic edge.

Then a sharp bang which fired some adrenaline into his system. He tried to fix his eyes on the driver, wearing sunglasses and a baseball cap. Bigsy tried to speak. Still nothing from his mouth. The car lurched again with strong forces as it made a sharp turn. His eyes moved back to a central position, and he saw the sky again and a cactus branch. He realised that his vision was returning and tried to speak again.

Another voice behind him said, "Don't speak right now. They have drugged us. It was pretty effective. Someone doesn't like us."

Bigsy remembered the previous evening. Then his body jumped involuntarily.

A loud explosion and a scraping sound of big metal from close to their car. They still seemed to be moving forward. Bigsy still did not know what was happening, but it was something furious.

"Okay, they're gone. Now we need to find somewhere to hide." The voice behind him. Bigsy recognised the voice. American. Clearly spoken, clipped and precise. Chuck. Oh, yes, he had met Chuck Manners the previous evening.

"Yeah, and what are we going to do with him?" said the other voice.

"No, he stays with us. Bigsy is a friend. I asked him to be here," came the reply.

Bigsy sensed the car edge forward and saw sparse cactus bushes replaced with a canopy of overhead cover. Then some stunning orange rocks. He realised that his senses were returning, but he still couldn't move his arms.

The driver continued driving, although without the urgency of the chase. Bigsy knew that he was drifting in and out of consciousness.

"We'll get into this shelter and wait for both of you to get your senses back." said the driver. "Chuck, you seem to be recovered, but the other guy's got a way to go."

"Yes, Mike," replied Chuck, "They have been quick to make

us. Almost like an insider told them."

"We should be okay here for a while," replied Mike. "And there are provisions in the car's trunk."

"A regular tourist, huh?"

They had stopped in an area set back from the main roads. An area surrounded by desert, but with a range of distinctive red rocks rising on all sides. The driver had manoeuvred the large, blue, softly sprung slab of a convertible car into an area giving shelter from the sunlight and an almost garage-like cave with a high overhead roof and on a downward incline back towards the nearest track.

"This is a good spot," said Chuck, "Mike, you haven't lost your field-craft."

"Look, you take it easy for a while, Chuck. Get recovered. I'll keep watch first; then we can have a chat, and then maybe you'll want to check the area. I think your buddy will take longer to recover from this."

Chuck's eyes flickered, "Yes, whatever they gave us was slow-acting but powerful."

# *London*

Jake was away for the whole weekend. Family business and somewhat stressful. Not just the travelling, but some of the entertaining and conversations of the weekend proved difficult.

Since Jake and his two friends had set up their business called 'The Triangle' there were a lot of questions asked around the family about what they all did.

Jake, Bigsy and Clare produced a good front story, but behind it all, they sometimes mixed up in quite complicated situations.

The creation of The Triangle led back to a time when one of their friends was murdered, and it dragged them into a complex web which led to them receiving a significant financial windfall. At the time there were no strings attached, but it meant they also became involved in another somewhat political situation. Jake couldn't explain any of this to his family and made up a bland story that they were advertising and media consultants.

Now, when Jake visited his family, they would ask questions about his life and fortunes, and he would make up answers which didn't always tally. It created a shifty impression of what Jake did for a living. Jake was convinced they thought he was selling drugs or doing something equally unsavoury.

Jake's prior background as a journalist didn't always help, because he would sometimes over-elaborate a story, which was then difficult to keep consistent if he was asked about it later. As a case in point, he had rented a family compatible practical hatchback for the weekend instead of his fancy Italian sports car. But then, he'd forgotten the colour of the hire car and neatly described something different when someone had asked, "What are you driving, these days?"

Now he was back in London at The Triangle's small offices in Hoxton. A weight had lifted from his whole being. It wasn't that he didn't like his family - far from it - it was much more to do with his need to keep them away from his business affairs.

Monday morning, and Jake flicked on the screen of his PC and waited for it to come to life. As it burbled through the start-up processes, he straightaway noticed a virtual sticky label attached to his desktop wallpaper. It was classic Bigsy. A note from Bigsy to Jake not sent by email or text or any of the standard methods.

Bigsy's computing background had devised a straightforward but secure way to send messages between the principal members of the office, but in a way that was not detectable by the usual snoopers. Bigsy had made the point to Jake that snoopers trying to hack into their system looked at the typical email and social media traffic and cookies. By having a completely separate system, they would be one step further ahead of anyone trying to pry.

Most of the time, they used it for shopping lists, but sometimes there would be something more significant. Now was one of those times. Bigsy's note said that he and Clare were contacted at the weekend and asked to go to Arizona.

Jake's eyebrows lifted as he read this. It was not a typical request, and he was slightly surprised that they did not phone him about this during the weekend.

Jake also realised that this must be a sensitive topic, which was why Bigsy and Clare were not making phone calls or emails about what was happening.

Bigsy's note continued that they had been contacted by a special friend who had disappeared. Jake knew immediately that this reference was to Chuck Manners. Colonel Manners was a contact that they knew from a couple of previous situations when they had got involved with the police and the military and some criminal types.

Chuck Manners was also elusive, and the strong rumours were that he had been killed after their last exploit together. Jake, Bigsy and Clare had never believed that Chuck had been killed, but they had been sure he had wanted to get away from anyone that might be looking for him.

Jake reached for his phone. "Ping me," he typed and then sent a message to both Clare and Bigsy. He was only signalling that he had read Bigsy's message and would now wait for them to make contact

# *Sedona*

Bigsy awoke with a start. He still felt woozy. He noticed it was dark and that he appeared to still be in the car. Earlier the roof of the car had been open, but now he seemed to be more enclosed. He attempted to move his arm, and to his relief, it appeared to be obeying him.

"Hello," he ventured. "Is there anyone here?"

He looked around and could see that he was alone in the car, parked in a small enclosed area surrounded by rocks. He worked out that they were still in the desert. He remembered that they were in Arizona. Then he noticed the driver of the car standing a few metres away.

Bigsy clicked down the door handle and eased himself out. He swivelled in the car seat and put his feet on the ground and gently pulled himself upright.

"Great, you can stand again!" said the driver. "Chuck has been able to walk around for a couple of hours. Can you talk yet?" he asked.

"Yes," replied Bigsy, slightly surprising himself that the words were coming out of his mouth. "What happened?"

"I guess you met with your buddy Chuck and have got sucked into something," answered the driver. "My name is Mike, by the way. I have known Chuck for many years. Let's say we shared a few moments."

"That was you driving a while ago?" questioned Bigsy.

"Yes, things were getting a little hot," answered Mike.

Bigsy took a closer look at Mike now. A wiry, slim build, deep tanned face that was still partly concealed by the baseball cap. Bigsy could tell that Mike was probably from a similar background to Chuck. Another ex-military type, American forces - no doubt - and perhaps some kind of special unit. There was a hardness to his face that Bigsy could see. The look of someone who has been in many fights and could stand his ground. Bigsy was glad that they were on the same side.

"We will wait for Chuck to get back." said Mike," He has gone for a scout around our location. I think you'll understand that I won't be saying too much about what has been happening until all three of us are together."

"In the meantime, you might like something to eat. Or at least something to drink? The trunk of this car has quite a few supplies."

Bigsy nodded, "Mike, thank you, that would be great. Water is my priority right now."

Bigsy made his way around to the trunk of the car. He was a little unsteady on his feet and realised that he had not recovered from whatever had affected him. Mike smiled and walked over and helped Bigsy open the back of the car.

Bigsy smiled. He could see that someone with a military mind had arranged the contents. There were several camouflaged bags arranged in the back.

"Yes, we have food, water and other items that might come in useful," answered Mike.

Bigsy lifted one of the bags. It was very heavy and seemed filled with some kind of mechanical equipment. Bigsy thought of guns.

"Not that one," said Mike, smiling. "The two on the left are the food and drink compartments."

Bigsy put his hand onto one of the other camouflage bags and could feel the outline of water bottles. He unzipped the top of the bag and pulled two bottles from it.

"Let's share one for now," said Mike, "I'm not sure how long we will be out here."

There was a small noise. A clink of a pebble hitting the edge of one of the large boulders.

"That's Chuck," said Mike, "He's sending us a message he is

nearly back. We've worked together a lot, and that's a typical way to warn one another when we're approaching the base camp. We'll tell you more in a moment, but we both worked together for quite a long time out here in the desert."

"Chuck recovered his senses a lot earlier than you. We had a chance for a good chat while you were still out of it. You seemed oblivious even when we were laughing. He's told me a fair bit about you, Clare and your friend Jake in England."

There was another sound; the crack of a stick being broken.

"Now he's just having a laugh," said Mike. "He can hear us already."

Bigsy looked around just as Chuck emerged from behind the rocks.

"Hi, Bigsy," said Chuck, smiling, "How's Rapunzel? Do you remember anything at all from yesterday? We were both given some kind of drug while we were in the bar."

"Hi, Chuck, I gather you recovered ages before me. I don't think I can remember as much as I should," said Bigsy. "I can remember flying here from Heathrow to Phoenix with Clare and then driving to the hotel with the fire pits in Scottsdale. I remember splitting up from Clare and even remember meeting you in the bar at the hotel. I think we also had something to eat?"

"Yes," said Chuck, "It was the dinner when things went wrong. Someone had intercepted us even before I explained what has been happening."

"But wait a minute," said Bigsy. "Where's Clare? She flew

out with me but was too jet lagged to meet again last night. She went straight to bed."

"Yes - although you called her room and told her you had run into me when we first met in the bar. And that we would eat something."

"Okay - so Clare knows that we met, but not much about whatever happened after that?" asked Bigsy.

"Correct, and we were in such a hurry to leave the place that we didn't have time to explain the circumstances."

"I presume Clare will be concerned?" asked Chuck, "Because we will need to extract her, but it may not be so easy to return to that hotel right now.

Chuck continued, "She wasn't seen with me, and I think I'm the person who's attracting the trouble right now. If Clare stays in the hotel, she should be all right."

"Clare won't move for a couple of days even if I appear to have gone." said Bigsy. "She already knows that we have met. She will think you have taken me somewhere related to your initial contact with us." said Bigsy. "But look - what about last night - I don't know what happened. I have a vague recollection of being in a car - this car? - and that some people were chasing us?"

"Someone was out to get us, or more specifically to get me, and you've got caught up in it," answered Chuck.

"I knew you wouldn't have contacted us again unless it was important," said Bigsy. "You know that most people thought you were dead after that trouble with the vaccine last year?"

"Yes," said Chuck," and I'm sure you'll understand it was best to leave it that way with most people. I'd always assumed that you would have suspected the truth - that I was still around."

"We worked out that you had escaped and changed your identity or something," said Bigsy.

"But it was obvious when you contacted us at the Triangle it was you. I left a secure note for Jake about your contact but have sent no emails or texts or used the phone about you," said Bigsy.

"As I said yesterday evening," said Chuck, "Thank you both for coming straight over here to assist me."

"You're welcome," said Bigsy, "and I'm reminded that there's never a dull moment!"

# *How did we get away?*

"So, look," said Bigsy, "I still don't know how we got away from whatever was happening at the hotel?"

Mike explained.

"There were several of us on the way to the meeting place at the hotel. I don't know who called us there. I wondered if it was Chuck, but he told me he hadn't requested the meeting. What I know is that it was one of the original team of us that worked together out here a few years ago. Anyway, I was the first to arrive. You and Chuck showed up soon after me, and I could tell you knew one another well."

"I didn't want to show my hand the first evening because Chuck and I arranged to meet the next day. It looked as if you guys were catching up. I could see you both talking fast in the bar before you got something to eat."

"I didn't spot you there," said Chuck, "And usually, I'd be good at this."

"It takes one to know one," said Mike. "But you said there was another person with you; Clare? I didn't see you arrive, Bigsy, and I wasn't aware that you were with someone else. I think it would be the same for anyone else checking out what was happening. I guess they will only look for you two, Chuck and Bigsy, because you sat together.

Bigsy commented, "Yes, and that was an accident. I didn't expect to see Chuck until the next evening. I only visited the bar because I couldn't get adjusted to the time difference and needed something before I went to bed. Clare had gone to her room. We'd arranged to see Chuck in the evening and Clare was going to check out the spa during the day.

Mike looked at Bigsy. "I couldn't work out what happened. Partway through your conversation, I could see you both looking tired, and I noticed that after this you both left the bar for your rooms."

"Bigsy, you mentioned your room number to Chuck when you were still sitting down, and then Chuck signed the bill for the meal, so I knew the room numbers for both of you."

"Old habits," smiled Chuck.

Mike continued, "I was suspicious that something was wrong but didn't know what had happened. I checked that you got back to your rooms safely, and that you were not followed. I could only follow Chuck because I thought if anything was likely to happen, it would be to Chuck, the trouble magnet.

Bigsy grinned.

Mike continued, "Sure enough, there were two guys on Chuck's floor, standing a few doors along from his room when he returned. I watched Chuck go in, but then saw the two other guys getting ready to break in. I knew that Chuck's drink or food had probably been spiked, so there would be very little resistance from him if they got through the door."

"Just as I was thinking this, I saw them use a small electronic key to enter Chuck's room. I had no choice but to pursue and, er, what's the word? 'neutralise' the two guys.

"Chuck was in no fit state to help, but he was still standing. I called him towards the elevator and then selected your floor, which was only one floor down because of the low-rise shape of the hotel. I didn't have the luxury of a special key and had to damage your door to get into the room. You were also in your room but looked as if you had passed out on the bed. I woke you again and got you standing. You were both the worse for wear, and I thought it was the tranquilliser drug effect, which had kept you both functioning but only just able to move. It was like talking to slow-witted zombies as we all got into the elevator and went down to the ground floor."

Mike continued, "An advantage of that Scottsdale hotel is we knew our way around its back-doubles because of earlier times spent there. It meant I could cut through to the car park lot with no need to use the main exit. I got you both into my car and you both passed out almost at once."

Bigsy watched as Mike paused. He had run through this story with Chuck, who also seemed to have little recollection of what had happened. Chuck seemed to be listening to the story, as if trying to remember more of the situation first-hand.

Mike continued, "My main aim was to get us all clear of the hotel as fast as possible. Unfortunately, my car wasn't low profile enough, and the guys I had left in Chuck's room had their buddies waiting in another car at the front of the hotel. I thought I got away from them and onto the main route towards the north and decided it was better to stop somewhere off the road in the dark. With you guys both needing to sleep it off, I had little choice but to wait until the morning for us to regroup and decide on a further move."

"My hiding tactic worked because they could not find us. Both of you were completely out of it in any case. I worked out they had spiked you both with slow-release sedative - something potent but non-deadly and I would need to let you both sleep it off."

"Then, at around dawn, I set off along the main road towards the north, and everything looked as if we were in the clear. not. After about an hour of driving, I noticed a fast car behind us and realised that we were being followed. I think this when Chuck came to and it could have been my erratic pursuit driving that helped shake him back into life. The guys behind were angry and trying to force us off the road or worse."

"I had to take serious evasive action, and this caused their car to turn over soon after we left the Interstate."

"I think that's when I first woke up," said Bigsy. "I remember being violently shaken."

"Yes, that would be us being chased," said Mike. "I don't think they built this car to go over the country routes at such a speed." He patted the side of the blue car, and Bigsy noticed there were a couple of added bends in the metalworks as well as light red flecking of mud from the rear wheels, sprayed onto the rear part of the vehicle.

Bigsy asked, "So the guys in the car that chased us...Who were they and what were they doing?

"That's what we were trying to work out while you were still out of it," said Chuck. "Mike and I were discussing this earlier. We've got a general sense of what is happening, but we don't know who is behind it."

"The fact they are at the hotel in Scottsdale suggests that they are now like bees around a honeypot looking for other people from our old team. I think it puts anyone else from the old gang invited to the hotel in danger."

# *Sleepers and Ties*

"What I can't understand," said Bigsy, "Is how Chuck keeps coming back to us when there's a problem? A year ago, we had trouble with the vaccines, and now again? Surely there are other people he could call on?"

Mike looked at Chuck, and they both smiled.

"Go on, tell him," said Mike.

"Well, Bigsy, it's like this. Have you heard of sleepers?"

"What the things that keep railway lines apart?" replied Bigsy.

"Er no - and we call those things ties here in America - I meant sleepers like you see in spy movies."

"Oh, the people that take up life in a foreign country and then get activated?"

"Yes, that's the type of thing," replied Chuck.

"Only the way they show them in movies isn't the only way that it works. When you are an agent like me or Mike, part of the training and fieldcraft is to get some people that are entirely 'off the grid' that can be relied upon under challenging circumstances."

"You mean like Clare, Jake and me?" asked Bigsy.

"Yes, and you are a classic and, dare I say, excellent implementation. We are supposed to find people and also to make them a little grateful for their contact with us. In your case, it was easy because we had that large lump sum windfall from the first situation."

Bigsy nodded. He knew that the first time he'd met Chuck the result had created a lot of money for himself, Clare and Jake. He knew that the money they had received was 'no questions asked' because of the basis by which they had received it. The only person who knew anything more detailed about it was Chuck Manners.

"In the movies, the sleepers learn all about the culture of the place they are planted and then get activated for ideological reasons or because someone has planted a chip in their head," said Bigsy, "You know that Manchurian Candidate that was programmed to kill the President. Or terrorist cells that are awoken to go bombing."

"Yes, you are right, but the way we are trained is to find a small group of people we can rely upon. They should have a good degree of trust with us but are going about their routine business. You, Bigsy, Clare and Jake are like this, but as you you've shown, you would all come to my aid if I needed it. And you have plenty of access to cash, so you have the wherewithal to do it."

"Yes," Mike agreed, "I had a similar small team, in my case recruited via a sports network where I'd helped them win a large donation."

"The point isn't to use them all the time but to rely on them in a difficult situation. They are like sleepers because they are in effect activated, but the difference is that they still have the free will to decline."

"So, if Clare and I hadn't agreed to meet you, then you'd have been stuck?" asked Bigsy.

"Or I would have had to try my other group of friends in Canada," answered Chuck. "In fact, I contacted them, but you agreed to come along first. I'm glad it was you, actually," added Chuck.

"Good plan, except, of the three of us, one is still in the UK, I'm being chased, and Clare has gone missing," said Bigsy.

"Yes, we need to put that right as quickly as possible."

"And Mike, what about you? Have you also been working with 'sleepers'?" asked Bigsy.

"The difference for me this time was that I didn't realise how bad things had got until I saw what was happening to you and Chuck," answered Mike. "I haven't had the time or an opportunity to contact anyone. The message was signed by Esther to meet in Scottsdale, like Chuck. I knew it related to the work we'd done together and also that 'Esther' was a made-up name."

"Made up, but designed to ensure it would get our attention," added Chuck.

"So, what did you want us for?" asked Bigsy, "When you assumed that we thought you were dead?"

"Not at all. I didn't underestimate your thinking on this," answered Chuck, "I realised that you'd at least maintain doubt after what happened and that therefore if I made contact again, you wouldn't be surprised. Come on - you thought I blew up in a car. That would be shoddy."

"You are right," said Bigsy, "None of us thought you'd been blown-up, and that car explosion was a little too -er - big and isolated for us to believe in it. You were driving all that way to the marshes in a car filled with a big bomb. A crater the size of a tennis court. No remains. You averted a major London catastrophe, but it also gave you a perfect chance to disappear. It's annoying that you didn't tell us you were okay. In our hearts, we knew it anyway, though."

"I would not take any chances, nor create any new links to you so soon after that last little scrape," said Chuck.

"So, when your message arrived, we were pleased to hear that you were okay, although we were also sure that your contact with us would be because of some problem!" continued Bigsy.

"Correct," said Chuck, "Although neither Mike nor I have worked out what has been happening. Except that it to do with our old project out here in the deserts."

Ed Adams

# *Campfire*

"So, what would be the reason?" asked Bigsy, "Why are they after you? What was 'The Old Team' doing?"

"Okay," said Chuck, "let us check our logistics and then we can tell you more. I started to explain this last night, but I think both of us have a hazy recollection of what we said."

"First things first, we should check logistics," said Chuck. Mike nodded.

"We must use the backroads to get to somewhere where we can swap the car." Mike looked over to the parked vehicle, and Bigsy had a first chance to notice that it was quite a sleek and retro-looking convertible.

"Why have we got something that looks as if it should be in a movie?" asked Bigsy, "It is the most discreet form of transport?"

"It's mine," said Mike, "Or at least it is for this journey. I thought I'd hide in plain sight. It would have been almost more noticeable if I'd turned up in a black van or an F150.

Like I was working undercover. This makes me look far more like a tourist."

"It worked well to get me from L.A. to Scottsdale, I'm sure I wasn't followed, but that means that they've picked up on us when Chuck arrived."

"Or Bigsy?" asked Chuck.

"I don't think so," replied Mike, "I'm certain that Bigsy wasn't expected or known about. He's hardly part of our structure," said Mike," Oh, no offence, Bigsy"

"None taken," said Bigsy. He looked into the small fire. He wasn't sure of anything now. A day in Arizona and he was already under some form of attack, holed up in the desert, with a Machiavellian ex-marine and a new guy who looked like an outlaw.

Bigsy smiled to himself. The pain and dullness were beginning to wear off. The food that Mike had prepared out of a can had been good. A cowboy supper as Bigsy thought of it. Beans and sausages from a can. A much bigger can than he'd ever seen from the stores back in England.

"So, it looks as if they spiked our food?" mused Chuck.

"The symptoms you both showed were like a slow-acting tranq," said Mike. "You were both zoned out and tripping. But it wasn't just some magic mushrooms or peyote mixed in the food, it must've been a far more refined version of whatever."

"Yes, enough to knock us out, but after a delayed period rather than immediately," said Chuck.

"Yes," said Mike. "It meant you could eat, get to feel drowsy and then get back to your rooms before the full effect kicked in. Then as you drifted off to sleep, you would in effect be out for the count."

"Long enough to be extracted from our rooms with no resistance."

"Yes, although I don't think they were interested in Bigsy. Just in you, Chuck," said Mike.

"So how come I'm here as well?" asked Bigsy,

"That was because of me," replied Mike. "I'd seen you together in the hotel and had you both under observation since you met. I didn't want to show up too soon, and it is lucky that I didn't," continued Mike.

"All this adds emphasis that there's something significant going down," said Bigsy.

Chuck nodded. "Yes. Bigsy, that's why I'd asked you and Clare to come here, I needed to tell you I think I'm under some threat, although I don't know its source."

"So why to call Clare and me?" asked Bigsy.

"The same reason as last time. You are unknown and have no records leading back into the military or the secret services. I'd wanted someone who could make some enquiries for me but drawing no attention. It needed to be face-to-face because I don't trust using email or phone calls for this kind of thing. You know I'd disappeared too."

Bigsy nodded. He and Clare both knew they'd help right from the first moment they received the call from Chuck.

Mike looked across to Chuck. "I'll go get the SIMMs then," he said, "We're in burner country around here, so it shouldn't be too difficult."

"Burner country?" asked Bigsy.

"Yeah, ever since that TV show about a schoolteacher making MDMA out in the desert, we've an extra traffic across the desert of camper vans and beat-up looking cars. Some are doing it like a travel route, others might well be cooking."

"Welcome to the land of opportunity," said Chuck.

Mike strolled towards the car. "I'll be back in the morning; I'll find a gas station with a store. May just stay in a motel tonight. You two will be fine."

Bigsy wondered why they all didn't move to the motel.

# *Crossed Arrows*

Bigsy awoke. He could hear something around the camp. A crack of a twig. The merest hint of pebbles skittering down towards a gully.

Then he noticed a light. Within it he could see a shadow. A silhouette of someone. Slim, with a hair bun.

He turned to shake Chuck but realised he had gone. No, the shape wasn't Chuck.

Then a hand appeared around the tent fastening. Bigsy felt queasy until a voice said, "Hey Bigsy, I'd like you to meet Tom!"

Bigsy felt the relief wash over him. Instead of being stabbed by a spirit, he was about to meet one of Chuck's friends.

"Hello, Bigsy," said the second voice, "My name is Atsa Tahoma - but most people call me Tom."

Bigsy flicked his iPhone, and its torch lit the scene. Bigsy could see a tall, athletic man, with dark hair, pulled back into a bun at the back of his head.

"Hello," said Bigsy, " I won't lie, I heard you moving about, saw the outline of a face and thought we were being overrun."

"No, I'm alone. Chuck called me up when he arrived in Phoenix. He's been devilishly difficult to track down. He texted me last night with your current position."

"So, where do you know Chuck from?" asked Bigsy.

"I used to do some work with him," said Tom, evasively.

"I see," said Bigsy determined to get more information," What kind of things and was it here?"

"Yes, it was," said a voice from behind Bigsy, "Tom was one of the greatest guides to the desert, he taught me about desert craft, showed me where people had gone and showed me the spirits of his people. The Navajo", it was Chuck who took a couple of strides towards Tom. They embraced heartily.

"Man, it's great to see you," said Chuck, "You too, my friend," said Tom laughing and tapping Chuck's belly. "Not quite as wiry as before? Too many American treats?"

Chuck smiled, "I wish. And this version of me is with a morning jog every day."

Bigsy smiled while breathing in; he wondered whether Tom would wish to remark upon his shape next.

"Okay, I think we can relax now, Bigsy," he beamed towards Bigsy, who looked a little rattled, "I'm pleased to make your acquaintance." Tom looked towards the breaking dawn.

'Before me peaceful, behind me peaceful, under me peaceful, over me peaceful, all around me peaceful.'

There, I've said it." He looked towards Chuck, who grinned back.

"Tom's people are quite spiritual," Chuck explained," They know things about the Desert, its Spirits and the ways to live within it."

"And how to follow a set of map co-ordinates!" laughed Tom.

# *Esther*

Chuck, Bigsy and Tom sat on rocks a few yards from the car. The shelter of the rocks around the cave worked well to provide efficient cooling. Bigsy realised that Mike had an excellent desert craft to find this spot but couldn't help wondering if there was any undesirable wildlife in the neighbourhood.

"Okay," said Chuck, "I ran through this yesterday with Mike, who seems to know less than me about what has been happening. He'll be back anytime now, I guess. I doubt if he'd spend much time at the motel.

As if on cue, they could hear a car approaching. It did a complicated manoeuvre, so it was facing back along the track.

"Hey Mike," called Chuck, "Look who is here!"

Mike looked up and then bounded towards Tom," Atsa Tahoma - Tom - It's been a long time!"

# The Circle

They hugged, slapping each other on the backs.

"So, are you still tracking out here?" asked Mike, "Working for the military?"

"Yes," said Tom, "They seem to need a lot of help."

"Well, it's brilliant to see you," said Mike," But hey, I don't want to interrupt. I could hear Chuck spinning some kind of yarn."

Chuck smiled. "Yes, it's what I was telling you yesterday, Mike. I'm bringing Tom and Bigsy, up to date."

Chuck continued with his story.

"Ben Leitzmann, an associate of mine and Mike's from project Esther, was killed in a boating accident. I knew about this, although Mike didn't. And Bigsy, I know what you are thinking, a boating accident by itself may not be suspicious."

"And I'd agree. A tragedy, but there is a reason for my apparent paranoia about it though."

"Ben had tried to contact me just before this happened. It was indirect, in that he had notified me via a postcard from his hometown. It wasn't sent to me either; he didn't know how to get to me except via an ancient post box number."

Chuck added, "Ben's approach was a perfect tradecraft way to tell that something was out of the ordinary. Just a card, out of the blue, but with a way to contact Ben. It would be a classic 'Call me' type message."

"Although, because of my circumstances, it took two weeks

to reach me."

"Not just the US Postal system then?" said Bigsy, "And why you? and did he tell anyone else?" He noticed a small lizard flick across a boulder. Chuck smiled.

"Completely safe here," he said, "except for the scorpions."

Bigsy flinched.

"It's okay in the daytime. They are night creatures looking for spiders and bugs. And don't expect ones like you see in the movies six inches long. These little critters are more likely to be a couple of inches at most. My advice is just don't be looking under any rocks."

Mike was nodding his head. "Yes. There's only one critter that's bad called the Bark. It looks kind of transparent straw coloured and packs a punch. But we should be fine here. If you see any big ones like four inches or more, then they are the hairy desert kind. They also have a darker coloured body.

Chuck said, "Now you know why I had that black light last night. It wasn't to show up your dandruff, just to look out for the critters."

Bigsy could feel his toes curling inward as he heard about these unexpected co-residents of the area.

Mike continued, "And no, I got nothing from Ben or anyone else. Just the request to come to Scottsdale, which I thought was from Chuck. That's also why I was scouting before I made contact. In case there was another dimension to this. Looks as if I was right and that someone is out to get us."

"Yes - there's a group of us," said Chuck. "You know something Bigsy, what I'm about to tell you is sensitive. Tom knows too, because of the work he did with us when we were at the base. I'll only tell you enough to give you context, but I don't want to put you in more danger by knowing more than you need."

Bigsy nodded. Chuck looked at Mike. "Are you okay with this, Mike?" asked Chuck.

"Sure," said Mike, "Bigsy is your contact, and if you've hauled him from the UK then I guess he must be all right." Mike was reaching into his jacket for something.

"Okay," continued Chuck, glancing towards Mike's jacket pocket," Here's the situation."

"The reason I asked you and Clare to come to Scottsdale is also no coincidence. Mike can confirm that this location, or should I say the hotel we were in, used to be a bolt-hole that some of us know about from work we did together a few years ago."

Mike was lighting a cigarette. Bigsy noticed as Mike replaced the shiny Marlboro package inside his jacket.

"How come?" said Chuck. "That's new?"

"I used to, then I stopped. Then I fell into some bad company, I guess," said Mike. The smoke drifted, and Bigsy wondered why it was trailing towards him.

Chuck continued, "It's like this. We're just over the state line here from New Mexico, and you may know that's where some of the big deserts provide space to try out new US military ideas."

"Mike and Ben and I and another few of us were part of a project a few years ago which was testing some new defence technology."

"There are some big ranges in New Mexico that can be used for missile testing and it provided perfect cover for some of the things we were doing."

Bigsy asked, "So was what you were doing legitimate? Was it part of something you were doing for the US government?"

"Bigsy, yes it was legit and for the DoD. US Army Intelligence employed Mike and me. Tom was employed too, in manner of speaking. It was an offshoot of a special unit called IARPA which stands for Intelligence Advanced Research Projects Agency. We both had special assignments to look after some of the more specialised and secret projects."

Bigsy nodded. He noticed that Mike was now stubbing out his cigarette with his boot.

Bigsy said, "So what were you doing there? Were you guarding the area or something else?"

Mike chuckled. He was already rummaging for another cigarette.

"Not exactly," said Chuck, "We were there to try out the technology."

"I think you know that I've been involved with several missions inside and on the edges of what the US government does. This time, we were trying out some new weaponry supposed to be for use by some of our elite forces.

"Mike, Ben and I were all part of a team that was involved in the testing. In effect, we were the users of this equipment."

"So, what did it do?" asked Bigsy.

"The project was called Esther. I think the simplest way to describe it is that it was a kind of guided rocket system."

"The jargon name we used for this was spot rockets. They are a kind of guided missile that can be fired with remarkable accuracy. It works by putting an identifying homing beacon onto the target."

"Most targets don't take to being identified in that way, so there's another aspect. They make the homing signal to be a tiny unit which can be hidden. It works by pre-locating the homing beacon well ahead of the deployment of the missile."

"But surely the homing device needs to create quite a big signal?" asked Bigsy, "Just the battery packs alone, plus the transmitter would make it large?"

"That was what made this clever," said Chuck," The technology used leveraged other technology to make itself work. It used a device like a SIMM card from a phone and a tiny aerial to hook itself into either a cellular network or a wifi environment. In effect, it was piggybacking on someone else's communications infrastructure."

"I see," said Bigsy. "It could use the effect of wide cellular and wifi coverage to transmit. It still doesn't explain how it could work for a long time without a big battery. Sending out a signal would still use a fair amount of power."

"That was a clever part," said Chuck," They had made the homing identifiers the same size as paperback books. There was quite a lot of technology in a tiny space. First, there was a little computer. Then there was a little battery pack. And third there was a wire-wrapped aerial that looped around the inside edges of the unit, . Like a square shape."

"At the time we all thought this was a cool technology," said Mike.

Chuck added, "What I remember is that the units produced sent out a very slow pulse. They designed it for something like four pulses per day - to conserve battery. It was only trying to find out if it had been woken up."

"I see," said Bigsy, "Low battery use running a timer like on a watch and then an occasional big pulse to see if they had woken it?"

"Yes, Bigsy, I can see you are still the computer geek I remember," said Chuck, "The pulses were to find WIFI or a cellular network and to see if the device was polled. Every device had a unique identifier and only if it was called upon would it then power up into its targeting state."

"Brilliant," said Bigsy, "It would mean the battery could last, what one to two years, and still be able to run at full strength for maybe an hour or two?"

"Exactly," said Chuck," It was a way to deploy very stealthy targeting devices which could be powered up when needed."

"And what could they be used for?" asked Bigsy.

"There are more moving parts than I can describe," continued Chuck, "For example, the payload that can be delivered is configurable by this system. It's used to drive targeting of anything from a small tactical rocket launcher right through to firing armaments from something like an F-15 fighter plane."

Mike nodded," Yes, we got to test some cool things out in the desert. Although we were only allowed to make tiny bangs."

"It's much the same here nowadays, just the names of things change," added Tom.

Mike and Chuck grinned.

Mike added, "The delivery system missile or rocket needs to have the guidance capability to work with this device. That's what we were testing out in the Mojave Desert a few years ago."

"Yes," said Chuck," The transponder technology worked pretty well, and it relied upon being able to upload the co-ordinates of the small device to the guidance system. The cool part was that we could also use for moving targets once we had activated it. That's another reason why the devices are only activated just before use. It helps avoid detection."

Bigsy asked, "So did these devices get made?"

"Only the prototypes. There were still problems ironing out the linkages between the missile systems and the small transponders. It worked well with a reasonably sophisticated system like the payload you'd get on an F-15 or a big drone but was sketchy with smaller weapons like the field launchers.

"There was the main problem with the speed of response of the targeting over short distances. If you fire something from close by, there isn't time to change its direction. It is basic physics that you need some distance and a reaction time. It is like trying to make a bullet turn through 90 degrees."

"So, the DoD viewed it as a problem. The people sponsoring the research for this system wanted to use it for battlefield systems rather than long-range systems. They already have all kinds of satellite technology is to do the same things for the long-range."

Bigsy looked at Chuck. "But isn't this a Pandora's box? Once the transponder technology has been developed it could define targets anywhere? They could lay dormant for a long time and then be activated?"

"That's true, but without the payload part working properly, it wouldn't be viable," answered Chuck, "And that was the area still being developed when the program got canned."

"That's right," added Mike, "One minute everything was being tested and then everything just stopped. I think other technologies had overtaken this one and made it irrelevant."

"Yes, it was a budget cut decision," said Chuck. "In typical Government style, they were running multiple programs with similar aims. It was a bunch of advisors that came in, and the result was a cut. DoD decided this was a dead-end technology and had been superseded by more rapid response targeting. The long delays before the targeting system could be activated, the erratic nature of cellular coverage and so on killed the whole idea. Project Esther was shut down over a weekend."

# The Circle

Mike chipped in, "Yes, so Project Esther was quietly terminated, and we were all released with the usual heavy-duty secrecy agreements."

"And how many of you did you say there were involved with this?" asked Bigsy.

"There was only an internal team of six of us working on the user and testing aspects, and that included Mike, Ben and myself. But altogether there were probably around 35 people involved including the technicians and the scientists who were putting all of this together.:

Bigsy asked, "So is someone trying to get at you now because of this project?"

Chuck and Mike nodded.

Mike was on his next cigarette. He replied, "We're guessing that that is the least part of the reason. But some of it doesn't make complete sense because we are the people testing the weapons rather than the people inventing them."

Bigsy watched as Mike fiddled with a few small branches that he had made into a small pyramid shape. Then Mike took his cigarette lighter from his pocket. Bigsy noticed that it seemed to have a high setting, more like a minor blowtorch. In seconds the wood was on fire.

"It's not to keep us warm," said Mike," It's time for some proper coffee."

He walked to the back of the car and returned with a small coffee pot.

"You have to have some creature comforts out here," he said.

"I know that pot," smiled Chuck.

"You know one that looked very similar," said Mike.

"We don't look like a very obvious target, and, we are also harder to eliminate than a few scientists. I suppose we are the ones who used the stuff, but that's less interesting than the people who designed it?"

"My thinking too," said Chuck, "I'd have thought the people who know how to build it would be of greater interest than the people who have handled the systems. Although ironically, I suppose the individual scientists and designers wouldn't be as easy to round up as we seem to have been."

Mike nodded," Yes, the scientists and designers will have dispersed. Some went to Seattle, others to Washington, some to Chicago. Maybe a few to Houston. They will all have been reassigned to other projects."

"So how did you first get involved with this?" asked Bigsy.

"It was routine for me," said Chuck. "...And I guess so for you too, Mike? The military needed a group of professionals who could operate a wide range of weapons and didn't mind sleeping in the middle of the desert for weeks on end. We even had a cover story that we were just testing a new short-range missile in the desert. In that part of the country it is no big deal. They even set up a company as a spin-off of Lockheed, and gave the missile a name - ADONIL"

"Sounds like a headache tablet," said Bigsy.

# The Circle

"Oh, it's a headache for someone, all right," said Chuck.

Mike added," ...and that's why I guessed we were using Scottsdale as our meeting point."

Mike had been making the coffee. The pot had a traditional percolator which he had arranged over the fire. Bigsy noticed it was like a little ceremony. First, Mike had taken the coffee and pressed it into the metal container in the pot. Then he had rigged the pot so that it could brew the coffee. And finally, he had poured the coffee into three metal mugs.

"I know this is the Starbuck generation," said Mike," but you, Mr Englishman, need to try some proper cowboy coffee too.{"

Mike smiled as he passed the mugs around.

"When we all worked on the project, we would sometimes have some downtime. Then we'd get away from the base and out of the desert. It was better for us to do this under some kind of cover and we would usually go to Scottsdale to that rather nice hotel as a nearby base where we could let off some steam."

"We used to call it the convention centre. It was where we had our 'quotes' Sales Meetings." He moved his hands to make the symbol of quotation marks in the air.

"We would use the time to play golf and mess around but needed some cover and for it to be far enough away from the missile ranges not to cause suspicion. It's only about two- or three-hours' drive, but it's amazing that just crossing a state line somehow changes everyone's perspective about who we are and what we were doing."

"I see," said Bigsy, "So you'd go to Scottsdale or Phoenix, but you wouldn't go to say Albuquerque?"

"Way too near to the base," said Mike, "Albuquerque would be filled with other people involved in the business that would be conducted at the ranges. It was also just next to Kirtland, which has a huge Air Force base and the nearby Albuquerque International airport.

"I get it," chuckled Bigsy. "It's like not going to the nearest pub to the office when you are in London. But the distances are so much greater in America."

He looked at Chuck and Mike and laughed.

"You Brits have such a strange sense of humour," said Mike. He smiled and winked towards Chuck, "You know something. We were talking about the scorpions earlier. Did I mention the spiders? We have some cool spiders here too."

# The Desert

There's a man who sends her medals
He is bleeding from the war
There's a jouster and a jester
And a man who owns a store
There's a drummer and a dreamer
And you know there may be more
She will love them when she sees them
They will lose her if they follow
And she only means to please them
And her heart is full and hollow
Like a cactus tree
While she's so busy being free

*Joni Mitchell (23) - Cactus Tree –*
*October 12, 1967*

# *Scottsdale, AZ*

Clare had slept through until what she thought was late. She had woken up once at around 7 am UK time, which was still only midnight in Scottsdale. Then she had slept for another 7 hours. Her watch was still on UK time and said 2 pm.

She looked towards the large television in the room. She flipped it on with the remote control and waited for the menu system to start up. 7 am. It was still only 7 am. She was convinced it would be later. It felt a lot later. And she was hungry.

Maybe it wasn't such a good idea to go straight to bed after they arrived. Perhaps she should have joined Bigsy downstairs in the bar.

Clare remembered that she and Bigsy had made no specific plans for breakfast time. She'd told him she would try the spa and he'd said they could meet again in the evening. She knew his room number, and they had even swapped spare keys. Clare spared Bigsy the early morning wake-up call and instead arranged for her breakfast.

# The Circle

She pulled the curtains and looked at the bright light of the view. She could tell it was already hot outside. Hot and sunny. She was on the second floor of what looked like a low-rise block with a great view from its balcony.

Problem solved. Clare would take breakfast on the balcony. She wouldn't be meeting Chuck until the evening and that gave both her and Bigsy a chance to try the facilities of the rather luxurious hotel.

Clare reflected that it was always easier to fly from the UK to America because the time zones worked in favour of being able to get up late. The days before her flight had included time on the road with her musician friend Christina. The music business was all late and later nights. So, this excuse for a lay-in had been most welcome, and she could still feel semi-righteous that she was starting the new Arizona day early. She picked up the phone and ordered breakfast, being sure to include strawberries and maple syrup.

Then she showered and prepared for the day, ahead of the breakfast in her room. Maybe she would call Bigsy after all. If he was awake, they could share the breakfast on the balcony. She knew there would be too much for her to eat alone - this was America - and they could easily order extra coffee.

She called Bigsy on the hotel system. Clare knew that it was better to avoid using cell phones until they had contacted Chuck and understood what they were getting into.

Clare dialled Bigsy's room but could hear the standard hotel voicemail message. Either Bigsy is still asleep, or maybe he too had got an early breakfast and was out somewhere. No big deal and no need to order extra coffee.

Clare spent the day until at least mid-afternoon lounging in the hotel. Bigsy would make contact at some point no doubt with an update from Chuck.

The hotel spa treatments looked good. There was an excellent half-day special. The spa and the pool would be fine until she had to meet Bigsy and then Chuck.

# *Mount Ord Trailhead*

"Guys, I need to contact Clare," said Bigsy, " Otherwise we don't know what she will do. She knew we'd treat the first day as decompression and had already said she'd go to the spa in the hotel. She won't be looking for Chuck or me until early evening. But we don't want my apparent disappearance to alarm her."

"At the moment I don't think there will be any link back to Chuck," said Mike,", I was monitoring you last night, and I didn't work out you'd travelled with someone else. I very much doubt if anyone else will be able to. The main thing will be to stop Clare from creating a trail that links you three together, at least until she is away from the hotel."

Chuck nodded. "I think you are right, Mike. Although, I'd have expected to pick up on you being at the hotel early."

"Whatever," said Bigsy, "We must make contact and also pick up Clare. My hire car is also still at the hotel. Valet parked."

"I think I should call Clare. on her mobile phone number from a pay phone. I suppose I could use your phones, but I don't want to create any more links than we need to."

"You are right," said Chuck, "We must find somewhere to hide for another night and then to pick up Clare in the morning. It would be best if she can get your car too. We should check the maps for a good position for a meeting place."

"How about the airport?" said Mike. It is busy. It gives access to other vehicles - like a replacement hire-car. You can select a random incoming flight as the rendezvous?"

"I agree," said Chuck, "It's close to us here too, but big enough to make tracking us difficult."

"We'll get back to the road now," said Mike," We have left a very long gap here. We can find a different gas station from the one I used last night and Bigsy; you can make the call."

"Yes, said Tom, I can direct you to one; it is operated by Navajo, and I can ask there if anyone has been looking for you."

"What about cameras?" asked Bigsy. Mike and Chuck smiled. "Just smile," said Chuck, "We'll lend you a baseball cap and some big sunglasses."

"No need to worry about cameras," answered Tom, "Let me go into the gas station first. I can ask for a short-term blackout."

Mike had been packing the small number of items he had

retrieved, back into the car.

"Ready to roll?" he asked.

Chuck took the second front seat, and Bigsy and Tom climbed into the back. Mike gently revved the engine, and they picked their way through rocks back onto a track and back towards the main road.

"Bye-bye scorpions," said Bigsy.

"Don't get your hopes up too soon," said Chuck, "There's a lot of desert out there."

# *Elemental*

Clare had visited the elemental spa. There was a willow stream that ran through the area which the brochure said was inspired by a place called Havasupai, an oasis deep in the Grand Canyon where energy unites and restores.

The spa had a mesa rooftop pool under the deep blue Arizona sky. Clare enjoyed a private cabana and could look out towards the McDowell Mountains.

It had said 'take a half-day' on the brochure, and Clare had followed the advice trying the Desert Oasis, the open-air reflection atrium and also dawdled at the waterfall. To her surprise, the treatment room also had a private outdoor patio, so she had blended the experiences both indoors and outdoors.

# The Circle

Now she felt pleasant and relaxed, but thought it was probably time to find Bigsy again. And anyway, if they stayed a few more days, then maybe she could have another go.

She returned to her room.

Clare looked towards the room phone but saw that the red message light was not flashing. No messages. Bigsy hadn't called. He couldn't still be asleep. It was inconceivable that he would wait this long to make contact, and anyway she had called him at breakfast time.

It was now 2 pm, which would be around 9 pm in the UK. Clare also checked her mobile phone. She didn't expect messages from Bigsy there, aside from the text he had sent when he had found Chuck the preceding night.

Clare decided she would check in Bigsy's room and made her way to his floor. The door had a 'do not disturb' sign on it.

She felt into her jeans for the key to Bigsy's room. First, she tapped on the door. No reply. Again, a little louder. No reply and no sounds from within,

She opened the door, noticing the damage around the lock, and tapped again, this time on the open door to the side bathroom.

No-one.

Then inside the main room. It was just like hers, only a floor lower. Curtains were open. She had the best view.

Bigsy's case was on the bed. A few items scattered around,

which showed Bigsy had been in the room, but didn't look as if he had unpacked.

The bed looked as if it had received turndown service, but no occupant. There was a small chocolate in a wrapper. Bigsy's red backpack on the bed looked as if it had only been placed there before Bigsy headed for the bar. Bigsy could only have spent a few minutes in the room.

Clare realised Bigsy must have met Chuck. She wondered if they had gone somewhere that evening. It was unusual for Bigsy not to leave any message though. Clare would need to resort to using her phone to contact him, even if they had preferred not to use this form of communication.

She clicked her phone, ready to text. Then she noticed it. Bigsy's phone was one of the loose items in the room.

Highly unusual. Bigsy wouldn't go without his phone unless he was in a big hurry.

Clare would lay low in the hotel until Bigsy contacted her. She was sure that she would be contacted by the evening in any case. She chose not to contact Jake in this period, but in the evening to check the bar in case Chuck showed up.

Clare picked up the most important of Bigsy's belongings and put them into the small canvas laundry bag in the wardrobe. She would take them back to her room for safekeeping.

Then she left the 'Do Not Disturb' sign and headed back to her room.

No sign of Bigsy, no messages, but he had been with Chuck. That would be the explanation. The enigmatic Chuck had taken Bigsy somewhere as part of the reason they had been called to Scottsdale.

Clare would need to sit tight until Bigsy, and Chuck returned.

Clare looked through the items she had picked up from Bigsy's room. A small bag containing a laptop computer, the phone, two spare SIMMs, some connector cables, two different sets of keys, a small empty notepad, a few pens.

She moved the various items to the small safe in the cupboard in her room. She noticed it had a charging socket inside and charged Bigsy's computer while it was inside. She placed the other items inside the safe, except for one set of keys.

The set which said 'Hertz'. She would check out the car to see if there were any further clues. She smiled at the thought they referred to it as a car. When they had arrived at the car counter, they had expected the vehicle to be ready to drive away.

It hadn't been ready, and when they did eventually get it, the original one was enormous, like some van. They had made a fuss and had it 'downsized', which seemed highly amusing to the people working in the booth. They were much more used to people asking for something larger.

It was still a big vehicle and looked very capable of going off-road. Clare and Bigsy were both relieved to see the large-sized parking bays in America and could understand why everyone 'front parked'.

Clare walked to the parking area. They had valet parked the car, so it was fortunate that Bigsy had only handed over one of the two keys supplied. The car was still there. Clare thought that even this downsized car looked enormous. Clare peered inside. There was nothing to indicate that Bigsy had moved it. It looked as if he had gone wherever with Chuck in Chuck's car.

# *Gas station*

Bigsy looked out of the car windows as they drove along the highway. It wasn't a fast road, but one with long curves and undulations. Both sides Bigsy could see prominent red rock outcrops. Quite striking.

"Many people say this area is mystical," said Chuck.

"I can see why," said Bigsy. "The scenery is most impressive."

Tom nodded, "Around this part of the desert there is much of four colours," he said.

"You'll see the shadows of black, whites from the rocks, blue from the sky and yellow from the sands. When the conditions are like this, we sometimes call it the Ni'hodilhil First World."

"Ni'hodilhil First World," said Bigsy, "I must practice that one."

"On a spiritual day, you will see the four cloud columns. They are white dawn on the east, blue daylight to the south, yellow twilight to the west and black night to the north. It is said that only First Man and First Woman lived here, far apart on opposite sides of the plain."

"Like Adam and Eve?" asked Bigsy.

"These Mist People had no definite form but were to change to men, beasts, birds, and reptiles of this world," continued Tom.

"Okay, not like Adam and Eve then," said Bigsy.

"Once they found one another through the use of their fires and crystals, they were tricked by coyotes — one coyote who was formed in the water and the angry coyote who wore a hairy coat.

"This group attracted more to their number and the wasps, bees, and stinging ants arrived.

"Then more insects arrived in this primordial land, and all became chaotic with fighting. The man brought a big reed, which he planted in the east. It grew fast so that when the gods became angry with the first world and destroyed it, most creatures could escape to the Second World.

"Wow, that's quite a story," said Bigsy.

"Remember that's only one of four worlds," answered Tom.

"No wonder so many crystal gazers have migrated to the desert," mused Mike," Take Sedona as an example."

## The Circle

"The residential areas around here are well-heeled nowadays," said Chuck,"... not exactly where hippies that have made it come to, but you'll find a fair share of crystal gazers."

"It's mighty impressive," said Bigsy.

"But a long way from the ocean," added Mike, "Look, Tom, is this the one? This will do fine." He gestured towards a filling station ahead of them. There were already several other cars and camper vans filling up.

Tom nodded, "See the dreamcatcher outside of the door? That's not just for tourists, you know."

"I'll fill, you make the call Bigsy," said Chuck, handing Bigsy a pile of small coins.

Bigsy walked towards the payphone. He could see that the phone had a card slot but also a small coin slot. He realised he could fill it with small coins to make the call to the hotel. Chuck had given him several dollars' worth of quarters; he just hoped it would be enough.

He dialled and was connected. He asked for Clare's room and was put through efficiently. He hadn't needed to top up the call yet. Clare's voicemail.

"Hello, this greeting recorded at 3.30 pm. Please leave a message."

She had gone to the trouble to put her voice on instead of the standard message. Bigsy worked out that it would be for his benefit so he would know he was calling the right room and that she was all right.

"Hi, it's me. I'm with him. Meet this evening at the airport as if for the return flight. Park. Leave the bags in the car and meet me at the gate as if we are going back. Don't check-in. Don't call me. All Okay."

Bigsy was pleased; it was a short message. He knew Clare would understand it and he also knew that she was okay, based upon the message she had left. His meeting was a little improvised but gave enough for Clare but not a huge amount for anyone else who was trying to figure it out.

He still had a lot of Chuck's change as he made his way back to the car.

Bigsy also knew that Clare would not try to make any other contact with him. There was nothing more he could do until the next day when they would meet.

Bigsy knew that Clare would get to the check-in area around 2 hours before the flight time as if they were going back to London. This limited the amount of time they would need to spend there and also kept their options open about what they would do next.

"All good," he said to Mike and Chuck, "Clare will be meeting us later at the airport."

# *Missed calls*

Clare couldn't believe it. She'd headed downstairs to check with the front desk in case Bigsy had left a message.

That was precisely when he called her room. She had missed him.

In a way, she was still relieved. He'd got into a scrape already with Chuck but at least was in communication and making a plan for what they needed to do next.

Unfortunately, it blew a hole in the repeat spa treatment idea.

The message from Bigsy was very short. Clare knew this meant he was trying not to give too much away. She assumed it was a payphone. The message was clear enough, though. Get back to the airport with the car and meet Bigsy and Chuck at the departure check-in.

It was very short, and she knew that Bigsy was trying to avoid giving too much information away.

Clare looked at her watch, which was now on American time. She had about six hours. Include an hour to get to the airport. Two hours to wait. Maximum.

She hurriedly packed her own items and carried her bag to Bigsy's room. Then she scooped the few items of Bigsy's into his bag and using her bag as a support wheeled both bags to the elevator.

She wondered whether to check out but decided it might be better to leave the option to return to the hotel open. Also, if she was being watched, it would help keep any followers off guard.

At the valet area she explained that she was with Bigsy from room 317 and that she was getting the car brought around. No, she didn't have his ticket, but she had the other car key as proof. Bigsy "Mr Carter" was out, and she was going to pick him up.

The valet hurried away to get the car, and a few minutes later the luggage was loaded, and she was on the road. It was only about 35 minutes to the airport, but she'd allowed more time because of the chances of getting lost on the way. Although she had navigated for Bigsy when they had driven to the hotel, she had expected it to be tougher going back. It was simpler because she soon picked up the road signs towards the airport and then towards the terminal car parks.

She moved the vehicle into a short stay bay in the pickup area close to the terminal and crossed to the arrivals level in the terminal. She looked around as she did this, but then crossed via the escalators to the departure level check-in.

## The Circle

It was busy with people, and a few security people in uniforms. Nothing out of the ordinary. She spotted a small coffee shop in a corner and, after buying a newspaper, headed to the area and sat with a tall latte waiting for Bigsy to show.

She was sure that he would arrive around two hours before the flight time, so she probably had less than an hour to wait. She sipped at the latte.

Clare felt somewhat cut off from the action but decided it would be even worse for Jake. She called him to bring him up to date. Jake's mobile was ringing.

"Hi, Jake," began Clare.

"Clare," he answered, "It's about time I heard from you. Are you still in the US?"

"You bet; How did your weekend go, with the family?

"Don't ask, they were keen to hear what I was doing. I'm sure they think I'm selling drugs or something. How did you get on?"

"Well, we arrived at the hotel, both of us tired from the flight. I went to bed. Bigsy had a drink. I think he ran into Chuck. They've gone somewhere now. I don't know what has been happening during today, but I'm sure that Bigsy will try to make contact this evening.

"We'd agreed to have a day to chill before we met Chuck, I can only guess that Bigsy ran into Chuck in the bar yesterday or something."

"Aren't you concerned?" asked Jake.

"Not yet," said Clare, "But monitor the comms. I'm certain that Bigsy won't want to use too many phone calls or ways to trace or link us all together. Look, I'll call you as soon as anything develops. Meanwhile, I'll keep you updated via that stickies App that Bigsy has put onto all of our phones and laptops."

# *The I-17*

Mike had driven the blue car back onto the I-17.

They were heading south again, back along the road that Bigsy assumed was the same one they had driven in the other direction the day before. The road was busy with traffic, and Bigsy assumed this would this give them an element of cover.

"A little further and you can drop us off," said Chuck. "There's a big shopping mall, which will give us somewhere to be lost until it's time to get to the airport."

Mike nodded. The mall would be an easy place for a drop-off, provide anonymity and also give easy access to taxis to get to the airport later.

"Will you be all right with this car?" asked Chuck, "I think they know it now, so I wouldn't stick with it for very much longer".

'That's fine," said Mike, "It's on my list too. I don't want to jack something though, because that will add the cops into the equation. I need to move the gear in the trunk to something else but will probably head to a rental to get a replacement.

As a matter of fact, I'm planning to go to the rentals at the airport after I've dropped you off."

Chuck nodded. He also knew it was better for them to split up and that it was not sensible to wait at the airport longer than necessary. The shopping mall was a better location because it was both random and also had plenty of hiding places.

They drew up to the entrance to mall and Bigsy looked at Chuck.

"Er- is this the right place?" asked Bigsy. It was a large mainstream mall just to the side of the I-17.

"Right now, there is no right place," said Chuck. "We need somewhere to stop until we get to the airport."

"I guess it is then," said Bigsy.

His eyes searched along the signage, and he spotted the words 'Food Mall'.

"Okay - I can lead us from here," he said, grinning, "There's a food mall and also restrooms to freshen up."

"Hey Mike - Thank you for everything - it's been a strange 24 hours," said Bigsy, shaking Mike's hand vigorously, "You take care now."

Chuck looked at Mike, "We'll need to stay in contact until this has played out." said Chuck. Mike nodded. "Yes. What will it be?"

"We'll use gunfight at the OK Corral," said Chuck, "It seems kind of appropriate."

Mike nodded, "Que te cuides, Chuck. You take care now."

"Hasta luego, Mike," said Chuck, "See you later!"

Mike tapped the gas, and the car eased away.

"What was all that about?" asked Bigsy. "The OK Corral? Very cowboy."

"It's if we need to get in contact, we'll use Amazon and add comments in the sale of that DVD. It'll only be for the next week, but it is a quick way to communicate without it being very obvious what we are doing."

Bigsy nodded. Another piece of field craft in Chuck's trade.

But now it was time to check out the Food Court.

# *Phoenix Airport*

Chuck's plan to get a taxi from the shopping mall to the airport worked effortlessly. There was a full cab rank outside the mall, and the journey to the airport was only about 25 minutes.

The three of them, Chuck, Bigsy and Tom, had arrived with about two hours to the departure time for the British Airways flight to London and made their way to the area by the check-in desks. Bigsy looked for Clare while Chuck and Tom looked for anyone that may watch them.

They had agreed that they would separate when they were in the airport and would only meet up again once Bigsy had met Clare and they were walking back to the car.

Soon enough Clare spotted Bigsy and left the cafe to walk directly towards him. She could see that he had seen Clare, but only signalled with his eyes to follow her outside and back to where their rental car was parked.

Clare understood immediately and without showing recognition, made her way quite slowly back towards the short stay car park. Bigsy couldn't see Chuck anywhere but was sure he would be following.

Clare found the payment machine, paid for the parking ticket with several dollar bills and then walked towards the car. Bigsy held back until Clare had opened the car and then stepped forward to sit in the back seats of the car.

Before they even started talking, Chuck appeared and climbed into the front seat next to Clare. Tom slid into the rear seat, next to Bigsy.

"Just drive," said Chuck, "We can do the proper greetings later."

"He's right," said Bigsy, "We need to be away from here."

"You know what," said Chuck, "it's probably better if I drive for the moment."

Clare climbed out of the car while Chuck shimmied across into the driver's seat. Tom climbed into the back next to Bigsy.

"You don't give a girl much time to catch up," said Clare.

"All in good time. This should only be precautionary," said Chuck, "And me driving is only in case we are being followed and need to take some evasive action. I know these roads… And say hello to Tom, he is a great friend of mine and a wonderful person to have assisted us here in the desert."

"Well, hello Tom," said Clare, "Hey and good to see you all. I was just starting to get worried!"

Chuck gently moved the car towards the exit from the car

park and then out into the confusing ramps and exits from the airport. He soon took them back onto the I-17 and was heading north towards Flagstaff.

"I'm starting to know this area's roads," said Bigsy.

"When we are out of this area we can stop, swap drivers and have a proper conversation to bring Clare up to speed," said Chuck," I'm sorry it has started like this. At the moment I'm keeping a lookout to make sure we are not followed."

"Did you get our bags?" asked Bigsy, "There were quite a few important things in my room."

"All taken care of. They are in the back of this huge, so-called car. I took everything loose from your room and put it in your backpack, then had all the luggage transferred to the vehicle by the concierge," said Clare, "Although I've left us checked in at the moment."

"That's good," said Chuck," If anyone is checking for us, it will take another day to realise we have gone."

"Yes, I'll check out by phone tomorrow," said Clare.

"We have quite a few tales to tell already," said Bigsy, "It's not been dull. How about you?"

"Spa treatment," said Clare, "I didn't realise anything serious was happening until I got your voicemail. I thought you were with Chuck and had probably gone to pick up something."

Chuck smiled, "You know guys, I'm very grateful that you have come along to assist me with this. I still don't fully know what is happening, but I'm getting more of an idea."

# The Circle

"So where are we heading right now?" asked Clare.

"Mainly north," said Chuck, "and then, Tom, I think we'll be heading east into the desert. I think I will need to visit the area around which I worked a few years ago if we are to get to the bottom of this."

Tom nodded agreement," Yes, we must head for the bases. Don't worry though; there will be plenty of opportunities for concealment."

"Concealment, chases, mystery; Chuck, it's fun, as always, being around you," beamed Clare.

Chuck answered, "Originally I'd hoped to keep it very simple with you running some anonymous interference for me. But whoever is after me has already seen us together. Well, they have seen Bigsy and me together. Oh, and they have also seen Mike, who you haven't met, Clare."

"Okay, you must slow down and explain properly," said Clare," I can tell you've been living it fast. We also must update Jake with what is happening,"

Clare noticed that as they drove further north, the scenery changed from the suburbs of Phoenix to a more arid landscape. They could tell that they were on the edge of the desert. The fast road was mainly straight, but every so often there would be a split between the northbound and southbound carriageway is which would sometimes appear to be a good quarter of a mile apart.

Bigsy looked from the back seats of the so-called car that the rental company had given them. Even this scaled-down one was more like a small van. Huge by British standards with sliding doors for the back section. It also had a brilliant air-conditioning system which kept everyone cool.

"I can see why this size 'car' is so useful now," he remarked, stretching his legs out in the back.

# Navajo Nation

She heard about a place people were smilin',
They spoke about the red man's way, how they loved the land
And they came from everywhere to the Great Divide
Seeking a place to stand or a place to hide

Down in the crowded bars out for a good time,
Can't wait to tell you all what it's like up there
And they called it paradise, I don't know why
Somebody laid the mountains low while the town got high

*The Last Resort - Glenn Frey / Don Henley*

# *Dangerous bends*

Clare watched the scenery as Chuck continued to drive north at a steady speed for two hours and then turned east onto the I-40. She could tell that both Chuck and Bigsy were tired and that this drive was their first chance to unwind, maybe since they had left the hotel back in Scottsdale.

"We will keep going along this road for about a couple of hours," Chuck said, "By then we will be around 250 miles from the Scottsdale hotel. It is far enough away for us to be harder to trace. And it's also in the right direction for us heading towards the ranges. It will be good to take a break then."

"I think you and Bigsy are way ahead of me about what's happening," said Clare. She considered asking Chuck if he would prefer her to take over the driving, but he seemed engaged with the task on these smooth roads.

Chuck signalled and pulled off of the main road and into what looked like a 1950s motel. Clare thought it looked like a classic design and would have made a good venue for a television series.

"This will be a great spot for us this evening," said Chuck.

By now the sun was setting, and there was an orange glow

across the scene. They climbed out of the car and Chuck led the way into the small reception of the motel. As they walked across, it amused Clare and Bigsy to see a dozen Prairie dogs lined up along the roadside, like so many inquisitive meerkats. Chuck asked for four rooms and after a short discussion paid with cash.

"It's for overnight," he said," And we will leave here early tomorrow morning." Then he turned to Bigsy, "Meantime, we should find somewhere to eat, and we can try to explain what has been happening, to update Clare."

Across from the motel was a small diner, and they walked across to the entrance. They ordered some burgers and coffees and talked about the last couple of days events.

In the room's corner, a television was playing the local news. A traffic incident showed up. A blue convertible had crashed off a bridge and into a river. Bigsy noticed it first.

"Chuck you'd better look. Is that Mike's car?" he whispered. Chuck stood up and walked closer to hear the sound better.

"Bigsy, it's happened again. That was Mike. He's gone like Ben. The news report shows his car crashed clean off the bridge and into the river. It was a 100-foot fall. They have not found the body yet, but there's no way that Mike could have survived that. Remember, this was the second attempt to get Mike. I thought he should have changed that car. It was too distinctive. Although, strangely enough, they are not mentioning anything about the car's content. Mike's trunk was 'fully loaded'."

"If they think there was something suspicious about the car, then they may hold the information back on purpose?"

suggested Bigsy. "…And I presume there's no link back to us?"

"Nothing," said Chuck. "I was very careful when we left the car to check for lost belongings. There will be fingerprints and so on, but not anything more obvious to create a fast and direct link to us."

"I wondered about those other bags in the back," said Bigsy, "They felt kind of heavy."

"Yes, weapons," said Chuck, "Mike had a one-man army provisioned into the trunk of that car."

"That news means they won't give up looking for me," said Chuck.

", I think we could give them the slip after we stopped at that shopping mall and then switched to this car. They would need to be very on the ball to keep up with that switch. I think we were also very careful around the airport, so I don't think they have followed us. I think we have an advantage as long as we don't do the things they will predict."

"But what about going to the military ranges?" asked Clare, "Surely, they will expect that?"

"Maybe," said Chuck, "But it is a huge area to monitor."

"But what about phones and other things they could use to track us?" asked Clare.

"They don't have my cell phone identity, nor either of yours. I didn't give that information to Mike either," said Chuck, "At the moment we are clean."

"They don't know about me, either," said Tom, "That could also be useful later on."

"It's a pity that Bigsy has already been linked to me," said Chuck," Although I don't think they could link Clare at the moment. When I asked you guys to come over to join me, it was to help me find information without it being detected. Look, Clare, I think we need to bring you up to date."

Chuck recounted the previous events to Clare, and Bigsy and Tom added what information they could remember.

"Well we still have one advantage that neither me nor Jake is known to your pursuers, Chuck," said Clare, "As Bigsy has been seen with you, it could compromise him being involved in the next stage."

"So, here's what I think is happening from the way you describe it. You, Chuck, and some of your ex-colleagues have been called back to this base where you used to work. We know it's something to do with this special missile guidance but that the project was cancelled." Clare twisted the top of her coffee mug around through a quarter turn.

"I'm guessing that this guidance technology has resurfaced even if it is defunct and superseded. For some reason the people that know of its existence are being eliminated. Although it's strange because you guys were users of the technology and different people were its inventors." She moved her coffee cup another quarter turn.

"Agreed," said Chuck. "I was thinking the same thing. We were also the people that knew where the individual scientists had gone after they finished their work on this assignment."

"We were each responsible for the re-allocation of between one and three of the lead scientists. I had to take one to Seattle and another one to Washington. Mike had a couple in Portland, Oregon and I think he had another one somewhere in New York."

"That part was more-or-less babysitting them until they got to their new roles. Kind of breaking the trail back to New Mexico."

"So," said Clare, "Maybe they are trying to track down the originators of the technology?"

"That's a good point," said Bigsy," But why would they tried to restart this after all of that time?"

"I'm not sure," said Clare," But I wonder if it's because some of the ideas were in the original design were perhaps ahead of their time?"

"That's a good point," said Bigsy, "If some of the systems worked too slow or were maybe  too large then the technology will have moved on."

"That's it," said Clare," Maybe with a modern design they can make everything smaller and faster?"

Chuck said, "Yes, I think you're right. The idea was to get the little transponder devices to the size of a credit card. Then to male them about as thin as a credit card too. The early ones we used were about the size of a paperback book, so they were hardly discreet."

"Chuck, you know I spend quite a lot of time working with

technology. Computers and the like?" said Bigsy.

"I expect nowadays they could shrink that device down to the size you say. It's like the credit cards that can be used for remote payment. There's a little computer inside the credit card and also a large aerial that runs around the edge of the card. I expect for these devices they would also need a small battery, but it will also need to last for I'm guessing several years."

Bigsy picked up a piece of paper and drew a small sketch. It was a credit card with a microchip on it and an aerial around the edge. He added a small circle about the size of a coin that was the battery.

"There," said Bigsy, "My back of an envelope design for the transponder using today's technology."

Clare looked at the picture and then at Bigsy. "I think you've just drawn something like a transit card?"

"Yes, it's like the Oyster card used in London, but with a self-contained battery," said Bigsy, "all stuff that is readily available nowadays. Which reminds me, I've always wanted to take one of those Oyster cards apart."

"If you are right, then this introduces a whole new small form of targeting device. Such a small targeting device could be planted pretty much anywhere and could remain undetected for a very long time," said Chuck.

"Although, for regular military use nowadays, they still would not be much good. The speed of activation was a bigger problem. The slow pulses sent out to preserve battery. The reliance on phone carrier signals or Wi-Fi. I can understand why the system was scrapped."

Chuck continued, "By comparison, we already have pretty sophisticated laser targeting devices which can be used to light up a target from the ground for detonation by either a military plane or even by a drone aircraft. It's much more usable in a field situation."

"So maybe this is not something for the military?" questioned Clare.

"Maybe for others. I think you are right," said Chuck, "Maybe this could be something very interesting to terrorists or assassins."

"I can see what you're thinking," said Bigsy, "It would be possible to set up a target for future use."

Clare nodded, "but I suppose that even Google maps could be used for some of that nowadays. For example, to type in the coordinates using the GPS grid?"

"Yes," said Chuck, "That's pretty much how it works in a battlefield nowadays, although the grid can be inaccurate on purpose within a war zone area. These little devices could be used to set up a target which could be very refined such as a person or a vehicle, and it could be used even when GPS is switched off, such as in a war zone."

"But what about the other parts?" asked Bigsy," You know, the part that goes into the warhead or another device?"

Chuck said," Yes, that was a big problem with the work that was going on. The response time of the system was both technical and physical. I mentioned this when we were together in the desert Bigsy. It wasn't easy to make the missiles change direction, and every device needed a different setup of connections. It was a big problem. No standardisation."

"But, of course, if you are a terrorist you don't need all the kinds of weapons to work. You just need one or two," said Bigsy.

"Correct and also scary. I'd partly forgotten what it was like working with you two, "said Chuck," But now it's all coming back."

He smiled.

# *Saddle up*

Bigsy remembered that Chuck had suggested they made an early start the next morning. He realised for Clare this was easy. She'd relaxed in the previous hotel with the added benefit of being pampered in a spa.

Bigsy considered his condition by comparison. He had been drugged, hauled around the countryside, slept rough, been in hiding plus the worry of finding Clare again. It had taken its toll, so the current bed felt soft and welcoming.

There was a loud knock at the door of his room. He looked at the clock. 6:30am. The time that Chuck had suggested for them to leave.

He looked through the spyhole. It was Chuck holding two cups of coffee.

He opened the door.

"Here you go Bigsy. A cup of Joe to set you up for the morning. I'd rather we moved from here like we said and took breakfast on the road. Can you be ready quickly?

"'Saddle Up,' as Tom might say. I suggest we go for about half an hour and then find some breakfast by the roadside."

Bigsy nodded. "Thanks, Chuck. Give me a few minutes. Have you checked that Clare is also ready?"

"Clare is already in the car," said Chuck, "We gave you the extra beauty sleep."

"Okay, give me 15 minutes, and I'll be ready to go," said Bigsy.

A few minutes later, as he walked outside, Bigsy noticed how hot it already was, even on the short walk to the car. He hadn't been convinced about the air conditioning in the room, but now he was outside he realised it had been doing its job.

Tom was sitting in the front passenger seat, looking alert and ready for the day. They exchanged greetings as Bigsy grunted and climbed into the back seat, next to Clare who was dozing. Then Chuck pulled away into the light early morning traffic. Bigsy noticed there was more traffic heading the opposite way to their direction.

Bigsy noticed as they moved away from the motel and scattering of other small buildings, they were soon back in the desert. A flat and arid area, with distant hills to the left-hand side of their direction of travel.

"So how far are we travelling today?" Asked Bigsy.

"It's about 2 hours for us to get into the right area, but we will then need to take some care," said Chuck. "I will also want to stop somewhere to pick up a few extra supplies before we head towards the ranges."

# *Esther's end*

The noise of them chatting woke Clare.

"Good morning, Clare," said Bigsy," I see you were up bright and early."

"Yes," replied Clare, "I set the alarm and then Chuck brought me a coffee."

"It didn't work too well," said Bigsy.

"I think yesterday's spa worked a bit too well," replied Clare.

"So, Chuck, you'd better tell us some more about your experiments in the desert. I've had a chance to think about it now, and I can't imagine why anyone would want to restart something that has been superseded.

Surely all the technology is pretty well understood nowadays?"

Chuck continued, "I'll explain a little more of the history. The testing was handling a range of ship defence systems, before the new transponders for the Project Esther came along. We were not involved then, and the systems were routine. They were important but routine."

"It all started with traditional stuff. The scientists were looking at ship-based weapons as part of a defence shield.

This was big guns, vertical-launch missiles and variations of cruise missiles like the Tomahawk."

"The ship defence systems needed to stop smart missiles being fired at the ships. You may have seen it when a ship fires a whole bank of missiles to take down something incoming. It's a kind of brute force system, but it stops the incoming missile from destroying the ship."

"They often refer to them as layered systems, with both missile defence and large calibre guns to stop the incoming."

"Since the work on those naval systems, they have become common as land defence systems too. They are sometimes referred to as 'Air shield' systems and have been used to protect country borders from incoming short-range missiles."

"I've seen that," said Bigsy, "I've seen the Israelis using that defence shield."

"That's right," said Mike," An early system was the one the Israelis call Iron Dome. They designed to it intercept and destroy short-range rockets and artillery shells fired from distances of 2.5 miles to around 50 miles away when the trajectory would take them to an Israeli populated area. They used it a few years ago, but now it claims to have intercepted over 1,500 incoming rockets.

"Israel are not the only ones, the technology has been sold to many countries as part of land-based layer systems, I think it is also called SkyHunter nowadays," said Chuck

"That's right," said Tom, "We had some big half-track systems with boxes of rockets delivered to the base. They were called SkyHunter. Among the Navajo it created quite a wave, because of our Sky hunter legends. I don't know why the American DoD want to name its craft and weapons after Native American Indian Tribes. Cherokee, Apache, Iroquois, Chinook, Kiowa, Tomahawk"

"There was even the experimental SM-64 Cruise, which was called the Navaho with an 'H' - notice the spelling," added Mike.

Chuck continued, "But that's only a part of the story. As is often the way, it was the discovery of a spin-off that caused me and the rest of our small team to be called in."

"So, did you work with the ship and land systems?" asked Clare.

"No, not directly," said Chuck, "We were only called in when the systems were flipped from defensive systems to ones that could be used offensively."

"Where you attack rather than defend?" this gets a lot more sensitive," said Bigsy.

"Yes and No," said Chuck, "It's inevitable with these systems that the research and the results get repurposed. Some of it gets very sensitive, when certain sets of components are linked, and it makes a whole new type of delivery system."

"By delivery system I take it you mean weapon?" asked Clare.

"Er - Yes," said Chuck, "Excuse my jargon."

"They had been solving a problem because incoming anti-ship cruise missiles were becoming increasingly sophisticated."

"They were trying to devise new transponders or waves to confuse the incoming missile so it would think the image of the ship was somewhere else. In effect, the incoming missile would be tricked to think an electronic shadow was the actual ship. So, the clever incoming missile would aim itself at a virtual ship instead of the real one."

"That's where the original transmitters were designed, as kind of cloaking devices to protect the ships."

"Basically, they didn't work because they needed such a powerful signal to be sent to ensure that the incoming missile caught it early enough"

"They were trying to make it harder for the extremely fast and agile missiles to lock on. Remember these things are flying at up to 5 times the speed of sound, so there is a very short reaction time. Which is why the transponders need such high power, because they needed to send their false image far enough out for the missile to have a chance to react.

"I see - like a many mile range or something?" said Clare, "so that they could trick the fast-moving missile?"

"Yes," said Chuck, much like a 75-mile protective bubble

around the ship. A dome above the water, if you like," said Chuck.

"Yes, remember that 75 miles is only just over a minute travel time at Mach 5," said Mike.

"So, the smart guys moved to a different technology to protect ships, called field-effect lasers. They disrupt the missiles with particles of light. Photon beams."

"Woah," said Bigsy, "This is starting to sound like science fiction."

"No, it's all out there," said Chuck, "Sailing the seven seas."

"Meantime, the scientists flipped the logic of the original transponders. From units requiring a massive bubble of energy to defend, they could turn it on its head and use it with a tiny amount of energy to drive a highly targeted attack."

"That's when we were called in. They wanted a small team try out a selection of weapon systems with the prototypes of the new technology."

"That's when your paperback book-sized units were in use?" asked Bigsy,

"Yes," said Chuck, "With the idea that they could be made smaller and faster. We were using them with a range of weapons, from small rockets, jet plane and eventually through to drone-based delivery."

"I personally worked with the initial field-based weapons, the short-range missiles and so on. There were others in the team beginning to use the jets and drones around the time this attack-based part of the project was cancelled."

"And again, why was it cancelled?" asked Clare.

"Simply put, it was funding," answered Chuck, "but I think there were probably a couple of underlying reasons,

"Firstly, as an approach, it was already superseded for use in the battlefield because of other laser and GPS targeting."

"Secondly, and I think sensitively, and this is my personal opinion because there were political reasons for discouraging the use of this on drones. The US had positioned drones as surveillance devices rather than as weapons. This pushed it into a whole other area and one that had a lot of political ramifications."

"Anyway, the project was stopped, and everything was bunkered away like you see the old warplanes waiting to be scrapped."

"Like a deadly car park of old technology?" said Bigsy.

"More like a large pile of freshly manufactured scrap metal," said Chuck.

# *Homing in on the range*

"I should probably tell you something about the ranges as well, "said Chuck. "I expect you have heard of Los Alamos?"

"Yes," said Clare, "It was used for designing the original atomic bombs."

"It was," said Chuck," but it is still used as a major weapons development environment. The leading site is tucked away around a town, but there are several locations outside of Los Alamos in the desert where we used to run tests. We also used an area to the south-east of Albuquerque. There's a massive airbase in Albuquerque and it's also a big storage facility run by the DoD."

Clare asked, "So these were your test areas?"

"Yes," said Chuck, "And don't misunderstand the scale. We are talking about some vast areas. Some parts are public access, even tourist spots. The Native Americans mainly use some, and some fenced off as military spaces. There's a lot of space out in these deserts."

"But wouldn't somebody notice if you are doing this kind of thing?" asked Clare.

"The environments and areas around Los Alamos are a kind of open secret," said Chuck.

"Quite a few people in the area work at one of the bases and they are used to planes and rockets as part of the testing. By the way, we don't need big explosions to test things. We just need to know that the armament has reached its target."

"But before we go to Los Alamos, I'm going to make a diversion," said Chuck, "I'm going to go to visit one of Tom's buddies who can help us with some, let's say, precautionary measures."

Bigsy had been looking out of the windows of the car and could see that at intervals along the road were various signs for Indian jewellery and other artefacts. Soon Chuck took a turning to the left following one of the signs towards the jewellery. Clare and Bigsy looked a little surprised.

"Are we being tourists and buying souvenirs?" asked Bigsy.

"You can if you like while I visit my contact," said Chuck.

He pulled up in a car park by two slightly makeshift shacks. They were both selling jewellery and other native American Indian paraphernalia.

A brown dog was sniffing around at the site, and a couple of other tourists were climbing back into another SUV.

# The Circle

"A chance for us all to stretch our legs," said Chuck.

"I might just have a look at that jewellery," said Clare.

"This is part of the plan?" asked Bigsy.

"Yes, we'll be seeking a particular person who can help us now," said Chuck. He and Tom climbed from the car and moved over to start talking to a woman selling pictures. They spoke for around 10 minutes, and Bigsy could see that the woman was giving some kind of instructions to Chuck.

Chuck also bought three small crystals which he brought back to the car.

They waited patiently for Clare to finish looking at the jewellery items and noticed that she also returned clutching a small bag.

"Successful?" He asked

"Yes, I have got a little necklace which has a depiction of Kokopelli on it. It's a great souvenir of this area," said Clare.

Chuck and Bigsy both looked at the necklace and agreed.

Tom smiled, "Yes, Kokopelli is a special deity. Kokopelli is the humpbacked flute player. A God of harvest and plenty. It is thought that his sack was made of clouds full of rainbows or seeds. Kokopelli is said to be a wandering minstrel with a sack of songs on his back who trades old songs for new.

"Kinda' like Aladdin, except with songs instead of lamps!" said Bigsy.

Tom smiled again, "I think you'd find that Kokopelli was somewhat raunchier than Aladdin. Not everything is modelled in the tasteful jewellery that Clare has obtained."

Clare asked," Is this where I'm supposed to blush?"

"OK," said Chuck - "We need to continue now we've just found the location of the person we need to visit. It's about another 7 miles from here across the back roads through part of the desert."

They drove on, and in the distance, Bigsy could see several rocky outcrops quite high and the route that Chuck was taking seemed to lead into them.

They soon arrived at a small house. There were a couple of old vans parked in the front area and a couple of dogs sitting tied with ropes by a small broken-down fence.

Despite the scorching temperatures, there was smoke coming from the chimney of the house.

"Wait here," said Tom. "I'm going to see my friend alone."

He climbed out of the car and walked across to the stoop of the house. He tapped on the glass and waited. A tall, dark-skinned man appeared with shoulder-length hair. He smiled as soon as he saw Tom and stretched out both arms. They slapped one another on the back, and it was clear that they knew each other quite well.

Clare looked at Bigsy," What you think is happening?"

"My guess." said Bigsy, "Tom is getting some kind of

weapons. This guy can help supply them. They are probably buried in the back garden."

"I think both Tom and Red are more sophisticated than that," said Chuck.

They waited a few more minutes and then Tom came out.

"Guys," he said, "I'd like you to meet Kilchii Bidziil – 'Red'. He already knows Chuck and when we all worked together, he was also assigned to help up when we were out in the desert. He knows it like the back of his hand."

"Hi," said Kilchii Bidziil, "You can call me Red - and welcome to my home. I am alone here at the moment, but my family will return in a couple of days. They have been visiting Santa Fe for a festival. I had to stay around here for a couple of reasons. I didn't expect to add to them that I'd be seeing Tom."

"Red can help us in a couple of ways," said Tom. "First, I think he will be able to provide us with some additional ironware in case we need it."

"Guns?" asked Bigsy, "You know that is not Clare's or my thing."

"Yes," said Chuck, "but it is purely precautionary. I don't want to find ourselves in the middle of something and not have any form of defence."

"The second thing that Red can help us with is to get into the complex and the ranges undetected."

"Er- isn't that kind of thing impossible nowadays?" asked

Bigsy. I thought there would be so much security around anything related to defence systems and the US Government?"

"Correct," said Chuck," but that's why Red can help. He and others from his tribe have ways to walk through walls."

"But for that to work, I'll have to invite you to my hogan," said Red.

"Is that the local secret society?" asked Clare.

"No," said Red, "it's my real house in the desert. Come. We will go immediately."

"So, will we walk?" asked Bigsy." What? When we have your Dodge?" Asked Red. "Let's go."

Chuck took the driving wheel again, and Red sat in the front. Bigsy and Clare discovered that there was a third row of seats in this so-called car. They headed off further along a trail, which soon became a single track and dusty. Then they took a sharp right and drove very slowly for another 20 minutes.

In the distance, Bigsy could make out a small conical structure. It appeared to be made from logs.

"That's my hogan," said Red," and it's where we will be spending the night.'"

"Wow," said Clare," this is amazing."

"It is my proper home," said Red, "Nowadays we have houses like the one where you met me, but the tradition of the Navajo is still of a nomadic people."

# The Circle

Chuck added, "Red is a shaman from his tribe. Tonight, we are in his place and will follow his ways."

"Thanks," said Red," although it is strange nowadays because I also get called up on email about being a medicine man. You can imagine that I do a lot of that from the house by the roadside. Coming here is a bit more of the real deal."

"I hadn't thought of it like that," said Bigsy, "but I suppose the world moves on."

"Yes, you'll have seen along the road that we sell jewellery, run casinos and do other things to keep current and make a living.," answered Red.

"Most of us are used to living in two worlds, aren't we, Tom? There is the modern world where we use mobile phones and the Internet and satellite TV of course, and then there's the old world where the commune with the spirits."

"So, if I emailed you and asked to see a shaman, would you be able to do that?" asked Bigsy.

Red smiled, "You know something, quite a few people do exactly that, and you know something else, they get what they have asked for, and they pay a fee."

"Some would say it is entertainment in the same way that the casinos are entertainment," said Red.

"But that's not why you're here, and we have two things to do. One is to find the instruments that Chuck has requested and the other is to spend a night with the spirits."

Ed Adams

# *Starting a fire*

Red started to prepare a fire. He stacked logs in a pyramid shape and outside of this created further logs in a circle. Then he retreated into the hogan and brought out some smaller twigs.

"These are very dry. They will start the fire," he explained, "We need to light it but one of you should do this. He gestured towards Clare. "Clare, I think you should have the honour to start this fire."

Clare looked worried, "I don't think I've ever started a fire from scratch."

Red laughed," Don't worry, we will use the white man's world to start the fire. Here is my zippo lighter."

They all laughed. Red demonstrated how to flick the lighter. He handed it to Clare. He kneeled close to Clare.

"Look," he said, "Put the flame there."

He guided Clare's wrist.

There was a crackle. The small twigs caught fire. Clare stepped back. They all watched, and in a few moments, the fire had taken. It was still light, and they could see black smoke curling along with the orange flames.

"That's perfect," said Red.

"We will let the fire take hold and then we will begin the ceremony."

"Chuck come with me. I will get you the equipment."

Chuck and Tom followed Red into the hogan. Clare and Bigsy could hear clanks and sounds from inside the structure. After about 10 minutes Chuck reappeared carrying a cylindrical camouflage bag. It looked heavy, and he moved it towards the car. Then Tom emerged carrying another similar sized bag. It also looked heavy.

"It's probably best that you don't know what is in this bag," he said, "Some of it might have been borrowed from the US government."

Red returned and sat and sat by the fire.

The darkness was already descending. It was possible to see a few stars already in the dwindling light.

"Now it is time for your alibi," said Red.

But first, you must say goodbye to Tom. Chuck has asked Tom to go back to the desert, to keep an eye on what is happening, and to tell you if there is anything strange."

# The Circle

# How the people caught the sun

"Now it is time for your story," said Red. "But first, you must say goodbye to Tom.

Chuck has asked Tom to go back to the desert, to keep an eye on what is happening, and to tell you if there is anything strange."

Tom walked around the circle, looked each of them in the eyes, hugged them and said, "Walk with beauty"

Bigsy could see Clare looking slightly tearful.

"Walk tall," said Bigsy to Tom.

Tom smiled, "Yeah, and walk straight; I know that one!"

He laughed as he walked back towards his 4x4. I'll be seeing you guys!" and with that he took off is a cloud of desert dust.

Red continued, "The reason you visited me was to sample my hogan and hear one of my stories. Remember this well in case you are asked about the encounter by anyone."

He looked up towards the dark night sky. A red spark from the fire cracked and spiralled upwards. He began.

"Saynday's world was dark, and he kept falling over things. He began to get angry because the darkness made him clumsy.

Then, just when he was losing his temper he crashed into his friends, Fox, Deer, and Magpie.

Magpie flew straight up in the air, but Fox and Deer were hurt when Saynday tripped over them and did not try to move.

"Look where you're going, can't you?" Fox demanded.

'It seems to me you could do better than that," said Deer.

"Well you try it and see how you make out," Saynday snapped, sitting down by a prairie dog hole.

All of them were fed up with the darkness.

"What we really need is some light," Deer said, "I can't tell if I'm eating grass or weeds. Sometimes the weeds taste disgusting and make me feel sick."

"Well, at least you can find something to eat," said Fox.

"How would you like it if you had to run after your food and catch it in the dark? Something I thought was a rabbit turned out to be a bear, and nearly ate me."

"What about you?" Saynday asked Magpie.

"Well," answered Magpie, "I can fly up in the air. When I get extremely high, I can see a little rim of light over in the east." '

'There is light, then," said Saynday. "What we have to do is figure out a way to get to it, so we can find our way around and be sure of what we are eating." '

'Well, you work it out," remarked Deer. "You're the one who's supposed to be smart."

The little prairie dog, by whose hole they were sitting, burrowed deeper in the earth. She was afraid that if Fox could see her, Fox would eat her instead of a rabbit.

"Now, then," said Saynday, "if the light is so far away that Magpie can see only a little rim of it in the east, it will be too difficult for one person to get it alone.

We will have to line ourselves up like a relay race. Fox, you can run hard and far. Go to the east and get into the sun people's village.

When you get to know them and they trust you, grab the sun and run. Deer can carry it next, and then Magpie. I'll put myself last, because you're all better runners than I am."

Fox started his journey to the east. At first, he stumbled around in blackness, but finally he began to see the little rim of light on the edge of the world that Magpie had talked about.

# The Circle

The light grew ahead of Fox, and sometimes he had to stop and put his paws over his eyes, for fear it might blind him. When he did that he rested, too, to get ready for the big race.

Eventually Fox came to the sun people's camp, and he saw that they were playing a game. The men were lined up on two sides, and each side had four spears.

First the leader on one side would roll the sun along the ground then the opposite leader would.

While the sun was rolling like a big ball, the men took turns with the spears trying to hit it. Fox watched very quietly.

One side was ahead, and when the losing side took their turns with the spears, Fox said, under his breath, so only their leader could hear him: "Good luck to the losers."

That time the losing side scored more points than the other, and again Fox wished them luck, and a third time when the score was even.

When his side won, the leader came over to Fox, and asked, "Who are y
"Never heard of him " said the sun camp man. "What are you doing here?"

"Just going along," said Fox, "trying to see the world."

But he had to shut his eyes then, because the sun was so bright. Remember, a fox always sees well at night, and the sun is reflected in his eyes in the darkness.

"Why don't you stay here a while?" asked the man.

"You are pretty lucky. We can teach you to play our game if you promise to play on our side."

"All right," said Fox. "I'd like to learn the game."

Fox stayed in the sun camp for four months, and though he never did get used to the brightness, he did learn to play the spear game. When he got good at it, and the game was going fast, Fox stabbed his spear into the sun, put it over his shoulder, and ran. He ran as hard and fast as he could, with the sun people right behind him.

Just as Fox was about to drop from running, he met Deer. Deer grabbed the sun from Fox and ran as fast as he could, with the light growing and glowing all around him.

The sun people were not used to the darkness they were running into, and they began to slow down, but Deer didn't. He just tore along, and as he began to lose his breath, Magpie dived down out of the sky and grabbed the sun away from him.

Now the other side of the world was getting darker and darker, was becoming bright.   When Magpie dropped down to the earth and gave the sun to Saynday, they had all the light there was in the world, but the sun was so hot it had burned black streaks on Magpie's feathers, which had been all white before. Now the sun became a problem.

Nobody knew what to do with it, and there was so much light all the time nobody could sleep except Fox, who was used to it.

"Maybe we'd better put it in the tipi," Saynday decided, "that way, it might not be so bright."

But the tipi didn't seem to darken the sun enough.

"Put it on top of the tipi, so we don't have to look right at it," suggested Fox. But that was no good, because the sun set fire to the tipi and burned it right to the ground. "Oh, throw it away," said Magpie. 'it's just getting to be a nuisance." "All right," Saynday agreed.

"Now stay there and travel around the world," Saynday ordered the sun.

"Spend part of your time with the people on the other side, and part of it here with us."

And he pushed the sun to the west to start it going around the world. And that's the way it was, and that's the way it is, to this good day.

# *As above, so below.*

"Tonight, our ceremony is being one of protection for each of you," said Red

"We should link hands. Clare should sit opposite me."

Bigsy and Chuck looked at one another and then at Clare, but Bigsy noticed that Chuck had already linked hands with Tom.

They all linked hands around the fire. By now the flames had subsided, and there was a gentle glow from the centre. The sky had turned black and was speckled with stars.

Red began.

"We sit around the fire; the fire that is the sun within the Earth.

"We form a circle. The circle that has another edge outside of us.

"We use the fire and the Earth and the stars to absorb their beneficent power and strength into our minds and bodies hearts and songs just as the plants, animals and other beings are now drawing power and strength during this time.

"We ask for the circle to be filled with the light and enlightenment needed to grow.

"And we ask for the circle and the outer circle to extend to those we need to protect.

"We do this in the relationship of Earth, Sun and Moon bringing this unity with the larger web of being and becoming.

"Within you and without you. As above so below. As without so within.

"Allow us to shine to the greater Pattern."

Bigsy looked up. The sky was clear. There were no stars. It was dawn. He looked towards Clare. She was also sitting cross-legged, looking at the sky. Red and Chuck were nowhere to be seen.

Then Tom appeared. He was carrying two 2 cups of coffee. He handed one to Bigsy and the other to Clare.

"What happened?" asked Clare.

"One minute we were having a ceremony and the next minute it was morning."

"Yes, Red is good with the spells. I only woke myself a few moments ago," said Tom.

Red emerged from the hogan, "Good morning everyone," he said, "it is still very early, but it is a great time to see the desert and where the eagle flies."

"Red," said Bigsy," I don't think I knew what happened last night. I remember the ceremony and a sitting around the fire but then nothing until this morning."

"That is part of the magic," said Red, "As you commune with the spirits of the desert and ask for their protection you can be sure that there are powerful forces at work."

"Sometimes it is easier for a two legged to take on these powers while they are sleeping. I think that is what the desert wanted. I don't think you will feel any different, but you will start to notice some things change as you go about your quest," said Red.

Bigsy looked around him. There were marks on the ground behind him where the others had slept around the campfire. Bigsy assumed they were symbols that represented animal spirits.

"What are they?" asked Bigsy, to Red.

Red looked, "They are some clues for you as you go forward. They are symbols from the spirits. Each one has a meaning. The Elk, the Lynx, The Caribou and the Hawk."

"These will be spirits that will guide you in your mission with Chuck."

"And what do they each mean?" Asked Clare.

Red looked. If you see these symbols, as you would on a totem pole, they have particular meanings. The meanings are representative of the animal.

# The Circle

The elk shows strength and agility, pride, majestic independence, purification and nobility

The lynx is a keeper of secrets; a guardian listener and guide
The huge Caribou is a symbol of travel; of mobility, and nomadic adaptability to adversity

And finally, the hawk is a messenger bringing great intuition, victory, healing ability, recollection, cleansing, visionary power and guardianship.

"I think if we have these spirits to help us, we would be in good shape," said Bigsy, smiling towards Red.

Red replied, "but now I think you will need to be on your way."

"Red, these are from us," said Chuck he extended his hand and placed something into Red's palm.

It was the three crystals that Chuck had bought at the shack by the roadside in the desert earlier the previous day.

# *Albuquerque*

Chuck slowly drove them back towards the main road. It took about 30 minutes to get onto a normal road surface and then another 20 minutes before they were back on the highway.

"What's just happened back there?" said Bigsy, "One minute I was watching the flames around the fire and the next minute it was dawn."

"I know," said Chuck," There are some powerful forces here in the desert. I've experienced this kind of thing before with Red and although you don't have to believe it, don't be surprised when something returns from the evening later.

Clare asked, " What's in the back, Chuck? It is something we can all get into trouble for, if the police stopped us, for example?"

"Not necessarily," said Chuck," but it's still better that you don't know."

Today before we make any plans to go into the missile ranges, I'd rather check some things. We are close to

Albuquerque now, so I suggest we stop there for the rest of the day. Find a hotel and use the Internet to check a few things.

Tom suggested a hotel in the centre of Albuquerque. Bigsy smiled at this idea. The chance of a decent night in a hotel, not in the car or a wooden shack or a ramshackle motel would be excellent.

"Good Plan," said Bigsy.

They could already see the sights of Albuquerque appearing, and Chuck headed for the middle. There was a very central hotel with an adjacent parking lot. He pulled the car in, and they walked the short distance to the hotel. It was a pleasant environment with a huge atrium and an expensive look about it.

"This looks fine," said Clare smiling. She noticed that Chuck was carrying a small camouflage bag, which she assumed had been inside the larger one.

"And I will get this," said Chuck as they checked in. He asked the receptionist if they could pay cash for what would be an overnight stay. Chuck rummaged into the camo bag and pulled out some hundred-dollar bills. He counted them out and handed them over for the rooms.

"I suggest we all freshen up then meet in the bar to discuss our next plans. Bigsy, I may need your help with some of the internet things."

Ed Adams

# *Hotel Parq Central*

As well as the main bar there was a row of booths along one side of the hotel atrium. Each one was different and featured some kind of unique ambience.

They picked one which seems to have a Japanese theme and sat down with a couple of laptops. One was Bigsy's and the other was a rather military-grade device carried by Chuck.

"Okay," said Chuck. "Tomorrow will be when the fun starts. We will visit the base and try to find out what has been happening to my colleagues. Tom will guide us in. I expect there's more to it than the old experiments from eight years ago. Some of that equipment that Red's people provided will help us get into the base. "

"Is it guns," said Clare.

"Not exactly," said Chuck, "It contains uniforms and badges. Red talked about walking through walls. I think we need to walk through checkpoints then the easiest way is to look as if we belong on the inside.

"So how have Red's people come by this equipment?" asked Bigsy,

"Simple really," replied Tom, "Red still sells a few items to people on the inside of the base and to assist this it is helpful if he has some ways of getting in and out easily."

"Is that not a major security flaw?" asked Clare.

"Kind of yes, and kind of no," said Tom. "The Navajo guards that work at the base have excellent field craft and great fighting skills. They also still speak the Navajo language. This provides a ready-made code for communication. You may have heard about this being used back in the Second World War?"

"It means if we get into the base using the material supplied by Red, then the base guards will know that we are friends of Red."

"I just hope this works," said Bigsy.

"Do not forget that you'll have me along too," said Tom. "I don't traffic material into the base like Red, but plenty of the people across the security control will still know me."

"But this evening we must check the status of my colleagues," said Chuck, "I know that Ben and Mike were both killed. That leaves three others. We need to find out if they were contacted. Bigsy, this is where you can help me."

Chuck started up his computer and logged in to an email system.

"These emails are not stored on this computer, they are

installed in a secure site," said Chuck.

"You can see this the message sent to me that first told me that the project Esther links would be re-established."

"And you can see the message that asked me to come to the hotel in Scottsdale. It doesn't mention the hotel by name but uses the slang that we all used for when we worked at the base."

"The convention centre?" asked Bigsy

"Yes, that's what we called it. And it was an accurate description often," said Chuck.

"Okay but the location is vague enough to mean that if you didn't know the slang, then you wouldn't even have a clue about which country to visit."

"Exactly," said Chuck, "It either means somebody has been leaky with their email communications or that somebody from our team has let it be known where we would meet."

Clare asked, "So the other three people. Have we checked on their whereabouts?"

"Not yet," said Chuck, "I didn't have time to piece this together when I first arrived and then after the hurried exit from the hotel this is the first chance I've had to carry out any research."

"So, what are the names? ... Klaus Wegener, Barbara Somerville and Tony Capaldi"

"Let's start with Wegener," said Bigsy. "It's the most unique sounding and the easiest to track down on the Internet."

He typed it into a search engine on his computer and a recent news item from Vancouver came up as the first result.

"Man dies in lake," it said. Bigsy scanned the article.
"It says that Klaus died trying to rescue a dog in a lake," said Bigsy.
"Two weeks ago," said Chuck.
"There is a clear pattern here," said Clare.

Bigsy searched for Barbara Somerville and Tony Capaldi. Barbara Somerville's name was too common and there were many hits.

"I don't think we can tell whether Barbara Somerville is the same one," said Chuck, "And anyway there doesn't seem to be any mysterious accidents listed in the recent past for that name."

They looked for Tony Capaldi. Again, there were some mentions, and it looked as if it was several different people.

"Tony also had a nickname," said Tom, "Try again and add in 'Buckeye'."

"Huh?"" Said Bigsy.

"Buckeye, well done for remembering that, Tom" said Chuck, "He was from Ohio."

"I'm none the wiser," said Bigsy.

"Buckeye is a nickname for someone from Ohio," explained Chuck, "it is named after the buckeye tree."

# The Circle

"I've never heard of it," said Bigsy.
"Me neither," said Clare.

"OK - but let's try it."

Bigsy typed the name again and added 'Buckeye'.

To his surprise, a name now rose to the top of the list. It even had a picture.

"That's him," said Chuck, "although the picture is probably quite old."

They read the entry, and it described him as a lecturer now based in Columbus, Ohio and working at the Ohio State University.

"That's great," said Chuck, "we should be able to trace him easily from that."

Bigsy was already typing in the web site address for the university.

"Let's try the Employee self service area," he said.
"I will not hack into it, but I think we can use it to get some information."
He flicked through a few screens and made some notes.

Okay. I have a plan. Here's what we need to do.

Bigsy explained how they would call the University about a personal package that needed to be delivered to Tony Capaldi.

"I don't need to know more than whether he is there. We'll need to do this tomorrow morning when there are some admin staff on the faculty."

"We also need to get some up to date satellite images and maps of where we are going tomorrow," said Chuck.

They used the mapping functions to produce area maps, which Bigsy saved to a memory stick.

"Now to go to the hotel offices services to get four copies of everything printed," Chuck grinned.

"That story of Red's" asked Clare, "It was quite haunting."

"I know, said Tom," He's a medicine man, some say shaman, so he should be good at telling it."

"You know there's a next part? We all learn it. It is passed down from generation to generation."

"Remember you were in a hogan? The wooden shack construction? That's a woman's hogan.

"First Man and First Woman wanted a hogan. They wondered where to build it.

"The Talking God helped to build the first hogan. This was a male hogan. lot was like the forked stick hogan we have today. lt had a doorway facing east. This let in the early morning light.

"The Talking God explained that the male hogan was only for ceremonies.

"What, like a church?" asked Bigsy,

# The Circle

" Yes, kind of like a church," continued Tom

"First Man and First Woman still needed a home where they could live. With the help of other beings, next, they built a female hogan.

"This hogan was made of mud and logs. It was shaped like a circle. This was the place where the people lived and worked.

"That's like the one we were inside," said Clare, "with a hole in the roof to let out smoke."

"That's right, said Tom, "Hogans are energy efficient, timber structured with doors pointing to the sunrise.

"By now, First Man and First Woman had become human. They were like us. For food, they ate wild plants and animals. The Holy People sang songs and gave prayers to let plants grow. Then the people planted their own food.

"Then came the four seasons. In the spring, the plants came up from the ground. In the winter, the plants died and were hidden under the snow. The plants grew into crops like corn, beans and squash.

"But all was not well.

"There were monsters who hurt people. Horned Monster chased people and killed them with his horns. There was a monster that kicked people off the edge of a cliff. Another monster killed people by staring at them until they were under his spell. Then he ate them.

"First Man and First Woman could not stop the monsters. They did not know what to do. Then one day they looked up.

They saw a cloud over a bluff. First Man went to the top to see what the cloud was. In the cloud was a baby girl.

"First Man lifted the baby into his arms and carried her down to First Woman.

"The Holy People helped First Man and First Woman raise the baby girl. They named her Changing Woman. In time, Changing Woman grew to be an adult. She had twin sons. One was named Child Born of Water. The other was called Monster Slayer. The twins grew to be tall and strong. One day they went hunting. They looked down and saw a hole in the ground.

Smoke was coming out of the hole.

"Hmm, that's usually a bad sign," said Bigsy.

Tom continued, "They looked closer and heard a voice say, 'Come in.'

"They climbed down into the hole. At the bottom, they found Spider Woman.

"The Twins always wondered who their father was. They asked Spider Woman about this. 'The Sun is your father,' she told them. The Twins decided to meet their father. They left Spider Woman and went toward the Sun.

"It was long, hard trip. Many things tried to keep the boys from their father. Finally, they reached the Sun. They told him about the monsters that were hurting people. The Sun promised to help get rid of the monsters.

"Before the Twins left, their father gave them weapons and

knowledge. "Use these to kill the monsters," the Sun said.

"So, the Twins left. Monster Slayer used his new weapons to kill many monsters. His brother helped.

"It included killing the giant, and Monster Slayer stripped off his helmet and coat-of-mail and put them in his two big baskets, to carry home to their mother. Then the younger brother, Child-of-the-Water, cut off the giant's scalp, whence he got his other name, the Cutter.

"When the twins got back, they found their mother making baby-tracks of corn-pollen, as a prayer for the return of her sons. She also had a long piece of turquoise, which she held up to the Sun. When smoke arose from the upper end, it was a sign that the boys were in danger. When drops of blood appeared at the lower end, it was a sign they had killed their enemies.

"The next morning the Slayer went out alone and killed the great one-horned Monster which had tried to eat him up. The next day he went to Winged Rock, where the harpy which had pursued him dwelt; and so on each day he went out until the last of the monsters was dead.

"But just when he thought the land was freed of all evil, he spied four ugly strangers. They were Cold and Hunger, Poverty and Death, and straightway he went to destroy them.

"Cold was an old woman, freezing and shivering.
'You may kill me if you wish,' she said. 'But if you do, it will always be hot. There will be no snow, and no water in the summer. You will do better to let me live.'

"'You speak wisely, my grandmother,' he answered; and so

we still have the cold.

"'If you kill me,' said Hunger, 'the people will all lose their appetites. There will be no more pleasure in feasting and eating.' So, the Slayer let him live.

"Poverty was an old man in filthy garments.
'Kill me,' he said, 'and put me out of my misery. But if you do your old clothes will never wear out, the people will never make new ones. You will all be ragged and dirty, like me.' So, the Slayer spared his life.

"Death was old and bent and wrinkled, and the Slayer was determined to kill her.

"'If you slay me,' she said, 'your people will never increase. The worthless old men will not die and give up their places to the young. Let me live and your young men will marry and have children. I am your friend, though you know it not.'

"'I will let you live, my grandmother,' he said. And so we still have Death."

Tom had been leaning forward while he told the story. Now, he leaned back on his chair.

"Wow, great story," said Clare, "The sun providing weapons, the four old women of death, poverty, Hunger and cold. The roaming badass monsters. The twins Child-of-water and Monster-slayer!"

"It's more than a story," said Tom, "It's a belief in our culture."

"Yes, and it differs from, say, the four horsemen," said Bigsy.

Tom agreed, "Yes, and it is a well-repeated tale among Navajo and other Native Americans."

"Thank you," said Clare, "Thank you for sharing it with us."

# *Legal document*

The next morning Bigsy could hardly contain himself. They had breakfast and then waited until after 9 o'clock when they will be sure that there would be people present in the administration block in the University in Columbus, Ohio.

They decided that it would be best if Clare made the call which she did with a straightforward message. It was to explain that Tony Capaldi was to receive an important legal document that had to be signed for personally. It would be delivered later that day, and could we be sure that Mr Capaldi would be available to receive it.

The admin staff confirmed that although Capaldi worked at the University at they could not get out more specific address information. They noted that he was away for a few days but would be back the following week.

Clare thanked them for this information and hung up.

"Well, he works at the Uni," said Clare, "But is not there at the moment."

"I'm sure all thinking the same thing. Capaldi is already in Scottsdale or on the way unless something has already happened to him," said Bigsy.

"Unfortunately, I agree," said Chuck, "But this is where we need some of that behaviour that Red was talking about. The need to know whether Somerville and Capaldi are being chased or whether they are the chasers?"

"Yes, but it has given me an idea," said Bigsy. "If Capaldi is on his way to Scottsdale, we can page him there at the hotel, maybe try Somerville too."

"Good idea," said Clare, "But we must distance ourselves from this. What about Jake? He can call the hotel and then advise us of the outcome."

"That's great," said Chuck, and it should still preserve the gap between us via communications monitoring. I'm sure that those following Mike, Bigsy and I won't know anything about Clare, Tom, nor the link to Jake."

"So, what's the message for Barbara Somerville and Tony Capaldi?" asked Bigsy.

"That this is a courier and we are trying to get their papers for the conference delivered," answered Clare.

"They won't know whether this is something they have shipped or whether it is something from the organiser of the conference. We should say that there has been a mix up with addressing and they are now to be shipped to the hotel in Scottsdale, but would they confirm that this is correct."

"Perfect," said Chuck. We should be able to find out whether they are in the hotel in Scottsdale.

# *Chucking it down*

Clare rang Jake again. This time it was from Chuck's room and on the hotel phone system.

"Hey Jake," said Clare

"Hey - I've been wondering, you know," replied Jake, "so what has been happening?"

"Plenty - Bigsy ran into Chuck. Chuck was about to be inconvenienced by two gangster types, but then Chuck's colleague from their desert days showed up in the hotel. His name is Mike. All three of Mike, Chuck and Bigsy high-tailed it out of the hotel pursued by the two gangsters. Mike's driving appears to have thrown them off the trail, but we are still worried that they might follow us.

"They went into hiding in the desert, where they met another ex-colleague, a guy called Tom, who is Navajo Indian."

"What?" said Jake, "This is sounding a little far-fetched?"

"Nope," said Clare, "Then we drove off into the desert and met one of Tom's buddies, a trader named Red who got us some new hardware for the mission. I know it included military uniforms, but I think there might also be guns."

Jake interrupted, "America, Land of the Free."

"Land of the NRA more like," said Clare, "Well Red is a shaman and took us to his hut - which is called a hogan, by the way, where we were treated to a night under stars and spells. It was all very mystic. Now we are in Albuquerque in a nice hotel, where I've just come back from sipping cocktails."

"Wow," said Jake. "That's an impressive 36 hours. You certainly know how to pack in adventures."

"You know what," said Clare, "I don't think we've even scratched the surface yet."

"Do you want me to come out there?" said Jake.

"Jake no. I think it is better that you stay in the UK. I think you can be very useful to us by helping us to track down some of the information about what is happening."

"Okay, but you will have to tell me more about the direct situation for me to help you."

"Sure," said Clare, "It appears that Chuck and another few military types were involved in protecting some scientists back about seven or eight years ago. They were working on guidance systems for weapons and targeting systems that could guide in a rocket. It was like a souped-up homing device that could be planted on the target.

# The Circle

"The project was called Esther. The scientists were based in Los Alamos although the testing was done in deserts all over Arizona and New Mexico. We are only less than 100 miles from the area now.

"Anyway, the people that Chuck worked with seem to have been picked off over the last few weeks. The latest casualty was Mike, who we were with until yesterday, when his distinctive blue car crashed off a bridge and fell 100 feet. Another guy died in a fishing incident. Another one drowned rescuing a dog.

"Then some men came for Chuck, but he managed to wriggle free, with the help of Mike. Chuck reckons that only two of the original team he belonged to are left now."

"So how can I help?" asked Jake.

""We've set up a little test to find out whether the others have been invited to the same hotel as the rest. Chuck and some of his buddies were invited to a reunion of some kind associated with the original project - Esther it was called. Now we want to find out whether two of the are present.

"Their names are - get your pen ready - Barbara Somerville and Tony Capaldi - both part of the old Esther project and both known to Chuck."

"We'd like you to call the hotel and to ask for each of them. Say you are a courier company and want to know whether to deliver the conference papers to the hotel or to another address. It should be enough to flush them out.

"Then ring me back to let me know what has happened."

"Got it, said Jake, "It sounds as if you are having a great, if somewhat dangerous, adventure out there."

"Adventure? It is one of the scariest things I've done in a while, " answered Clare.

"Hey, how's the weather?"

"Scorching hot sunshine 42 Degrees" answered Clare.

"It's been chucking it down here in London," said Jake, "I was out drinking with my buddies yesterday afternoon - you remember David and John - it was hilarious. They were soaked through and looked like two drowned hipsters - they even made a walk-along iPhone video around Canary Wharf. We all stopped at a bar for some light refreshment."

"I must explain 'chucking it down' to Chuck," said Clare.

# Ministry Moments

"Power is in tearing human minds to pieces and putting them together again in new shapes of your own choosing."

-    *George Orwell 1984*

# *Penny for the Guy*

Jake saw whether he could piece together anything from what he had been told. He started by checking out the names they had given him. He found the same contact in Columbus University. Also, some papers by him related to electronic surveillance systems.

He tried typing in Esther. But found nothing related to the project. Then he tried the leading Los Cabos site and soon found quite a range of topics related to shooting things at one another.

But the emphasis seemed to be more around nuclear research and around guidance systems. Jake tried a more comprehensive search and found some other sites which described similar technologies to the ones that Clare had mentioned.

But it was also clear that newer space-age technologies had superseded most of these systems with laser beams and photon guns. Jake thought it was all getting a bit Star Trek.

He went out for a walk around the streets of London. It was a shopping expedition for some milk and coffee, but he decided it would also be a way to clear his mind.

# The Circle

It was early November. The trees had turned golden, and there was a covering of further leaves on the ground. He also noticed curious obstacles where the council had already begun sweeping the leaves away into bulbous plastic bags.

Jake approached the garden area in the centre of Hoxton and noticed some kids with a Guy Fawkes on a small trolley. He thought for a moment. This wasn't a common sight anymore. Maybe the thought of a terrorist set to blow up Parliament had become a little too realistic.

'Penny for the guy' had very much disappeared from the streets. Then he noticed the kids behind the brightly coloured Papier-mâché masks were older than he had first thought. Students with some kind of enactment of the childhood scene. He walked closer and could see they were advertising a show at a nearby theatre.

They had cleared part of the path and had that old trick where they had put a couple of pound coins on the ground and were watching passers-by attempting to pick them up.

As someone spotted the coin, they would pull it with a nylon fishing line, and it would jump towards the Guy.

Jake stood at a distance and watched them doing this. They were being remarkably successful and about every two or three minutes someone else was being caught.

A girl from the group spotted that he was watching and walked over with a leaflet about the show. "It's simple," she said, "very low budget marketing to the right audience for the show. We use something small to attract attention. Everyone we catch takes the leaflet. It sure gets attention."

Jake smiled and took the leaflet. He continued around the square. What he had just heard had given him an idea about what was happening in New Mexico.

He stopped at a small shop to pick up some groceries and then headed back to the office.

…

Clare's phone rang. It was early evening. The number showed as Jake's mobile.

"Hi Jake," she said.

"Hi Clare, I've been thinking about your situation with Chuck. Suppose that technology isn't used anymore because of all this new stuff. Suppose the military has decided it's a dead end. That doesn't mean it isn't something that somebody else could use. I think sometimes a simpler technology could still be very useful."

"What do you mean?" asked Clare.

"There are still many people who couldn't use fancy laser guns but would find a simple technology that could deliver something to a target very interesting."

"What like terrorists?" asked Clare.

"Exactly," said Jake, "Or any hired guns that need to create disruption without the expense of a full army. What's the word, Asymmetric warfare?"

"But I thought the homing devices that Chuck described didn't work?" said Clare.

"I agree," said Jake," but we shouldn't forget that this was designed several years ago. There's been enough progress with most technologies to mean that this could work now."

"We should ask Bigsy," said Clare, "I'm sure you are right, Jake, and I am confident that Bigsy will know what is possible regarding the way such a transponder could be designed now. He almost implied that the technology could be scaled down to the size of a credit card - he said an Oyster card - with an extra battery added to it.

Jake said "Yes, and that's one thing I can't figure in all of this. If someone like Bigsy can figure out how to build the transponder - even at a general level - then what is it about this that means it is so sensitive?"

"I think I need to take your news to Chuck," said Clare, "But first, did you find out anything more specific about the project Esther and those two people?"

"I rang the hotel. They knew about both of the guests, although they said that Barbara Somerville had cancelled. They said they were sorry for the loss. Someone has died, but they were not saying who."

"For Capaldi, they seemed to think he was booked in but uncontactable. I must try again."

"I'll keep looking. Let's sign off now and pick up when one of us has more news. And, hey, Clare. You take care now and take care of the others!"

# *The four winds*

It was 7 pm, and they were all sitting together in one of the small booths in the hotel. This time the booth looked middle eastern.

"It's more like something out of Scheherazade or Aladdin than something that I'd expect to see in the middle east nowadays," said Chuck.

Bigsy nodded. He'd been on an assignment to Turkey once to fix a bank's computer systems. It didn't look like the booth — not one little bit.

Tom looked around, "Some of the symbols are quite like Navajo," he said, "Look. The four winds, spirits in the sky, water, the elements."

"But no magpies, foxes or deer?" asked Clare.

"So, you were paying attention!" laughed Tom, "Don't forget to tell the story to a friend. Pass it along in the Navajo way!"

Chuck smiled, "I brought us together this evening so we can explain more about the military situation around the

Albuquerque area."

"As well as Los Alamos, there is another facility in the same area. It's called Kirtland Air Force Base. It's linked to the Albuquerque main airport called Sunport.

"Okay," said Clare, "I guess you were based there as well then Chuck? - And you too, Tom?"

Chuck replied, "Not exactly although we were all very aware of its presence."

"If Los Alamos researches then Kirtland handles implementation. The base is called a material command base. In practice, that means it's the nuclear weapons centre for North America."

"You'll have heard of the original Manhattan project when the first nuclear bombs were being constructed and tested? That was all done around this area, and back in those days they flew the scientists in and out via the old Kirtland base."

"I guess you might say 'welcome to nuclear central'" said Chuck.

"I'll tell you more about the base. The NWC is the center of expertise for nuclear weapon systems, ensuring safe, secure and reliable nuclear weapons are available to support the National Command Structure and Air Force.

"The NWC's responsibilities include acquisition, modernisation and sustainment of nuclear system programs for both the Department of Defense and Department of Energy.

"There are two main wings to the NWC - the 377th Air Base Wing and the 498th Armament System Wing.

"Wow - not the easiest numbers to remember," said Clare.
Bigsy smiled, "But these things sound heavy duty."
Chuck continued, "Oh yes, they are:

"The 377 ABW provides munitions maintenance, readiness and training, and base operating support to many Federal government and private sector tenants.

"Among these is the Defense Threat Reduction Agency's Defense Nuclear Weapons School, the mission of which is to provide nuclear weapons core competencies and chemical, biological, radiological, nuclear, and high explosive (CBRNE) response training to DoD, other Federal and State Agencies, and National Laboratory personnel.

"The Defense Threat Reduction Agency was the part that we were working for when we were involved in the tests, although we didn't operate at the air force base. We were further out into the desert,

"The other one is the 498th NSW is responsible for the sustainment of nuclear munitions and cruise missiles, including operation of two munitions maintenance and storage complexes (at Kirtland AFB and Nellis AFB, Nevada) and the 498th Missile Sustainment Group at Tinker AFB, Oklahoma. It encompasses the entire scope of nuclear weapon system support functions to include sustainment, modernisation and acquisition support activities for both the Department of Defense and Department of Energy.

"So, you were working close to some big explosives then," said Bigsy.

"Yes. Most of them are within 100 miles of us."

"I can see why they have been put in the desert," said Clare.

"To put it in context, there's over 20,000 people working at the Air Force Base; we are going to a different site, to a low-key admin building.", said Chuck.

# *War Chalk*

They arrived at the Los Alamos site and followed the plan with Chuck changing into the uniform and then using the access pass to gain entry to the building. It worked well, and it surprised both Bigsy and Clare that there had been so little effort required to gain access.

Chuck looked the part wearing the uniform and knew the best things to say at the entrance. He'd arrived by taxi and used the pretence of meeting a particular person to get through to the cafe area within the building. Because he had an access pass, there was no problem for him to do this and he was not treated as someone that needed to be escorted around the site.

Chuck bought a coffee and sat down for around ten minutes, by which time he looked part of the establishment. Then he made his way to the restrooms adjoining the cafeteria and after a short time, moved towards the back of the building. He could see that the cafe area had back doors and that they led towards the area he had seen on the map.

He noted this and retraced his steps towards the admin block.

# The Circle

It would be easy enough to get to the right area, but he was not sure how he could gain access to the files he wanted.

He approached the area and asked one of the administrators about the project. He said he was only looking for the year of the record- nothing more and could he borrow the file.

The administrator said she would need to check whether it was still restricted but came back a few minutes later with a folder.

"There's no restriction on the basic file," she said, "but there's also nothing in it. Here - you can take a look," She handed him a manila folder which contained a couple of typed sheets. It provided a two-line description of the program and a summary of its status as 'Closed - No further action - Technology superseded'

He looked at the folder again, and at the sheets. Nothing untoward.

This had been very easy but had given no information. As he was handing the sheets back to the administrator, he noticed something on the cover. It was two halves of a circle with the word Esther2022 written above it.

Chuck recognised the symbol immediately. It was a warchalk. Something he had not seen for several years but was once a way to communicate about access to private networks. They had started in the days before wi-fi and internet signals were pervasive and were a way that hackers signalled to one another about networks they had found.

This was clearly a pointer to such a network, which Chuck suspected would give further information about the project.

He realised there could be a problem though; that the signal was only available from within the facility.

He returned to the cafeteria and to see if it was possible to gain access. He had his phone and could try with that.

A few minutes later, he had a second coffee and was accessing his phone, very much as if he was reading emails or doing any of the normal corporate things people did while they were waiting.

He tried the node, and to his surprise, he found it immediately. It was not broadcasting its presence, but once he had typed in the identity, it let him in without asking any security questions. He looked at what it provided. It was a code GC1G655. That was all it said. He wrote it down and flipped off his phone. He would leave now and based on what he had found, he could exit through the front door rather than climbing through the cafeteria and over the bins. Much tidier.

He was sure the combination of the warchalk and code was what he needed but he didn't know what the code referred to at all.

# *Vauxhall Cross*

In London, Jake continued to review the various web sites and contact names they had given him. The work related to what he assumed was Project Esther was available. The technology had moved along and that the Esther project had been parked.

He had also tried further searches for Tony Capaldi and found him listed for both his work at the University but also some other work related to radiofrequency spectrum.

This was consistent with him being involved with the transponders, but his work seemed to have veered towards educational systems including ways to provide peer communication amongst devices.

This all looked mainstream to Jake and not suspicious although it provided the tie in with the earlier other work.

He decided also to look at other related papers and content that might shed some further light on what had taken place. Everything pointed the same way that Chuck had described it. The technology was superseded, and the more space-age sounding laser guns and something called a dazzler, which was about as close as it got to making ray guns for real.

The other names Chuck had provided him didn't feature.

Jake noticed that there were many references to GOT (which he realised wasn't the TV show). It referred to Go Onto Target systems and semi-active homing used to send a signal from the target to the incoming device.

These systems were using variations of SSKP Single Shot Kill Probability enhancement, and this gave Jake a few more ways to search around for information. It comprised systems to light up a target with laser beams and then fire a missile. Jake decided it was a variation of the homing system that Chuck had tested.

None of what he discovered was helping Jake to find out the reasons for the interest in Chuck and the others. Jake had been working on this for several hours and could feel his eyes gazing over.

# *Amanda Miller*

There was a sudden noise as the office security phone bleeped. Jake flickered back from his reverie. A visitor to the office? He looked at the entry phone picture.

A dark-haired smart-looking woman dressed for business looked into the camera. Jake thought she had piercing eyes.

He answered the door via the speakerphone.
"Mr Lambers?" Asked the woman.
"Er yes" answered Jake, "How can I help you."
"May I come in?" she asked.
"Who are you?" asked Jake.

"I'm from security services. We are aware of your little excursion to America and the items you are uncovering," she said. "We need to ask you a few questions."

"Can you show me some proof?" Asked Jake and the woman produced a very official-looking badge and also a smaller pass card which had SI6 written large on it.

"You'd better come in," said Jake and buzzed her in.

"I've brought a couple of colleagues," she said. She gestured behind, and Jake could see two policemen standing wearing bullet-proof vests.

"I'm not expecting any trouble because we want to help you," said the woman.

"You've been creating quite some interest with your use of search terms: Esther, SSKP and even Go Onto Target were the technological equivalent of looking for 'how to make a bomb' on the internet.

Your internet location was intercepted and monitored. Not just by the British, but by at least a couple of other agencies."

"Am I under arrest?" asked Jake.

"And why would that be?" replied the woman.

"Precisely, "Said Jake, "What if I were to say 'No, I won't come along'?"

"It would be better for you and also for your friends with Colonel Manners in Arizona," said the man.

"How do you know this?" asked Jake. He was sure they had been careful.

"Your activity with your computer led us to realise that something was happening. We have been monitoring you for the last 24 hours."

"I'm not sure that is legal," said Jake.

# The Circle

"I'm not sure that some of the things you have been doing would be classed as legal if we want to get particular about it," said the woman.

"Okay," said Jake, "Just give me a minute."

He looked into the office, picked up his keys, his phone and a small memory stick.

He would go with them but wasn't sure if this was his brightest move.

They walked outside to a waiting black Jaguar car.

"Please get in," said the woman.

Jake sat in the back on one side; the woman sat in the back on the other side. One of the policemen sat in the front passenger seat, and the other sat in the remaining empty seat in a second car.

As they pulled away, Jake noticed that there were also two motorcycles with police officers which now moved to the front of his car, then another vehicle dropped into a gap in front. He was now in the middle of a three-car convoy, led by two motorcycles.

"Thank you for co-operating", said the woman, "I think you can see it was a lot simpler that you've agreed to come along voluntarily. My name is Amanda Miller. I work for SI6. You seem to be tripping a lot of wires with your recent investigations. I hope you've only tripped wires that we can see."

"You must tell me more than this," said Jake, "I won't deny accessing the sites, but I've not done anything wrong, and everything I've looked at has been in the public domain."

"Agreed," said Miller, "but you and your friends have stirred a hornets' nest. I think all of you are now in danger."

# *Route SI6*

Jake recognised the route from Hoxton down towards the Embankment and then along to Vauxhall Bridge, where they turned left. He assumed they were heading for the SI6 building on the south side of the Thames and, sure enough, they took another left and then down a slope into an underground area.

Jake noticed that the route had been continuously moving which implied he had received some priority treatment based on being part of a cavalcade of police cars. He thought this was a new record to cross this area of London.

He looked across the back seat to the woman, "Okay, Ms Miller."

"Call me Amanda."

"Okay, Ms Amanda Miller, why are you so insistent on bringing me here?"

"I think you and your friends have got caught up in something

163

which has international dimensions. Not that you are in the USA, but that there are other forces at play."

"Okay, and the reason you need to bring me here?"

"In the short term, it is for your protection. We will want to ask you some questions, and I notice that so far you have been very cooperative. It would be better if it stayed that way. We want to protect you and your colleagues while getting access to the information that you uncover."

They led Jake from the car and into a reception area. There were conventional office security systems in use. Glass barriers and swipe cards. There didn't seem to be anything robust about the entry security,

He followed Ms Miller through the barrier and into another room.

"I must ask you to leave your phone, keys and other personal belongings here," said Miller. "The people over there will look after them for you and give you a small token that you can use to release them later."

"And if I say No?" Asked Jake.

"Please, Mr Lambers, please continue to co-operate. We have your interests at heart."

Jake noticed that other people were entering the room and going through a similar process. He remembered doing Jury Service once and that there had been a similar process to stop mobile phones from being used in the courtroom.

"As you can see," said Miller, "This is a routine procedure.

# The Circle

We need to know you are not photographing or recording things inside the building."

Jake emptied his pockets, keys, phone, the memory stick.

"What about my money?" asked Jake.

"You can keep that," said Amanda, "Although I'll be buying the coffee."

The woman behind the counter scanned Jake's wallet with a small device. There was a beep. "It'll be your Oyster card," she said. "They have aerials inside them."

Jake opened the wallet and flicked through the cards. The Oyster card was in there. He removed it, and the security woman tried scanning the wallet again.

This time it was clear. "I'll add the Oyster card to your stored items," she said.

Jake nodded. A significant security risk - his Oyster card.

"That's fine," said Amanda. We still have to go through the metal detector, which is just like the ones at airports. Jake walked forward and to his slight surprise could pass through this with no beeps.

"Good," said Amanda, "You are on the inside now. Let's go to somewhere where we can talk."

Jake thought about this. He was now cut off from everyone he knew, and after speeding across London in a matter of minutes, he was now inside the centre of the UK security machine.

"Here," said Miller, "I have a room for us."

Jake expected to enter a grim grey walled room with a table screwed to the floor and some mirror glass. Instead, he was now in a small conference room. There was a coffee pot, some cookies, a picture of a field and an oval table surrounded with about a dozen chairs.

At the front was a screen and a whiteboard, also on the wall was a sliding flipchart.

"I'm sorry - I couldn't get a smaller room at short notice," said Amanda," but I hope this will do. And won't be off-putting. A couple of others will join us and want to ask you a few questions."

# Cold Stone Creamery Jelly Belly jelly beans *(TM)*

Jake watched as two other people entered the room.

A blonde man, early thirties, well-tailored, carrying a slim computer. A woman, similar age, bright coloured outfit and Jake guessed she was of a Caribbean origin.

"Hello, my name is Richard, Richard Brookfield and this is my associate Harriett Delancey. We both work for the The National Counter Terrorism Security Office."

"Look, I'm not a terrorist," said Jake - "I still don't know what this is about,"

"No, we know you are not a terrorist, and that your two associates in the USA aren't either. Colonel Manners has some interesting attributes, but we wouldn't class him as one either."

"So why have you brought me here?" asked Jake.

"It's for your protection," answered Broomfield. He looked across the table to Miller.

"Amanda, have you explained what we think is happening?"

"No," answered Amanda, "I thought we'd wait until we are all together."

"Harriett, can you start this for us?"

Harriett leaned forward and pressed the remote-control unit stood in the middle of the table. There was a whirr and then an overhead projector flickered into life.

'Tony Capaldi
Mike Chambers
Ben Leitzmann
[Redacted]
Chuck Manners
Barbara Somerville
Klaus Wegener '

Harriett pointed to the list of names displayed.
"Colonel Manners and his sub-team comprising Mike, Ben and Klaus were assigned to Project Esther a few years ago. There were two specific scientists who were at the heart of this process. Their names were Barbara Somerville and Tony Capaldi

"They worked on the guidance systems that we can see you have been researching on the internet. After they cancelled the project, the scientists were re-assigned, Barbara stayed in the service, but Tony left and took a role in the University of

# The Circle

Columbia.

Although the technology wasn't much further use to the military, it became apparent to the two scientists that it could be used as an element in asymmetric warfare, if the size of the targeting devices could be reduced.

"Is that when they devised the credit card-sized units?" Asked Jake, "we found out about them and Bigsy could even describe how they would be set up to work."

"Yes," said Harriett. She looked towards Jake, "The clever part of the design was more about the way it could hook itself into a nearby network. This also meant they could pick its coordinates up by a remote sensing system."

"Because the units also have on-board batteries, we could leave them for a long time. Up to 5 years, they could broadcast a signal back to any adjacent Wi-Fi or mobile telephony mast."

Jake asked, "but they have superseded the technology, why would someone still want it?"

"That's the point, no one is very interested – no one until it became apparent that the transponders were being produced in bulk."

"We intercepted some signals from China where a manufacturing plant was producing batches of these transponders to the size of a credit card. Think about it for a minute. Mail order missile attacks. Send the unfortunate target a card. Then set loose a UAV-launched rocket.

It took us a while, but we intercepted a sample of these which was being couriered to somebody in Beijing. Our trail went cold, but it's also around the time that some upcoming Colonel Manners associates were being chased and some of them eliminated."

Jake asked, "but if you knew all this, why didn't you do something about it to intervene to stop people from being killed?'

"Firstly, this was out of our jurisdiction," said Richard, "and secondly we think this could be part of some major conspiracy."

Jake smiled despite being in a difficult situation, "Yes, I can understand that if it involves Chuck Manners then there's something big in the background."

Harriett continued, "We need some help now, and because it already involves Chuck Manners and your little team, and we think this may be the fastest way to find out what is happening."

Jake asked, "You just said that this was outside your jurisdiction. If that's the case, how can you help us when part of this is happening in America, and it sounds as if the rest of this happening in China?"

Richard answered, "Things have moved on fast since we uncovered what was happening here, you'll have noticed how we moved you from your offices to our building and that we seemed to be able to clear most of London's traffic to do this. That wasn't for effect. We are treating this as a very high priority item, not just here in the UK but also in the US. You won't know yet, but the Department of Defence are also involved, and we have a direct link with them for this."

There was a crackle and Jake knew the phone system on the middle of the desk was live. It had the regular little tell-tale lights on it, but they were all switched off.

"Hello Mr Lambers, my name is Captain Garcia and I have been listening in on this call. As the man says, I am from the United States military and based in our counter-terrorism unit in Washington."

Jake looked startled, "Can you just do that?", he asked, "Just listen in on the conversation like that without telling anyone?"

He realised what he just said was a little bit naive in the circumstances, but it just blurted out. After all, he'd just been transported across London in a police convoy and was now, he wasn't sure, captive inside MI6 or SI6 or whatever they called it nowadays.

"I guess I got to get used to all of this," he said, "Things are moving fast. How much of this can I tell Chuck and the others?"

Amanda answered, "We want them to know what is happening, but we want to tell them without it being a phone call from you."

"The reason is simple. At this stage, we think it is very likely that whoever is chasing Chuck will have started to make the connections with Bigsy and Clare as well and that this will inevitably lead back to you Jake."

"But we are also sure that they have no idea that we are tracking them from MI6 or from the US antiterrorism group."

"We don't want to give the game away I'm sure you understand, so this means they could be a small gap before we can somehow advise Chuck and the others about our presence."

"So how you do it?" asked Jake, "Will you send somebody to meet Chuck."

"Yes," said Amanda, "But we'll need something from you to help him believe that we are genuine and not another trick being played."

"I see," said Jake, "You'll need something that only I know that you can pass on to the others as a form verification?"

"Yes," said Amanda, "and something recent, not something that could have been looked up on the Internet or from some pub conversation."

Jake thought for a while. He tried to single something that only Bigsy and Clare would know about. Something recent and probably trivial but something that they would remember. There were a few possibilities, like his support for Fulham F.C., but he thought too many other people would know his team.

Then he remembered the thing he asked Clare to bring back from the USA. Daft, but also very memorable. Jellybeans. Not any jellybeans, the Cold Stone ice cream flavoured jellybeans that you can't get in England.

Jake spoke, "I'm not sure if I should say this. At least not say this out loud. I think the password you need will be 'Cold Stone ice cream jellybeans '!"

Amanda looked at Harriett. Harriett held her expression for about half a second and then laughed.

Amanda said, "Perfect. But please tell me this is something recent!"

Jake said, "Oh yes, I asked Clare to bring some back from this trip. You don't think I'd be telling too many people about this do you?"

Harriett asked, "Are they delicious then?"

"The best," replied Jake.

# *Los Alamos*

Bigsy looked out on the morning. It surprised him to see it had been raining overnight. There were still some puddles on the ground by the car park at the side of the hotel. There were early signs that this would be another sunny day. Bigsy wondered what it would be like to live in an area that was an arid desert.

He prepared for the day and repacked is a few items into his small bag.

Bigsy left his room and headed for the breakfast area. Clare and Chuck are already seated. "We need to plan the day," said Chuck.

"But first, you must say goodbye to Tom; It is too risky for him around the base with us. He's still known, and it would be more than embarrassing for him and his people to be caught with a group of interlopers. I've suggested to Tom that he go back to the desert, to monitor what is happening, and to tell us if there is anything strange."

# The Circle

Tom walked around the circle, looked each of them in the eyes, hugged them and said, "Walk with beauty."

Bigsy could see Clare looking slightly tearful.

"Walk tall," said Bigsy to Tom.

Tom smiled, "Yeah, and walk straight; I know that one!" He laughed as he walked back towards his 4x4. I'll be seeing you guys!" and with that, he took off in a cloud of desert dust.

Chuck continued, "We are going to the base this morning. I have worked out that only one of us needs to go inside. That will be me. I know my way around and if someone challenges me, I have the right language to be able to get out of most situations without drama."

"I assume that means you won't need too much of the heavy stuff from that camouflage bag?" asked Clare.

"That's right," said Chuck, "I'll be using a uniform and the ID card to get into the base. Once inside I can walk around easily. I know where I'm going and can keep my time on-site as short as possible.

"What will I do?" asked Bigsy.

"You'll be my getaway car," said Chuck, "although I hope I won't need it."

"I assume from that you will not be taking the car into the site?" said Bigsy.

"That's right," said Chuck, "I'll take a taxi to the base. It will look less suspicious if I show up in a taxi."

"So, I assume we will park somewhere close by?" said Clare. "That's right," said Chuck, "Look at this map."

He showed them an extract from the Google maps they had made the previous evening. It showed an aerial view of the site and several main office complexes.

"It would appear," said Chuck, "we will not be going to their most secure environment. The project was stopped and is off of the radar now. They are far more interested in the new laser guns and photon systems."

Chuck pointed to the map. "See. This area has a setup for testing rail guns and other high energy devices. All we need is a little office block over to the west of all of this. That's where anything we need would be stored. "

They looked at the map. It was a small complex considering the work that took place.

"Of course," said Chuck, "You can't see most of the site because there is quite a large underground complex. We need not go anywhere near that for this little excursion."

"The main extra thing I need is to find a spot where I can be met later," said Chuck, "I don't want to rely on a taxi to take me back out again."

He scanned the perimeter area and pointed to a small area to the north of the office block he would be entering.

"There," he said. "That's our best opportunity. I'm using the low-security area of the site where deliveries or the catering or made. It has still got fences, but look. There are all kinds of carts and general rubbish behind this area. I'll be using one of the carts to help me get over the fence. As long as you are there, we can be away in a few minutes."

"To be honest, I don't think they'll even notice. I expect this site has been sleepy for years. I wouldn't fancy my chances across the way at the main accelerator site though."

Clare and Bigsy looked at one another, "Do you think we will be safe driving this automobile to where you have showed?"

"Look," said Chuck, "There is a regular car park about 200 yards away. I think you need to park there and drive towards me when I am leaving the site. I can be in the car in a moment."

"I don't want to be in the site for over one hour. I want them to think I am at a meeting and for us to be away before they expect me to check out again."

"By then, we will have what we need. They may have a good photo of me, but they know me anyway. Frankly, if I am recognised it could also be a signal to both the good guys and the bad guys that we are on to something."

Clare asked," So do you think this is part of a bigger conspiracy?"

"Undoubtedly," said Chuck, "I think Jake is right that this is some small breakaway team that is picking up this outdated technology."

Bigsy nodded, "Yes, it's hardly ancient if it's only been

around for a few years and could still be dangerous in the wrong hands."

"It's almost showtime," said Chuck, "But I don't want to be seen in the uniform until we are almost at the site. We should leave here in civvies. I'll get changed when we are very close to the base. It'll take us about an hour from here. I'll drive."

# *Tonto (Jay Silverheels)*

Bigsy looked out of the front windscreen of the car. He'd moved forward when Chuck had left. Clare was seated next to him. They had been watching the time, wondering when the moment would be to go to the side of the Los Alamos establishment which Chuck had described.

Then, to Bigsy's surprise, he saw Chuck walking towards him. No-one following, no dramatic chases, just Chuck in the uniform.

Chuck smiled and walked around to the rear door on Clare's side and climbed in.

"Let's go," he said.
Clare turned backwards as Bigsy manoeuvred the car away.

"So how did it go?" She asked," That all seemed undramatic,"

"It was," said Chuck, "The admin area was pretty much unsecured as part of public information, and I almost think we could have got the same information from the internet. The Public Access to Information Bill can explain a lot of things," he added.

"But if we'd gone to the internet, we would not have discovered the additional information that I got by turning up in person," he added.

"What was it?", asked Clare. "There was a marking on the folder containing the information. It was quite 'old school' but effective. A symbol that told me there was a hidden wi-fi network in the vicinity. I went back to the cafeteria, logged on, found it and it took me to a home page with a code reference on it."

"What kind of code reference?" asked Bigsy. He was driving.

"Not anything I've seen before," said Chuck, "Here it was an alpha-numeric string 'GC172NM' It looks like a plane marking or something," said Chuck, "I think G is Great Britain." "So, it could be G-C," said Bigsy?

"I think 172 is a type of plane too," said Chuck, "The Cessna is one of the most common civilian plane types - it would be a needle in a haystack to look a British Cessna with G-C markings."

"I don't think we are on the right track at all," said Clare, "although I suppose there is that big air force base to the south of here."

"Not the place to find Cessna though," said Chuck. "Tank busters maybe and F-15s, but not little civilian pop-pops."

"Okay," said Bigsy, "We should find somewhere to regroup. I think we'll need some internet time to make more sense of this."

# The Circle

Bigsy had been driving out of Los Alamos, and now they were on a long strip of road with a ribbon development of modern shops and stores.

"There will be somewhere along here where we can stop, have a drink and score some internet," he said.

Sure enough, within another mile, they were at the approach to a sprawl of individual stores.

"This is fine," said Chuck. He gestured to the Coffee House Cafe. "Look Burritos," said Bigsy. "This is fine."

"They pulled off of the main road and into the parking lot. As they climbed from the car the temperature of the day startled Bigsy and Clare. "Whoa, it is hot," said Bigsy.

"Welcome to the land of air conditioners," said Chuck. They walked into the cafe. Clare ordered three coffees, and Bigsy added some orders for Burritos and a side of nachos.

Bigsy fired up his computer.

"Okay, let's start by doing the obvious thing," he said, "He typed the code from Chuck into the computer's search engine."

To his surprise, there was an immediate hit. "Wow," said Bigsy, "I think we are on to something. The code appears to be like a map reference."

"It is not GPS," said Chuck

"No, it is a 'Geocache'," said Bigsy, "People use geocaches to set trails for hikers. This is a reference to a particular cache."

"This seems more likely than the Cessna idea," said Clare, "Where is the Geocache located?"

"I don't know yet," said Bigsy," but it's got a name. Er - a slightly crazy name. 'Tonto Number 2' according to the search."

"Let me find a geocache site."

He typed in Geocaching Maps, and to his surprise, a map of the west coast of the United States appeared covered in little symbols.

"Hmm," said Bigsy," This could take some while."

 The map covered the area around San Francisco and was covered with little symbols which Bigsy took to be Geocache locations.

He zoomed in, and there were even more locations shown.

"This could be like looking for a needle in a haystack," he said.

Clare pointed to the top of the map. "Look," she said," it says 'Search'. Let's type in the code."

Bigsy typed in the letters, and the map swirled to a different location. It was difficult to tell where it was because the symbols more or less obliterated the place names. Zoom Out, said Clare let's see if we can find something we recognise.

Bigsy zoomed out, and they could make out that the area of

the map was in the locality where they were travelling and seemed to be centred on Santa Fe.

Okay, now let's zoom right in, said Chuck, to see where this cache is located. Bigsy pressed the button a few times. The map got more crowded, but then it started to clear. They could make out an aerial grid of streets, still with a surprisingly large number of locations shown.

Then it started to clear as they got to a level which began to separate the individual markers. They could make out the city and an airport. It was Santa Fe. They were looking at a map of the very centre of Santa Fe inside a hotel called La Fonda.

"Look," said Clare, there's another cache close by as well. GC272NM. At that Chapel.

"Yes, we have found the location," said Chuck." That's the place where something has been left which will tell us what to do next."

"Isn't this becoming like a treasure hunt?" asked Clare, "Why doesn't the person just put the information in one place."

"It's very deliberate," said Chuck," This is to create a chain which needs to be followed and also to ensure one person only holds that information. Like a cell. I'm sure you've heard of that idea before?"

Chuck and Bigsy nodded. Something was being hidden and there was a difficult process to uncover it.

Bigsy was busily typing in another reference 'Tonto Number 1'.

"I've been chaining along these Geocaches. This seems to be the last one in the series. It's at a hotel in Santa Fe." He dialled up the hotel on his computer.

"That looks nice," said Clare, "Another winning combination! Let's go check it out. It's only around 35 miles from here."

# Part Two

# Route 66

You'll see Amarillo, a-Gallup, New Mexico
Flagstaff, Arizona, don't forget Winona
Kingman, Barstow, San Bernardino

Would you get hip to this kindly tip
And take that California trip?
Get your kicks on Route 66

*--Bobby Troup*

# *La Fonda*

It took around forty minutes to drive to Santa Fe. The route headed to the east and then in a curve around towards Santa Fe.

Both Clare and Bigsy were taking in the scenery while Chuck was driving. There was plenty to look at; this was a rugged country. A mix of mountains, valleys, and desert scenery. All baking under 35°C temperatures.

They arrived in Santa Fe. Both Bigsy and Clare were expecting it to look like a typical American city with a skyline of skyscrapers as they approached. Instead, they were surprised to see it was quite a low-rise environment and that the central area comprised Pueblo like structures.

As they drove into the centre, they could see many people walking around the varied shops and cafes. There was a square near the centre, and Chuck looked around for somewhere to park. Then Clare pointed, "Look, 'La Fonda', that's our hotel."

It was just to the edge of the central grassy square. It had a small entrance, but there was a valet parking spot outside. Chuck manoeuvred the car to the entrance.

The valet asked if they needed any help with their bags, but Chuck refused," We'll take the bags. Thank you, but please park the car for me." He gave the valet banknote.

"I think this place would be difficult for us to park in if we were not staying at this hotel," said Chuck. "This means we can be very central but may slow us down when we need to leave."

"I hope we won't need to be leaving in that much of a hurry," said Clare.

Bigsy looked around and could see that Santa Fe was geared up as a tourist destination. It seemed very Spanish but along one edge of the green square was a kind of Native American market. He was too far away to look at it closely, but could see that they were selling jewellery, clothing and other first nation artefacts.

it reminded him of his time only a day ago with Tom and Red.

"Let's get in here," said Chuck, "And then we will need to find the treasure chest," he joked.

Clare also looked around as they walked into the hotel. It was deceptive; the inside somehow seemed much larger than the outside. It was because they had set up some shops along the outer facade of the hotel. Inside it appeared to cover most of a block.

"Wow," said Clare, "We are getting to some fascinating places! I feel like we are on vacation while we are being chased."

# The Circle

"Don't get too comfortable," said Chuck, "Once we have found the cache, we will need to be on our way again."

"Maybe it will take us a while to find it," said Clare, smiling.

Chuck arranged the check-in and once again paid with cash.

He looked at Clare and Bigsy, "You know I'm paying for all of this with cash to reduce our electronic trail?" he said.

"I'm guessing I know what some of the contents of your big bag is then," said Clare.

Chuck nodded, "Yes, set aside for a rainy day; yours is not the only stash of money that I know about."

They walked through the busy corridors of the hotel towards their rooms. There were various side rooms and a cafe and a restaurant together with a central atrium area.

"If we are looking for something here, it could take some while," said Clare. Bigsy nodded.

"You know what," said Chuck," I think whoever has hidden it here will have found somewhere obvious to protect it. No one will look here unless they know about the cache.

"When I get to the room," said Bigsy, "I will look at the Internet again and see whether I can get a more precise positioning for this cache,"

"Great," said Chuck," but I think we all owe ourselves time some downtime now. We should rest this evening and be fresh for an early start tomorrow."

Clare looked at Chuck, for the first time she could see that he looked tired.

"Good plan," she said, "We can meet in the restaurant this evening for something to eat and then take an early night."

# *Cache*

Bigsy unpacked when he got to his room, he didn't have much by way clothes because they'd only expected to be in Arizona for a couple of days. He visited the small market to pick up a couple of tee-shirts to add to his available options for the next few days.

Before that, he checked the information about the geocache. He found a website he used and once again zeroed in on the area, this time going directly to the hotel. To his surprise, the geocache he had found on the search didn't show up when he attempted to look for it directly. As a comparison, he looked at another nearby geocache. He remembered that there was a chapel shown on the map almost next to the hotel.

Loretto Chapel. He zoomed into the map to find the chapel, and sure enough, there was a geocache shown at this spot.

Then he tried the name he remembered from searching for the geocache inside the hotel. He typed in the code again, and this time the geocache appeared. It looked as if it was almost central within the hotel. Pretty much in the area of the atrium where the restaurant was situated.

Bigsy decided that he would look at the restaurant on the way to the stalls selling tee-shirts in case he could see anything. It would impress the others if he'd already located the geocache.

The restaurant was busy, and he skirted the edges looking for anything obvious that might be a hiding place. Bigsy realised that this location was bustling and that it was unlikely that anything would remain hidden for long because of the sheer volume of traffic of people through the room.

He also considered that it would be unlikely that a lot of treasure hunters would be allowed to wander through the restaurant area unchallenged.

He left further investigations of this type until he met with the others, but he could at least tell them it was the restaurant area that they needed to examine.

Instead, he walked out of the hotel and across to the area selling the tee-shirts.

He'd taken his backpack for shopping and his small laptop computer.

One tee-shirt with an iguana looked good and another which said Santa Fe also looked good. He decided not to become distracted with all of the other things on offer and was about to head back to the hotel when he spotted the Loretto Chapel. As this was another spot with a geocache, he thought he would look inside in case it was easier to find the geocache at this location. It might give him some ideas about how these things were concealed.

# The Circle

First, he looked at the inside of the chapel as if he were as a tourist. He considered he was here working at the moment. The featured aspect of the chapel appeared to be a unique wooden staircase that had constructed without the use of nails and which had the same number of steps as Jesus' age.

He looked around inside, and similar to the hotel realised that there were many hiding places but also very large foot traffic which should make concealing and keeping a geocache tricky.

Bigsy decided to go back outside the chapel and found a small cafe where he could sit with his laptop and a cold drink and examine the way that the caching worked. He typed in the code for the geocache at the chapel again and this time found a site which had more information. It appeared that there were two caches at the chapel: the virtual cache and another physical one.

For the physical cache, there was a further clue in the information. It was written in code, but also included the key to the code on the same page. Bigsy worked out that this was so that people travelling a long way to find the cache had a way to locate it if they were stuck.

He sat for a few minutes, decoding the instructions about the geocache in the chapel. It turned out that the instructions were for a location in the car park of the chapel and that the hidden information was on a magnetic sign for a reserved parking area.

Bigsy realised this was a whole world it had never involved him had never with. But he could learn fast.

He headed for the car park at the chapel. It was really for

staff members and quite small. He found the reserved sign and although there were quite a few people around, he could see a small box attached to the back of the sign magnetically. Inside the box was a small logbook that people had signed. There was also a code to verify that people had genuinely found the cache.

"Great," thought Bigsy, "Now I know how this works it should make it a little easier when we are trying to find the geocache in the hotel."

Armed with this new information, he made his way back across to the hotel and straight for the restaurant where Clare and Chuck were already sitting eating something that looked Mexican.

# *Loreto Chapel*

"Bigsy!" said Clare, "You were gone a long time. I thought you were getting a couple of tee-shirts?"

"I did, said Bigsy, "but I also had a look at the geocache in the Loreto Chapel next door."

"Wow," said Clare, "was it easy to find?"

"Not especially, "said Bigsy," I had to use a clue. The one in this hotel doesn't have an entry like the one for the Loretta."

"The entry for the chapel included a kind of code which explained where to find the geocache. It was very precise and explained that it was in the car park magnetically attached to a sign on a fence post.

"The actual chapel was very busy, and it would have been difficult to hide something in it, and I am not sure that the people running the chapel would have taken too kindly to a lot of treasure hunters running through their building looking for hidden items.

"So, do you think that will be the same problem here?" asked Clare.

"I do," said Bigsy, "and unless we can find something like the clue at the Loretto Chapel, then I think it could take us a long time to find this."

"I suppose the other thing we can do is ask someone?" said Clare.

"Good point," said Chuck, "If they have a regular traffic of people looking for this thing, then maybe the staff will know about it?"

"We should ask," said Bigsy, "but I doubt whether this item is as known as the one across the way at the chapel because it seems to have been concealed from the geocache maps. I only found it because I knew its reference number. When I searched the maps, it doesn't show up."

"That's a neat system," said Clare," It means anyone could hide anything on a map but unless you know the reference you won't be able to find it."

"Yes," said Chuck, "this is good fieldwork by whoever has hidden this item. Tonight, I think we should study this room but then tomorrow only one of us should ask about the geocache. Ideally alone so that we don't draw attention to our full group."

"That's great," said Bigsy," and tonight, I will continue to check on the Internet in case I can find any other ways to locate this geocache."

# Breakfast in Santa Fe

Bigsy returned to his room. He tried a few more ways to access the information about the geocache. There was nothing just the two references to the geocache in Santa Fe and the other one at Kirtland airfield near Albuquerque.

He decided he'd had enough for one evening and that it was time to get some sleep.

Next morning, he woke early. 6:30 AM. He realised it was still an effect of the jetlag because of the time zone differences between the UK and the US. He had still only been in the country for about four days but had almost no proper sleep during that time and he was quite shaken up with the various sleeping arrangements.

Chuck and Clare had agreed that they would all meet in the morning at 9 o'clock. Bigsy decided he would go downstairs to the restaurant and take an early breakfast in any case.

When he needed to meet the others later, he could drink coffee while they ate. He knew that the restaurant would have great breakfasts and was in the mood for something with lots of American styled peppered potatoes and lashings of bacon maybe also a fried egg on top and some strawberries. That would make a good starter. Then perhaps some of those pancakes piled high and dribbled with maple syrup.

He took a quick shower and then headed to the breakfast room. It was quiet, and they showed him to a large size table in the middle. As he had hoped, there was a good buffet, and his dreams of a fry up could even be improved upon with some of the other things on offer. Although he wasn't sure about what looked like apple crumble being served for breakfast even if it was coated in cinnamon.

And the deep-fried bread with eggs yet more cinnamon also looked a little too much after the sugar frosting had been applied.

Maybe his appetite wasn't quite as large as he thought.

He'd picked up a copy of USA Today from outside his hotel room and brought it along to read during his solitary breakfast. He could see the other early folk tucking into their food. There were individual people on business and small groups that were vacationing.

The room was interesting too and the wall had many small squares with what looked like small motifs from native American Indians, maybe with a Spanish twist. He had seen some similar signs before and recognised the similarities with the symbols that shown him after the night around the campfire.

# The Circle

But then he noticed something unusual. One of the small panels looked different from the rest. Instead of having an ethnic motif inside it; the five-inch square seemed to contain something else. Bigsy the realised it was a quick code. The thing used for guerrilla advertising in the UK. One of those little squares that comprises binary dots that somehow make a website address when you point a camera at them and have the right software.

Bigsy realised that maybe this was the hidden geocache. He felt in his pocket for his camera phone and decided he would get close enough to take a picture of the square. It was at a low level in a corner. He decided that it would be simplest to walk across to the corner and take the picture without attempting to hide what he was doing. Fortunately, that part of the group had not yet been filled by the waitresses allocating tables.

He walked across to the square, took the picture and continued on his way towards the metal containers with the hot food.

He'd noticed that there was also writing on the bottom of the code. "Santa Fe Electric," it said. This was probably just a sticker related to the electricity contractor.

He put his phone back into his pocket and picked up some food. It would be better to check what he had got when he was back in his room. He didn't want to draw too much attention to what he had been doing.

Bigsy settled into his breakfast, reading a newspaper for around 15 minutes before leaving the breakfast room and returning to his room in the hotel.

Now he could see what was on the quick code. Maybe he would have information for Clare and Chuck, or perhaps he would be just be able to read the local power meters.

# *Quickcode*

"The problem with technology," thought Bigsy, "is that it's never as simple as it makes out."

Bigsy had got the photographs he took from his camera displayed in front of him. He looked on his camera for the software that reads quick codes and realised he didn't have it. He would now need to download it from the Internet.

The problem was that the special program would not capture the picture he'd already taken. He would need to make a copy of the quick code and then take another picture of it after he downloaded software.

This was all turning into something of a nightmare. He persisted, downloading the special phone App so he could read the quick code. Then he transferred the picture to his PC and displayed it as large as possible. Then using the special software on his phone, he took another snapshot of the code, this time using the special software.

"If this turns out to be a meter reading point or an advert for a CD then I'll be annoyed," Bigsy thought.

Moments later, the quick code revealed a website, he read it on his phone but decided it would be easier to type it back into his PC. He re-entered the web address, and sure enough, his PC displayed the site.

At the top the text looked to Bigsy like an advertisement for a weight loss program using tablets. Instead of abandoning this, Bigsy took it as a good sign. It was what would put most people off browsing further through the site. Clearly an advertorial.

He scrolled through around three pages of unconvincing photographs and text about how these tablets were the most fabulous way to lose weight and came to a section which seemed to break away from the main topic.

"Bingo!" Said Bigsy.

It was a block of text which was related to the project Esther. He read through what it said…

"Project Esther was cancelled because the technology wasn't was not fast enough to be deployed. Everyone involved knew that within a few years, processing speeds would increase, and a dangerous form of missile homing could be created.

"Someone involved with the project has reactivated it within the last few months. They are brokering a deal to sell three components. First, the transponder units which can now be manufactured to the size of a credit card. Second, a new and crucial component which allows the credit card transponders to hook onto a nearby Wi-Fi or cell phone link to transmit their information. Third, the device that is required within a missile or other guided device that can lock onto the transponder.

"My investigations show that the reason for the relaunch is financial. Someone is trying to cash in by selling the design. A small terrorist unit is buying it. They are planning to target key individuals and some locations in both the USA and mainland Europe.

" I have had to go to ground now so they cannot trace me. This is my way to pass the information along to whoever finds this from the original project Esther team. I think it involves someone from that team in this conspiracy."

The message was unsigned and after this block of text went back into more advertisements for weight loss products.

"Brilliant," thought Bigsy." We are a step closer to understanding what is happening. Someone is trying to sell the design that the labs came up with a few years ago. And it is to terrorists."

Bigsy looked at the clock. It had taken him some time to fiddle around with the various software and crack what they said on the website. It was now a few minutes before 9 o'clock when he was due to meet Clare and Chuck for breakfast.

Carefully Bigsy selected the text that described the project and saved it into another folder on his computer. He decided to put the laptop into the safe in his room and tell the others the story over breakfast.

# *Shortcut to the museum*

Chuck was alone in the breakfast area when Bigsy arrived.

"Hungry?" asked Chuck.

"I've already had breakfast, thank you," said Bigsy. "I've been busy this morning. I think I have found the geocache and also decoded it."

"I don't think we should talk about this here," said Chuck.

" You will want to hear this," said Bigsy, "I won't describe the detail, but someone is trying to sell your old project to another group. They want to use it for bad things."

"Okay," said Chuck, "I think we need to move on from here then. We may have inadvertently led people to the information."

"Right," said Bigsy, "We can talk further in the car once we are on the road. I'll get Clare."

Bigsy made his way to Clare's room and tapped the door. There was no reply. He wondered if Clare had overslept or like him had gone out early.

# The Circle

He opened the door using Clare's spare key. Their original arrangement to swap keys was proving invaluable. Inside the room, he was surprised to notice that all of Clare's belongings had gone. It looked as if she had moved out. There was no message or other sign.

Bigsy was concerned by this and retraced his steps to the reception area of the hotel. He asked if Clare had checked out.

"Yes, Clare Richardson checked out about 7 AM," said the receptionist.

Bigsy went to his room, picked up his belongings and headed for Chuck's room. "We need to go," said Bigsy, "Clare has gone missing."

"What?" said Chuck, "Are you sure she has not just gone for a walk?"
"No, she has checked out from the hotel," said Bigsy, "I have already been to reception and also to her room. There is no sign of her."

"Okay, we must find her then," said Chuck, "We should check out and meet somewhere near here. I will arrange for the valet to bring the car to us. We'll meet across the way at the New Mexico Museum of Art. It is just far enough away to create a problem for anyone following."

Bigsy nodded. The museum was diagonally across the grass square. It was only about three- or four-minutes' walk but would be inconvenient for anyone following them by car.

Bigsy was anxious about Clare. He and Chuck could leave, but they had no idea where Clare was at this time.

From a distance, he could see Chuck asking the valet to bring the car across to the museum. He saw Chuck slip the valet a small selection of dollar notes and was sure that Chuck had made it favourable for the valet to do this.

Bigsy then checked out and made his way across the square.

# *Galaxy Defenders*

Clare had woken early at the hotel in Santa Fe around 6:30 AM. She thought it was the time zone difference that had caused her to wake early but then realised that someone was knocking at the door. She went to look through the security keyhole and could see that it was someone delivering room service breakfast.

Using the security chain, she slightly opened the door.

"Good morning, room service," said the waitress, "with the compliments of Chuck Manners."

Clare thought she had arranged to meet Chuck and Bigsy for breakfast at 9 o'clock? Maybe there was a change of plan and that everything had been brought forward. It wasn't unusual given the circumstances of the last few days.

"Okay," she said, "Please bring it in. Do I need to sign something?"

The maid brought the breakfast in and set it down on the

table by the side of the bed.

"I have been asked to give you a message," she said, "The message is from Jake."

Clare stiffened, "How do you know Jake?" she asked.

The maid continued, "This is the message…He said I should tell you that it is important you bring some jellybeans, not any jellybeans but especially Cold Mountain ice cream jellybeans."

"You have to be kidding me," said Clare.

"No," said the maid, "I am from British intelligence, and I have been asked to make contact with you and to tell you about what has been happening to Chuck and more recently to Bigsy. All three of you are in danger, but at the moment they do not know that you are connected with Chuck although they do know that Bigsy is connected."

"Please come with me now, and I will explain what is happening. The plan is for you to be told so that in turn you can update Bigsy and Chuck about all of this. We cannot go directly to Bigsy or Chuck in case we are detected. You are still independent of this and can pass on the message without suspicion. It will mean we need to take you away for a couple of hours and then arrange for you to be reunited with the others. By then, you will know what is happening and can tell them without suspicion."

"And if I say no?" asked Clare.

"You could say no," said the maid, "But I think it will leave you all in great danger. Additionally, the information we wish to give you should help you and us as well to resolve all of this."

"Can I speak to Jake, please," said Clare. "I need to know that this is genuine. I prefer to do this now in my room."

"Okay," said the maid, "Let me introduce myself; my name is Jennifer Burns and I work for MI6. Here is my identity card. She produced a card and showed it to Clare."

"This looks fine, but it could be anything," said Clare," I need to speak to Jake if I am to believe you. Jennifer flicked on her walkie talkie and asked for a line to Jake.

"There have been other people listening into this conversation," said Jennifer," They are arranging a line to Jake as we speak."

"Hello," came a voice from the radio "it's Jake."

Clare listened, and it did sound like Jake's voice. "Hi, Jake, where are you?" asked Clare.

"Clare, you won't believe this I am with MI6 in London. I didn't know they would go after you - I only told them the bonkers story about the jellybeans - as identification - about two hours ago. They took me from our office to their building on the South Bank at Vauxhall. I am still in it. I think I am in some kind of bunker but it's pleasant. Not a steel wall in sight."

Clare knew by now that this was Jake talking to her.

"They have asked me not to tell you about the situation - secret squirrel and all that - but someone, where you are, will explain it to you. I think they want you to go with them for two hours while they do this. The plan is to link you back to Bigsy and Chuck afterwards so you can pass on the message. It's big stuff that is happening."

"Okay, Jake I will do as they say. Look, are you all right?"

"Clare, I'm fine. I think we are now doing more to help Chuck than he could have imagined. Of course, he hasn't got a clue that any of this is going on at the moment."

Another voice cut in on the speaker.

"Thank you, Jake," said the voice, "my name is Amanda, Amanda Miller, I am with Jake, and we will take good care of him until they finish this. We don't want any of you to be hurt, but there is a very high stakes game in play at the moment."

" We are trying to get to the source and isolate it so we can shut everything down."

"And thank you for your co-operation with this Ms Clare Richardson we will look after you and we will do the same with the others."

Jennifer looked at Clare, "I'm going to switch off this speaker now," she said.

"Goodbye Jake, "said Clare
"'bye Clare," said Jake.

There was a click, and there was now alone again in the room with Jennifer.

# The Circle

"Look, Clare, I must ask you to give me your cell phone while you get ready, we can't have you calling Chuck and Bigsy about this. We must keep the isolation of you from then until after we have briefed you. We don't want them to react in a way that tips off the people are following Chuck. I'm sorry to have had to do this, but I hope you will understand we cannot take any chances."

Clare nodded, "I guess so. I am, at the moment, the messenger between you and Chuck and Bigsy. You're about to tell me some things that could save them from something unfortunate. I would be crazy not to cooperate with you. You have my support. Please, give me a few minutes to get my things together and then I will join you. She was already drinking the coffee and looking at the pastries in the breakfast tray.

"That's fine," said Jennifer, "I will wait outside for you for 15 minutes, then we must leave."

Clare readied herself to leave. She left a short note for Bigsy, thinking he'd try the room when she didn't show. Then she opened the door of her room and saw Jennifer patiently waiting along with two other men.

"We will go out through a side exit from the hotel," said Jennifer, "There is a car already waiting. We have already checked you out you need not go to the front exit at all."

They took some stairs from Clare's floor to the ground level and then exited through a fire door towards the rear of the building. A large black SUV was waiting for them there. A further black SUV was parked behind it. They were clearly a convoy.

"Er, isn't this conspicuous?" asked Clare, "Surely a beige Honda would have been better?"

"Yes, they are cars from our local carpool. I thought the same. Nothing says 'Men in Black Spy Movies' more than black SUVs. But don't worry," said Jennifer, "We are only going a short way across town to a location where we can explain more what has been happening."

"We have also arranged for one of our teams to follow Colonel Manners and Bigsy so that at the right time we can we reunite you all with one another."

Clare looked wistfully towards the hotel spa sign as they pulled away.

# *Leaving*

Bigsy exited the hotel first. He was carrying his backpack which now had a small extra content of tee shirts.

He made his way across the square through a garden area with a small bandstand and tourists who were taking photographs and sitting on the grass and various chairs surrounding the square. A guitarist was busking for small change from the passers-by.

"In London, he'd have a contactless system, not an upturned baseball cap." thought Bigsy.

Everything looked very pleasant and like the place that to take a short vacation.

Bigsy arrived at the entrance to the museum and could see his car already waiting with the valet standing by its side. He showed the driver his ticket and fished in his pocket for some change to give the valet another tip. Bigsy looked back across the square but couldn't see Chuck yet. He loaded his bag into the car and sit in it, waiting for Chuck to arrive.

A few minutes later, Chuck appeared but from a completely unexpected direction.

He threw his heavy bag into the back seat and jumped into the front seat of the car.

"Let's go," he said, "I think I'm being followed."

Bigsy manoeuvred the car away from the square. He drove cautiously, and there were many people around. Tourists ambled across the streets as if they were not intended for vehicles. Then Bigsy reached a set of traffic lights.

"Swap over here," said Chuck, "Let me take the wheel. I don't know who is following us, but I want to shake them off."

Bigsy jumped out of the car and walked around to the passenger side. As he climbed back in, he could see that Chuck was already in the driving seat.

"Fasten your belt," said Chuck, "I am going to lose these guys."

Bigsy looked back and could see another dark-coloured SUV about 10 cars behind. It had four occupants who looked suitably business-like.

"It could be that SUV," said Chuck, "but I think it's the guys in that taxi over there."
d out towards the ring road," said Chuck. "I will drive around like I'm lost on the way and see whether they continue to follow us. If they do, then I will find a way to lose them."

# The Circle

Chuck accelerated hard from the lights and changed into the same lane as the taxi. He was now around eight cars ahead. At the next right turn, he cut into the side road and then took a further right. He was now heading back in the direction he had been driving.

"This will help us eliminate anyone that is not following us," he said, "Not many people double back on themselves when they are going to a destination with a taxi."

"Have you been to London recently?" said Bigsy.

Chuck looked behind in the mirror and could see that the taxi was still following. A disadvantage of his change of direction was that the car was now much closer. There was another set of traffic lights about to change to red and Chuck accelerated through "That will inconvenience them, " said Chuck, "They can't jump those them, then took a left.

lights."

Bigsy noticed that there was now just one truck behind them.

Chuck continued to drive fast, beyond the speed limits for the side roads in Santa Fe.

"In a moment I will head towards the freeway," said Chuck, "Then we can throw some distance."

Bigsy nodded. Chuck seemed to know what he was doing.

# *Delta Seven loses it*

Clare's journey across town was sedate. On the way, there was a call from the radio in the front of the car. It was a call for Jennifer.

"Hi, this is Delta Seven. We have been following the Firefly. They have identified us and our starting to move out of our range. Damn, they just jumped a red light. We have had to stop. Now I can see them turning down another street. Don't think we should put on any lights around here.

Clare saw Jennifer's expression change. Jennifer looked troubled.

Then Jennifer spoke, "I think Manners is good. He has identified the people were following him. The problem about this, Clare, is that we were using the people following him to help us link you back together after we have debriefed you."

Clare said, "so does that mean they have given you the slip?"

Jennifer said "Yes, I don't think we can catch up with them

using just one vehicle and we have had to take two vehicles with us to make sure you are safe.

"We are sharing this mission with the Americans, and you can

He pointed to another car in a different lane at the lights. It was also several cars back in the traffic.

"I'm going to try to imagine that this was short notice to get everybody together. Speed was of the essence, and we got a good team with nine people and three cars.

"That's two cars for you and one for Chuck and Bigsy. They will have to look after themselves, which I guess will be easy with Chuck Manners there.

Clare said, "Okay, but this whole thing falls apart if we can't figure out how to get me back to Chuck and Bigsy."

"I agree," said Jennifer.

# Wagons roll

They say I'm crazy but I have a good time
I'm just looking for clues at the scene of the crime
Life's been good to me so far

My Maserati does 185
I lost my license, now I don't drive
I have a limo, ride in the back
I lock the doors in case I'm attacked

*Joe Walsh*

# *Interstate*

Chuck led the vehicle back onto the I-25 out of Santa Fe. He was now heading south-west in the general direction of Albuquerque.

"Look," said Bigsy, "I don't want to leave here without figuring out where Clare is. I know she left us that message in the hotel room about not worrying but: come on, we need to find out where she is."

"My guess," said Chuck, "She has been picked up by someone from intelligence services."

"The room and Clare's message are typical of the way they would work."

"If it was the bad guys, I think we would have found Clare already and I don't think it would have been very nice."

"To be honest I think the people following us were also from the intelligence services."

"If it was a hit team, for example, they wouldn't have been put off by a little red light.

"Frankly they would also have had someone on a motorcycle pith a shooter. This smacks of something that has been put together in a hurry by the local field intelligence team.

"So do you think we have just run away from some people that could help us?" asked Bigsy?

"It's possible," said Chuck but I don't think it was the right thing to do to wait around to find out just now, especially after Clare's disappearance."

"This way it gives us a chance to figure things out," said Chuck

"… and also, to figure out the best way to find Clare again, " added Bigsy.

"One advantage that I have in all of this is that I've seen a lot of these things before and know the way the moves work. If you think about it although you and I have been seen together by whoever is chasing us so far claimed has been separate most of the time," said Chuck.

"We have also not used our cell phones between one another so if someone has some surveillance, they still can't make the links. Also, the amount we have travelled has helped because it would require some determination to follow us around as much as we have been travelling."

Bigsy nodded, "I hope you're right Chuck, you seem to know what you're doing, I just will make sure we don't have any problems with Clare and that we remain safe."

"Absolutely," said Chuck, "The point that I brought you into this was not to put you into direct danger but for you to help me without drawing attention to yourselves."

"We've blown that, then haven't we?" said Bigsy.

# *Private Security*

After about 20 minutes, Clare's car pulled up outside an office block. It was a central hub and two wings diagonally at 90° to one another across a paved area.

Some flags were flying in front of the building, but Clare didn't recognise any of the logos.

"Welcome to our out-of-town office," said Jennifer.

"This doesn't look like a government building," said Clare.
"No, it isn't," said Jennifer, "It's a private security firm that is based here, but we have some facilities. It doesn't draw too much attention, and there's a reasonable selection of SUV's and cars with flashing lights pulling up as part of regular business here."

They walked towards the building, and Clare noticed that the guys from the other car were also looking and that she seemed to be surrounded by the others. It was not very obvious, but she knew that they appeared to be shielding her.

She looked towards Jennifer, who recognised it in Clare's eyes.

"Yes, that's right," said Jennifer," but this is so you don't get recognised."

"We're pretty sure we have not been followed here."

They entered the building and passed through a security screen. It was a full length 'air-lock' kind of device which Clare thought looked efficient at its job. She also realised that she was now effectively a prisoner on the inside of this building.

"Look," said Jennifer, "You are free to go at any time. We have brought you here so we can brief you about what we know. We will want you to brief Chuck and Bigsy and also Jake."

"We will want you to do it discreetly though so that anyone conducting surveillance is unaware."

# *Frosting*

Jennifer accompanied Clare into a briefing room. It had frosted glass walls and a central table, complete with a telephone system. One wall had flip charts, and there was a full projection system built into the ceiling.

"Is this being recorded?" asked Clare.

"Yes," said Jennifer, "and filmed. The record stays here though. They won't be removed unless there is an emergency."

"Okay," said Clare, "You'd better explain what is happening."

"We know that someone from Chuck's original team on Project Esther has leaked information about the project. We don't know who, although some of the original team members have started to turn up dead.

"From what we can see, Chuck is also on the hit list.

"We think he realised and that is when he asked you to get involved in helping him find out who was behind it.

"If this was a small team then Chuck and his associates could handle this alone, and we would never even know that it had happened," said Jennifer.

"In practice, this seems to be a much bigger conspiracy. We think someone is selling the technology from Project Esther to the Chinese. We believe the Chinese are ready to go into production. They would make clones of western armaments technologies.

"It would have several effects. It could undermine the pricing structures and bring down some of the well-established companies. They may not be as picky about who they sell it to. And they can make a tidy sum for whoever is behind this.

"It could be money motivated or ideological. We don't know that because the link to the people behind it isn't clear. They seem to be operating through a web of other people, from western countries. UK, USA, Switzerland and Holland.

"There are three parts to the Esther solution, and we've already briefed Jake about these. Chuck will know about this, although his knowledge could be a little out-of-date. One part is the transponder; the second is the guidance system and the piece in the middle is the unique communication link-up to make this all work.

"I don't understand why this would be so useful?" said Clare, "Surely a mobile phone would also make a homing device?"

"The difference with these units is we can set them up as passive units. They are small and don't give off any radio signals until we deploy them," answered Jennifer.

Jennifer continued, "They are also addressable uniquely, but unless you know the code for a specific unit then you can't turn it on. To start up a unit can take two days because they can be set to have a very slow poll rate. That is a deliberate part of the design.

"If they are to be used in an active war setting, they can have a much faster polling interval, but when they are to be used clandestinely, the rate can be set to be so slow as to make them almost undetectable."

"I see," said Clare, "so the transponders can be placed on things and left dormant for ages. Then they can be switched on and effectively light up a target."

"Yes," said Jennifer, "Imagine a scene where several politicians are gifted items which clandestinely contain the homing beacons. No need to trigger anything at that point, but one day in the future...Kaboom."

"That has to be illegal on so many levels," shuddered Clare.

"Exactly," said Jennifer. "And that's the problem now. If the design is refreshed and sold on to terrorists or state actors, it becomes, for them, an attractive way to create major disruptions."

"Wouldn't the people using it need the other two items as well? The special signal protocol and the guidance system?"

"Yes," said Jennifer, "and we think that is the deal being brokered at the moment."

"We think one person from Chuck's original team has gone rogue and is behind the trade. We think they invited everyone not already dead to Scottsdale so they could finish the job. That way only new allies know about this technology and its planned use."

"So, do you know what has happened to the members of Chuck's team," asked Clare. She could see now that a few pieces were falling into place.

We know that Ben and Mike were killed. We also know that Klaus Wegener died. Chuck has been attacked and Barbara Somerville and Tony Capaldi are unaccounted for. Capaldi we think was on his way to Scottsdale and Somerville's whereabouts are just unknown.

Clare told Jennifer about the signal that Chuck had found.

"Look, we also tracked down some information. We worked out that someone was trying to make contact and Chuck found a signal which gave us a code. I'm sorry but I don't have the code although I can try to remember it."

"Chuck found something written in Los Alamos - in an admin file - which pointed to a secret Wi-Fi system. He logged on and it gave him a code - we think it was a geocache code and that's the reason we were in Santa Fe. We checked the code on a map, and it seemed to be somewhere in the Fonda hotel in Santa Fe. That's where we were staying.

"We planned to look for the geocache today and try to figure out what was happening."

Clare looked at Jennifer, "Dis you know about the hidden code and the geocache already?" she asked,

"No, I can't say that we did."

"The thing was, when Bigsy tried to find the geocache on a map it didn't exist unless you already knew its reference... and the problem I have is that I can't remember the code. Bigsy has all of that information."

"It also had a name: 'Tonto' or something and I think there was another one like it with a similar name at Kirtland Airfield; the one at the airfield was on the map. Maybe you can use that to figure out the code?"

"There's a whole park and forest named Tonto outside of Phoenix. That's where the Lone Ranger companion's name came from," said Jennifer, "But can you remember any more?"

Clare thought back. She remembered they had talked about the code when they were trying to figure out what it might be.

"Oh yes, I can remember a part of it. When we were trying to work out what the code represented, Chuck said it sounded like an aircraft registration. It started with a G- like Great Britain. Oh, and they said it also had another connection with planes. It was like a Cessna plane type - a very common Cessna plane type, I think. But I can't remember the number."

"Okay," said Jennifer, "We can try to figure something out from that G, a plane type and Tonto, That's pretty good."

Her colleague was already typing Cessna into a search engine. Cessna - it says here Cessna Aircraft Company, wait the third entry is Cessna 172. It says it is the most prolific Cessna plane type 'in history'."

"I'm sorry." said Clare, "I think it was a three-digit number.

That might have been it, but I honestly can't remember."

"Okay," said Jennifer, "So we have G maybe 172 and 'Tonto'. Spencer, can you get onto it?"

"Sure," said Spencer as he left the room.

"What happens next?" asked Clare.

Jennifer said, "Look I think we've given you everything we know, and you have all of our information. What I want to do now is arrange that we have a way for you to communicate with us."

"We'll be giving you an additional cell phone the same as your one so you can charge it easily. This one will only have numbers to call me, and we have set it up so that is independent from your other phone."

"Okay," said Clare, "But I still need to get back to Chuck and Bigsy."

"I guess we can call them," said Clare, "I at least can call them using a landline to arrange a meeting point for me to hook up with them again."

"Sure," said Jennifer, "I think they will have left Santa Fe by now."

"Our guys thought they were probably heading towards Albuquerque."

"Okay," said Clare, "We stayed in a hotel in Albuquerque two days ago; maybe we could meet there?"

"Not a good idea," said Jennifer, "It would be standard for whoever has been following you to have asked the concierge or somebody in the hotel to keep an eye out for you in case you returned."

"You need to find somewhere different, but somewhere that's in that area is okay.

"There's a diner called Route 66 which is a tourist venue we could send them there and then arrange you to join them. We can get you to Albuquerque pretty, but you must take a taxi for the last part of the journey. We can arrange that as well and use one of our drivers to drop you off at the venue. That way if for any reason there is any trouble, we can still keep you with us."

Clare said, "In that case, we'd better get onto this then so I can make connect them."

Jennifer took Clare to another room.

"This is a special telephone," she said, "This is our special communications complex and we've it set up so that the call appears to come from a different location.

"We can change the area code to something like San Francisco."

 Jennifer spoke to one people in the room.

 Jennifer returned Clare's cell phone to Clare.

Clare said," I suppose you've copied all the numbers are on this already in a case? all my text messages as well?

Jennifer nodded, "Routine but it's still easier to ask you to give us Bigsy's number."

Clare read out Bigsy's number. Jennifer typed.

"Right you now have a direct connection to this cell phone as if you are in San Francisco."

The phone rang three times.

It was picked up.

It was Bigsy.

Hello?

"Hi Bigsy," said Clare.

"Hi Clare, are you all right?" asked Bigsy.

"Yes, Bigsy, it's a long story," said Clare. "I can't say anything on this call."

"I'm guessing you are heading back towards the town we were in two nights ago. The people I'm with had given me a suggested meeting place. They say don't go to that hotel again. The location is a diner called Route 66 and it is on the old Route 66 in the middle of town. I can be there in an hour.

"Hold on, I will just tell this to Chuck," said Bigsy.

Clare could hear the conversation.

"Chuck says it is 13:15 now. Allowing 90 minutes for you to get to here, we will be in the diner at 14:45 until 15:15. Chuck

231

has suggested we stay away from the venue until that short window."

Clare looked across at Jennifer who nodded.

"That's fine," said Clare, "I'll be arriving by taxi. People are driving me to Albuquerque and then swapping me into a local taxi. They are also driving the taxi."

"If there is any problem, they will stay until we are back together."

"That all makes sense said Bigsy. I'm just relieved that you are all right."

"Listen Bigsy. You need to take care. I have additional information for you when we get back together."

"Okay, nice phone spoofing, by the way!"

"That's all," said Jennifer, "We need to go now."

"Okay," said Clare.

"See you soon," said Bigsy.

# Get your kicks on Route 66.

"We're all okay again now?" said Chuck, looking at Bigsy.

"Yes," said Bigsy, "I think we've had a chance to cool off and I feel a whole lot better now that I know that Clare is safe and, on her way, to meet us again."

"I suggest we go to this diner, check it out its location and then find somewhere else to wait," said Chuck.

"Good plan," said Bigsy.

By now Bigsy was starting to recognise the roads around Albuquerque, and they were soon heading back towards the centre. Chuck was driving carefully and following the traffic at a normal speed.
The outskirts of Albuquerque were new housing estates and some low-rise malls by the side of the main route. Bigsy could see they were on the edge of the desert, and soon the landscape transitioned from arid to signs of trees and foliage.

Bigsy thought it looked as if man was sustaining most of this and that if the desert had its way it would soon overrun this area again.

As they approached the centre of Albuquerque again, Bigsy noticed that they were passing their prior hotel. Chuck soon took a left turn, and they were on a street which looked wide but had a selection of 1950s looking shops along it.

"Welcome to Route 66," said Chuck.

"Really," said Bigsy, "It does kind of look like Route 66."

"Although I'm not sure that we need any more kicks at the moment," said Chuck.

"The real Route 66 has been superseded by the Interstate," said Chuck," but because this is such a well-known route across America it used to be called the Main Street of the USA, so there are a lot of sections of it that have been preserved. It's like a tourist route now. This middle section in Albuquerque is an example where they have kept some look and feel of the old route. As long as there are enough tourists to sustain it, then I'm sure this will continue."

"But I guess you have to be determined to come here if you are in the US?" said Bigsy, "We seem to be right in the middle of the desert in New Mexico."

"Yes," said Chuck," That's what many people do, they will either travel from the East Coast or even from Chicago which is where Route 66 starts or they will start somewhere along the road and head across to the West Coast at Santa Monica which is the other end of the route. I reckon from the middle to the coast is the most interesting part."

# The Circle

"So, I suppose there's quite a few Route 66 diners along this road?" said Bigsy.

"Sure," said Chuck," but luckily, there's only one of them in Albuquerque." He gestured to the left as they drove slowly past a grey low-slung building which prominently displayed the logo Route 66 diner.

"I tell you what, Bigsy," said Chuck, "I'll buy you a milkshake there in about 45 minutes.

"What, a five-dollar shake?" asked Bigsy.

"I think they even do six-dollar shakes there," answered Chuck.

"Meantime I think we should get some gasoline and find somewhere quiet to wait."

Chuck drove on until they reached a Texaco gas station. Chuck stayed in the car while Bigsy filled the gas and paid with more cash.

"You know something else," said Chuck," We may need to think about whether we keep this car much longer. It's from the Hertz at Phoenix airport and as it's a hire car it will be fitted with a Lo-jack tracker device. So far, I don't think anyone has thought about this, but if they activate the tracker, it will make it very easy for anyone to find us."

"But so long as the car is going about its normal business, I guess we'll be okay," said Bigsy.

"Yes, it would be if the car was reported stolen or something like that, when the tracker would be switched on." said

Chuck.

"You know something," said Bigsy, "That may even be useful to us later."

Chuck started the car again, and they hauled away from the Texaco. He turned it around and they started back towards the diner.

"Look," said Bigsy, "The thermometer in this car says it's 120°F outside at the moment. I can see an ice cream parlour on the left. I say we stop there until it's time to meet Clare."

Chuck smiled, "You know something, I don't think the people I usually work with would expect me to be in an ice cream parlour. We should do it. I'm buying."

Chuck drove the car into the parking by the side of the ice cream store. It was somewhere they could wait for 30 minutes until it was time to meet Clare.

# *Taxi swap*

Clare's car had made its way back to Albuquerque. The driver had made good progress, and they were now close to the train station in Albuquerque.

"This is where we will make the switch into the taxi," said Jennifer.

"We've used a local car from here so that it looks more normal than somebody driving by taxi from Santa Fe."

"I'll be following in this backup vehicle just in case."

Clare picked up her bag from the back of the SUV.

"That's the car," said Jennifer and pointed to a lone taxi with its meter running.

"Look," said Jennifer, "The way we've done this means that no one should suspect anything. When you get back to Chuck and Bigsy, it will not be at all obvious that you have been with us.

Clare nodded, "I understand. We seem to have got ourselves into this deeply now. I will also need to contact Jake again to say that all is okay."

"It's fine," said Jennifer, "I think you should contact Jake in a way to keep the separation between your communications and those from Chuck and Bigsy.

"Remember, you are the firewall between Jake and the others. You are also the firewall between Bigsy, Chuck and us."

"I'm not sure that I should say thank you exactly," said Clare, "but thank you, and I hope we can work this through successfully for all our sakes."

"I know what you mean," said Jennifer, "I don't think any of us could have planned for this."

Clare was now in the taxi, and they moved away towards the main road. She could see that Jennifer was following in the SUV.

# *Quesadilla and meatloaf*

Bigsy and Chuck were sitting in the diner. Bigsy was marvelling at the authentic 1950s look of the place. At least he imagined it was a 1950s look.

'Nothing could be finer' it said on the menu. And it featured blue plate specials, too.

There was a soda fountain and a jukebox that was playing old records.

"Chuck, if we weren't in so much trouble this place would be pretty cool," said Bigsy.

They were both a little unsure what to order having just beaten their way through two large ice creams at the store along the route. "Maybe a sandwich?" said Pixie.

"I'll have a quesadilla," said Chuck to the waitress.

"Er, and I'll have a meatloaf," said Bigsy.

Chuck looked impressed, "Seriously?"

"And coffee, please," said Chuck.

"That's two please," added Bigsy.

Chuck had picked a table near to the back exit from the diner. It had a good view towards the front where people were shown to their tables.

It would be easy to see Clare when she arrived.

Chuck checked his watch it was 13:15. Precisely the time he had said. "We have given Clare a 30-minute window to get here," said Chuck, "if she is not here by the time, we said then we should leave."

"I'm sure Clare will be here," said Bigsy, "We gave enough time for her to get from Santa Fe. Even if she was swapping into a taxi on the way."

Bigsy looked towards the entrance to the restaurant, and at that moment a taxi was pulling up outside. He saw Clare climbing out the car with her luggage and walking towards the diner.

He also noticed the black SUV that was pulled up behind the taxi.

"Clare's here on time," said Chuck, "and it looks as if she's with someone."

"Will we stay here?" said Bigsy, looking panicked that he may not get his meatloaf.

"Yes," said Chuck, "We have to eat sometime, and we have at least two exits from this place."

Clare walked in and saw them immediately. Bigsy rose to greet her and they walked back to where Chuck was seated.

"There is a lot to talk about," she said, "Not here," said Chuck," Let's eat and then regroup somewhere."

"It's been quite a day," said Clare, "And I have somewhere for us to spend tonight."

# *Durango*

"Jennifer has given me an address in a place called Durango," said Clare, " It's supposed to be like a safe house we can stay in, and there is another vehicle there for us to use. It's only supposed to be around two hours from here, but I think it's across part of the desert."

"Jennifer has also arranged that one of her team will pick up the car we leave behind after a few days and have it taken back to the car rental depot."

"Now why would Jennifer do all of this for us?" asked Chuck.

"When I tell you what I have discovered, I think you will understand," said Clare, "But I know you don't want to discuss this while we are in this restaurant."

They finished dinner and went back to the car. This was the first time that Clare had been with Chuck and Bigsy. She could see that Chuck was looking all around and as he edged away, he studied the cars on both sides of the road and looked in the mirror to check that he was not being followed.

"I think the road we take to Durango is cross country," said Chuck, "When we get to that road we can easily see if anyone else turns off to follow us.

"So far, I think we are okay."

Clare explained what she had heard from Jennifer. Then Bigsy added what he had discovered from the geocache in the hotel back in Santa Fe.

"It is all consistent," said Clare. "Someone, from Chuck's old team, is trying to sell technology secrets to another group who we think is Chinese. They are trying to eliminate the people that know anything about this.

"Chuck and the list of suspects is getting ever shorter. So far Ben, Mike and Klaus Wegener have been bumped off that leaves just Barbara Somerville and Tony Capaldi.

"And we think Capaldi is somewhere in this area now having travelled from Ohio," said Clare.

"Well," said Chuck, "If we are at this safe house, then we are still within range of most of the places where the action seems to be taking place. To the south-west there's Scottsdale to the south-east there's Albuquerque and Kirtland Air Force Base, and to the more or less direct east, there is Santa Fe.

"In the middle of a circle," said Bigsy.

"We should also check with Jake," said Clare, "Jennifer emphasised tome to be the only person to contact Jake. At the moment the security services think that you two have been seen together, but they have not made a direct connection with me. Jennifer described it as a firewall between us. So, I should be the one to phone Jake. I should be the only one to phone Jake."

Chuck drove off of the main interstate road and onto a north-facing country road which twisted and wove its way across the desert. In the distance, they could see hills, and as they approached Durango, they noticed that the land was changing from desert to a kind of low mountain slopes greenery.

It surprised Bigsy that in such a short area the terrain could change so much.

"We have been driving right along the edge of the continental divide," said Chuck, "When we were on that main highway the country to the left of us was on one continental plate, and the country to the right was on another. Yes, we have been in proper earthquake country."

Busy smiled, "That's just about all we need!"

# *Kirtland*

Jennifer was driving herself back towards the Kirtland aerodrome airfield. The job she had just been on was not something she would typically do. They had asked her to step in because they needed somebody who could relate easily to a British woman, and they needed to make fast progress to make contact.

Jennifer was originally British but had left the UK when she was twenty-one as part of a UK Civil Service deal. She had eventually settled down in America. Nowadays she was dual-citizen and worked around a mixture of the Air Force Base and the laboratories in the area. There was very sensitive work conducted and more routine subjects added to which the open-access programs had meant that there was high foot traffic of tourists looking at some of their facilities.

Jennifer's day job ensured that security was appropriate for the different environments. She was part of a government team but also worked with private sector subcontractors from time to time. They had used a private contractor's offices for the interviews with Clare.

Jennifer had needed to improvise some of the situation but had also reached out to her bosses in Washington, D.C.

It had been a long and somewhat stressful day, and she drove home and pulled the large SUV into the car park of her apartment block in Albuquerque.

Indoors, she called Spencer to see whether he had made anything of the geocache code. Spencer replied that he had been working on it and the best clue had been the codeword Tonto, which Clare had remembered.

Apart from the obvious references to the Lone Ranger and other trivia, it turned out that there was a bridge called Tonto bridge on the route between Albuquerque and Winslow, Arizona. But it also showed up as a geocache marker somewhere on the edge of the Kirtland airfield. Spencer had asked around in his office and discovered that Lucas Wilson was a keen hiker who also used the way markers and geocache treasure trails. If Jennifer agreed they would go to visit the geocache at the edge of the airfield.

"Okay," said Jennifer," But you know what it's getting dark, please can we do this in the morning?"

"That's fine," said Spencer," How about I meet you with Lucas tomorrow at yours and the three of us take off to have a look?"

"That will be great," said Jennifer.

"Hey," said Spencer," Did you hear the other news?"

"What's that?" asked Jennifer.

"There is another security alert running at the moment. It's all confidential at the moment. I only know because I'm still inside the building. It's not in our territory but it links to what you have been looking at. Someone has killed Senator Williams, from Texas.

"It's being kept out of the news at the moment because of the circumstances. Someone fired a big incendiary device at his car. The Senator was on his way to a meeting when it happened. It was out on the open road and although he was in a short convoy, there was a direct hit on his car. All the occupants of the car, including the Senator were killed.

It's being explained at the moment that it was a light aircraft that crashed onto the road. They cordoned the area either side and from what I can tell it's made quite a mess. Look, Jennifer, I was only in part of your interview with Clare Richardson, but it sounds a little bit like the weapon you described.

Jennifer reeled with this news. This was something more significant than the run-of-the-mill situations she was used to handling at the airbase. Smuggling, drugs, unconventional foods being imported, cash in suitcases. But nothing like the events of the last two days.

"Thank you, Spencer," said Jennifer, "I need to get some rest, but I suggest we meet at mine around eight tomorrow to follow up on this geocache. Meantime please keep your thoughts about the Senator to yourself. We should try to find out more before we make any hasty connections.

"Are you still at the office?" asked Jennifer.

"Yes," said Spencer," I was just about to leave."

 "Maybe, please, you could pull some information about that Senator before you go," said Jennifer.

"Done already," chuckled Spencer.

# Bagels, Guns, Shacks and Oilfields

I'm a picker
I'm a grinner
I'm a lover
And I'm a sinner
I play my music in the sun

*Steve Miller – The Joker*

# *Einstein bagels for breakfast*

Jennifer was fixing some coffee when the doorbell rang. She flicked on the camera phone and could see Spencer at the main entrance. She buzzed him in, "Come on up Spencer."

A few minutes later Spencer arrived at her door, and she let him in.

"I'm just fixing some coffee," said Jennifer, "Would you like some?"

"Great," said Spencer, "But I've left Lewis downstairs in the car. Have you had some breakfast yet?"

"No," said Jennifer.

"It's lucky then," said Spencer, "That I brought this with me."

He held out his hand, and there was a bag containing two bagels.

"We got them from Einstein Bros," said Spencer, "We thought they would set us up for the hike. There's more in the car."

Jennifer smiled, "Did you find out any more about the Senator?"

"Yes," said Spencer," I brought that with me. They marked some of it restricted, but I thought you'd want to see it. I believe we have a connection with what is happening with our friends Clare and the others.

"Senator Williams was involved in quite a few things but the most notable was his connection with trade to China. He is part of an energy committee that oversees how energy is traded between the United States and other major countries. You can imagine that Texas has quite an axe to grind on this topic. Williams seems to be strongly opposed to the increased trading power of China. His argument was that they were ratcheting the pricing structures and the futures for most forms of fuel. He was about to make a speech on this topic at today's gathering in Dallas

"Some of that is in the newspapers and you see that there are reports now that he was killed in a plane crash. In other words, the story is being manipulated by people here in the USA.

"Another report says he was on his way back from Athens, Texas to Dallas. The thing is the road route he was on seemed to go around the other side of the big Cedar Falls reservoir. There is a much more direct route than the one he was taking. It was on this route that the accident occurred. I couldn't get any of the photographs of the accident without drawing more attention to myself. It was out of state, and there was a big security blanket over the whole thing.

"This smacks of a cover-up," said Spencer, "but it's been done professionally. It looks as if it's one of the agencies that have taken control. The best example is that there is a lack of press coverage. You'd expect some of the helicopters from the news gatherers in Dallas or Fort Worth to have been on this like a shot."

"Is this possible?" said Jennifer, "Surely the media would be onto something like this in a few minutes?"

"Normally, yes," said Spencer," But they seem to be taking particular care with this topic and protecting the story. It's hard for us to tell what has been happening from here and I didn't want to probe too deep in case someone picked up that we were interested.

"I thought the enquiries I ran were just those that would be typical of a nosy remote office looking at what was happening."

"You know something?" said Jennifer," I should have switched on the television this morning while I made the coffee. Sometimes I just like a few minutes silence before the day kicks in."

"Yes," said Spencer," Lucas and I drove over here, and it was one of the main stories on today's news, although the information still seemed sketchy.

"Spencer, that's great," said Jennifer, "I'm concerned that we may need to pass on what we know to others. I think we may be sitting on something significant. I'm wondering whether we should have let Clare go or should instead have rounded up Colonel Manners and the others.

"But that wasn't our instructions, was it?" said Spencer," I thought you had been told to let Clare go so she could continue to work with Colonel Manners and that this would draw out the people behind the attempt to steal the technology secrets?"

"You are correct," said Jennifer.

"So, do you think we are also now in danger?" said Spencer, "The very fact it involves us could mean that someone will look for us?"

"Yes," said Jennifer, "We shall need to tread carefully. I don't think we should put too much of our communications through normal channels until we are sure that they are secure."

"I also think we may wish to go to the safe house we sent Colonel Manners to? We said we would go there anyway to pick up their car and we know the one they have as a replacement. Unlike the hire car, this has one of our regular trackers on it, and it will be much easier for us to follow them in the new vehicle."

"We should assess after we have checked out this geocache," said Spencer, "I see you have your hiking boots."

"So how come you're not wearing a checked shirt?" said Jennifer.

"You should see Lucas sitting in the car downstairs," said Spencer, "He really looks the part."

Downstairs, at the car, Spencer introduced Jennifer to Lucas.

"Hi," said Jennifer, "I think I've seen you around the offices. I see you come prepared for a hike across the airbase."

"Hi, Miss Burns," said Lucas, shaking her hand, "I'm pleased to help with this, and Spencer has said we need to keep it quiet. Please rely on my discretion."

"That's right, Lucas," said Jennifer," Call me Jennifer, by the way, we don't know quite what we are facing here, but there is a chance that it is quite dangerous."

"I'm based in the office," said Lucas, "It's quite a change for me to get out like this."

They were in Spencer's truck. It was a 4x4 and had two rows of seats. Jennifer sat in the back seat and left Spencer sitting next to Lucas in the front.

"Okay, let's go," she said, "Hey, and these bagels are superb."

# *Tonto One*

Lucas had been researching the geocache information before they got into the truck. He knew he was being brought along as a specialist and wanted to make sure that he could help.

"I've checked the code references for this location," he said," It looks like a regular geocache. There's quite a few on the airbase. I guess they use some of them for orienteering by troops during drills."

"This one appears to be in a public area and is accessible by road, at least until we are close to it. They call this one Tonto one.

"The geocaches have a standardised structure - like a phone number has an area code. You were lucky to find the code reference from Chuck's base break-in. The one Bigsy saw at Loretta Chapel isn't anything to do with this trail, but the one that Bigsy found, with the 'Cessna' middle section and then the one that Chuck found from the base break-in are part of a little                                                  set."

"We should find one now on the airfield. It would make sense that someone with a military background has put one of them on the airfield. And I checked the Cessna reference yesterday. The number must be 172 - the most common type of Cessna plane.

"Isn't this complicated?" said Jennifer.

"Not really," said Lucas, "There is a standard format for geocaching numbers, and they hide some of them to not show on maps. Remember the people who do this - like me - are in it for both the orienteering and also for the puzzle solving."

They were on the outskirts of the main passenger airport for Albuquerque, which had been extended for military use.

"We need to go around the perimeter road," said Lucas, "It's quite a long route but should save us a walk."

They drove for another 20 minutes as they negotiated the edge of the airfield and looked back across fields towards the runways and the terminal buildings. To their left was a large expanse of semi desert and to the right was the edge of the grass strips and the adjacent terminal buildings about a mile or a mile and a half away.

Jennifer knew this area well because of her role at the airport. She also knew that the desert area was part of the military testing grounds and also housed some other secure facilities. This access road between the two was a very quiet and seldom-used route towards some storage sheds and other miscellaneous maintenance facilities.

"We need to slow down here," said Lucas. He was looking at a small GPS device which he had removed from his belt. "

"The geocache will be about 200 yards away on the right-hand side. I think it is outside of the fence, but only just," he said.

They slowed the 4x4 and looked for anything that could be the basis for the hidden information. There was a small sign attached to the wire fence. It was one of the regularly placed signs that said, 'keep out' and gave other general instructions and warnings about not trying to enter the airfield.

"Look," said Spencer, "There's something else across from that sign." It was a small roadside box. The kind of thing that was used to provide improvised firefighting in the case of a small brush fire.

"Yes, I think that is likely to be where the cache is hidden," said Lucas. They stepped out of the truck and walked across to the roadside box. Lewis looked around it quickly.

"It won't be very well hidden," he said, "They don't want you to be dismantling the facilities here. It will be something simple like a tin box or maybe something smaller, such as a film canister.

"This is it," he said. It was a small tin box, the kind that could hold cookies, it had been nailed to the side of the roadside box such that the hinge was at the top and the box was placed vertically. He flipped it open. Inside was a sheet of paper in a polythene wrapper and also a small black notebook and a cheap pen attached via a piece of string to the metal box.

"This is a pretty basic geocache," said Lucas, "Sometimes there would be a small toy or something like that included in the box as well. The main deal is that whoever has located this geocaching will take notes from the paper and also add their name to the little book. Then take a photo of the artefact and big tick."

"That way they can prove that they have visited because they will know what the content of the cache was and also, they will have their name recorded for posterity. "Okay," said Jennifer, "Let's take a look.""

The paper was a short poem:

*'the detonation sites at Yucca Flat*
*Frenchman Flat, the subsidence craters, the playa:*
*50 times brighter than the sun, hell*
*burst from the skies torched ancient Joshua trees*
*their teddy bear & oven-mitted hands*
*Buster-Jangle, Tumbler-Snapper, Plumbob*
*Ranger, Latchkey, Sunbeam, Tinderbox*
*devastatingly beautiful some called it*
*a letter from home or a firm handshake*
*from someone you trust*

*i had blood running out of both ears*
*out of both nostrils*
*while on the diving platform at the Last Frontier*
*the man in a T-shirt, the man*
*with no shirt; the two men underneath playing ping-pong*

*-Extract from Desert View Overlook by Rose Hunter.'*

They read the poem couple of times and looked for any obvious hidden messages. Spencer took a photograph of the box and its contents and the poem.

"We can look at this back at base to see if there is anything else hidden," he said.

# The Circle

"Should we take the whole box?" asked Jennifer.

Lewis looked a little distressed at this idea, "You don't do things like that with a geocache," he said, "It spoils the fun for everyone if the little gifts or the boxes get removed."

"Take it," said Jennifer, "We need this back at our office."

She opened the notepad and flipped through the pages. It reminded her of an autograph book most people had put one name and signature on the page and additionally added a code of some kind.

"Those codes are the names and reference numbers of the individuals involved in the geocaching fraternity," said Lucas.

"It is so that people can contact one another, although most people will do this online through the websites nowadays,"

Andy looked at the last few entries. Most people had taken the next page and simply added their name for this cache. There were only about two dozen names. Then she saw the last name. It was Chuck Manners.

"Look," she said to Spencer, "It's got Chuck's name here. Two things: firstly, I don't think he would have been here and secondly even if he had visited, I somehow don't think he would sign this."

"Not with a geocache collector number anyway," said Lucas, taking a look at the page.

Jennifer looked around. Busy trucks were moving around inside the airport perimeter fence, but there did not seem to be anyone expressly looking for them.

"We should get out of here," said Jennifer, "Back to the office."

# *Jake sifts*

Jake was prepared for the lack of further information from Clare and Bigsy. He had decided he would monitor the Internet chatter that was related to their presence in New Mexico and Arizona.

When the news reports of the accident involving the senator in Texas started to come through, Jake noticed that the way it was being reported was surprisingly sparse even on the American newscasts.

He tried US-based Internet papers for the Dallas area and picked the Dallas Morning News and the New York Times and looked at each of them for coverage. More in the Dallas paper, but the reporting seemed to be about a freak accident involving a plane crash. No pictures, which he also thought was unusual.

There was more information about the senator himself. That Williams had been a Republican senator and very active in the energy lobby.

It said he was born in Calgary, Alberta in Canada and that his parents had been working in the petroleum industry. He'd got an impressive resume and had studied at both Princeton and Harvard.

After college he was working in the legal profession, starting in a practice that also specialised in petroleum law. This was a very specialised field and covered many topics related to territorial claims and the legality of certain types of energy-related trading instruments.

Because of some cases he had been involved with and the rulings made, the Senator had also been cited as a mover and shaker in the specialised legal areas related to energy matters.

Some of this had highlighted him to the extent he had become involved around ten years ago with politics. Nowadays he was regarded as a mover and shaker and had made fast progress in the Senate to his current position.

All of that stopped yesterday. Jake looked for any recent activities that involved Senator Williams which could be linked to what happened.

The main news he found related to the Albuquerque area was things that he thought both Chuck and Clare knew already. They were related to the uses of the American base at Kirtland and the surrounding desert area.

Fundamentally it was now used for nuclear-related activities. There was both stockpiling of munitions and also further out in the desert there were various test areas.

Jake was sure that this was what Chuck had been involved with when he was working there. He also realised that Bigsy and Clare would know about this by now.

The question Jake was pondering was whether the various activities were linked and what had triggered the sudden interest in all of this.

Williams' recent speeches talked on reduction of energy sources in North America and ways this could challenge the economy.

He described a scenario where, in less than 15 years, there would be major energy shortages in both North America and many parts of Europe. This was unless specific steps were taken. The senator had outlined a three-stage plan which included the creation of new nuclear power generation sites but also extensions to windfarm and even more oil drilling.

The senator pointed out that it was possible to recover the situation for houses and industry based upon the use of nuclear power . For transportation systems, particularly the automobile, there would be substantial shortages starting to accumulate in around 15 years' time. Prior to that he forecasted massive increases in fuel costs out of all proportion to their current levels.

Jake read this and considered that some of it was making a political point rather than driven by accurate analysis. However, he thought there was a truth to the messaging. He noticed that the senator had not provided answers beyond how nuclear power would be affected and that there needed to be something to replace the current way that the automobile was powered.

Jake thought to himself that this was nothing new and he was surprised that the Senator had made such a name from these types of speeches.

He looked more at the conference that Senator Williams had attended. It had been run by an Asian foundation called the Centre for Asian fuel studies.

Jake realise that this could be a connection with what Clare had been describing. Some kind of link with the Chinese. The question was whether Senator Williams was seeking help from the Chinese or making general points that were part of his day-to-day speechmaking.

# *Safe shack*

The SUV bounced its last few yards towards the address that Jennifer had given Clare. There appeared to be a small house next to a huge wooden barn. Sure enough, as Jennifer had said, there was a red pickup truck parked outside the wooden barn.

"So that's our new car," said Bigsy, "Well, it looks just as shiny as this one."

"Two rows of seats again," said Clare, "I don't think you get that in England?"

"It'll be fine," said Chuck," although if I'm honest, the bright red colour is a little bit obvious."

"We'll be living the dream," answered Clare, "Well a girl, my Lord, in a flatbed Ford is slowing down to take a look at me!"

"Take it easy," said Chuck.

"But it means we'll be away from this car which somebody

may have been able to track by now," said Bigsy.

"Yes," said Chuck," You can bet that the one provided by Uncle Sam will have its own tracker."

Clare nodded, "I think we should move our stuff into the new truck now. Then we should take a look inside the house and make a decision about whether we stay overnight night or move on immediately. I want to give Jake call soon as practicable so that we can compare notes about what's been happening."

They pulled up to the front of the house. "It's a shack!" said Bigsy. "A safe shack!"

"Hold on a minute," said Chuck, "We Americans enjoy making homes out of timber, particularly in the country."

"It looks very homely," said Clare.

Chuck said, "Let's get inside. We can see how homely it is by whether they've left us any provisions."

They made their way cautiously towards the front door. Chuck turned the handle, and the door opened immediately.

"I somehow don't think this is one of their most secure locations," he said,

"I'm more interested in it being safe," said Clare, "And ideally somewhere that nobody else knows about."

"Yes," said Chuck. He flipped the lights and walked towards the kitchen. There was a small note on the table it said,

*"Jennifer sends her regards. There's easily enough here to cook a killer grilled cheese sandwich, love, bianca (shack keeper) "*

"Okay, it looks as if we found the right place. Let's take a look in the fridge," said Bigsy.

"Wow," he said, "There are beers, pizzas, cheese, bread, salad, milk, Coke, and look some chocolate cookies in a jar. This may not be the healthiest place, but I'm not going to complain."

He passed the cookie jar around, and both Chuck and Clare took one.

"Monsters," said Clare, "These are big cookies! But first things first, I need to call Jake to update him. I'm wondering whether I should also call Jennifer now that we are here and also tell her what Bigsy had discovered when he was at the hotel back in Santa Fe."

"You know something," said Chuck," I'm pretty sure that they will have this place monitored. I don't think we could be in here without them knowing about it. Let's call Jake as the priority."

Clare reached into her bag and produced her regular cell phone, "I'll put it on speakerphone when we call Jake,"

There was a pause while she selected the number and then

dialled it. They could hear it ringing — a proper British ring tone.

"Hi, Clare," said Jake, "How are you all?"

"We're doing okay," answered Clare, "but it's been eventful."

"I'm still with the guys in SI6," said Jake, "They've moved me to an adjacent building; it's more like a hotel room. "Good actually, but I don't really want to be spending much more time here."

Jake continued, "They told me about what they arranged for you, Clare. How you would meet with Chuck and Bigsy and all of you would move to a safe place outside of Albuquerque. I'm guessing that's where you are now?"

"That's right," said Clare, "There's some extra information too. Bigsy was able to find a note left by the geocache in the hotel in Santa Fe. It said that the main situation has been caused by someone selling out to, we think, the Chinese. We think they want to use that tracker thing as a terrorist weapon."

Jake replied, "Yes, I've been looking at that accident in Texas with Senator Williams. I guess you have seen that as well?'

"Yes, we did," said Clare, "and it looks suspicious the way it's being shown on television. It smacks of a cover-up. "

"That's what I thought too," said Jake," Although I don't think anyone unaware of our recent developments would think about it quite as suspiciously as us."

"When I checked Senator Williams records on the Internet,

his profile said he was a highflyer that has been involved in the energy lobby. He has also been warning the Americans that they will run out of energy in around 15 years. There seems to be some deal with China in the background of all of this. You may have seen that he was speaking at a conference a couple of weeks ago where he made a speech about this.

"I passed this information onto the SI6 people already," said Jake, "I guess it will be with your security people there in America by now as well."

"We have not contacted them since I left them to meet Chuck and Bigsy," said Clare, "We are in a safe house at the moment, but we are alone. I say that, but we are probably being monitored," said Clare.

Chuck nodded.

"Jake," said Chuck, "Did you find out anything else ?"

"No," said Jake, "but I am wondering whether that 'accident' was the start of a broader campaign?"

"These people, whoever they are, don't seem to value human life very highly. In the last few days, there has been a mounting body count."

"We need to let Jennifer know what is happening," said Clare, "I think it may be better for you to do that, Jake. If Jennifer gets the information from you, it will be through secure channels rather than us calling her by phone and potentially giving away our location to anyone that is trying to trace us - Oh, Hi, Jennifer, in case you are monitoring this!"

# Ed Adams

# *Second Amendment, 1789*

Spencer drove Jennifer and Lucas back to their office in Albuquerque.

"Well, this is a first," said Spencer, "I'm used to tracing a bit of drug trafficking or even people trafficking but this is a whole different dimension."

"Yes," said Jennifer, " That's why I'm not sure how much of this we should reveal to our bosses at the moment. Clare told us that Chuck has already been chased once and that his colleague Mike was killed. I think we may be stepping into a rather murky pool."

"I've rigged up this office as our control centre," said Spencer, "It's a bit improvised, but it means we can probably keep everything in one room. For example, I patched the monitoring of the safe house through to here."

"So, can we listen to a playback of what's been happening at the house?" asked Jennifer.

"Sure," said Spencer, "First of all, we can see that they all arrived."

He pointed towards some television monitoring. A single screen split four ways showed different views of the main room in the house. Spencer ran the pictures at high speed.

"Look," said Jennifer, "they are all sat down together now; let's slow this down and listen in."

It was Clare preparing to talk to Jake. The others were huddled around the small cell phone that she was using as a loudspeaker.

Jennifer listened as they talked to Jake. She also heard them say that they would not speak to Jennifer again at this time. She knew she could contact Clare at any time on the additional phone but thought it wise to wait until she needed to do that. She also heard them discuss that Jake would send information to Jennifer via the back channel through her departments.

"Spencer," she asked, "Has anything arrived from the UK?"

Spencer looked at his other screen and replied, "Nothing at the moment. I think that conversation was only about an hour ago. I don't know how long it will take for this kind of thing to be relayed."

Jennifer looked at Lucas.

"Look, Lucas, thank you for your help with this so far. You now know more than anyone else about what is happening here. I want to ask you if you can join us for a few more days. I can square this with your department head, but it means that

272

we can limit the number of people who are involved in all of this. I know you said you were mainly office-based, but I can also see that you spend time on the trails. This could all be useful for us over the next few days."

Lucas nodded, "Yes, I will be pleased to help. This makes a big change from my normal day job."

"Some of this might be dangerous," said Jennifer, "Both Spencer and I can carry pistols and have been trained for firearms. I think this will put you at a disadvantage if we are out in the field."

Lucas said, "Yes, I agree, I have not been through the training here for any of that. You should know though that I was in the Army for three years and when I go out on the trails, I sometimes go hunting. I'm used to using both small arms and a rifle."

"Okay," said Jennifer. "Let's not get carried away here but you do need to be prepared for some rough stuff as we go on."

Spencer asked Jennifer if she was going to tell her boss what was happening now.

"Yes," said Jennifer, "I think we need to give him the general outline, but I think we can keep it fairly simple. "

"We have met one American colonel and two stray Brits who have been attacked. We have given them some temporary shelter last week while we work out what has happened."

"We don't need to say anything about Senator Williams or the geocache at this stage. We can explain that the other guy in Britain, Jake, is a good friend of the two Brits. The fact that the Brits had taken him into protective custody is nothing to do with us."

"Okay," said Spencer," I guess that would hold for about one day."

Spencer had switched on a television in the room that had been prepared. It was now showing some footage of the so-called crashed plane that had killed the Senator Williams.

"Honestly," said Spencer," This all looks a bit too neat. Somebody has gone in afterwards to make this scene."

He checked the local road summaries for the area around the reservoir in Texas. Sure enough, the road was still closed for several miles either side of the incident.

"My guess is that they have removed the site of the crash away from where it happened. I think there will be two sets of wreckage. The real set which will look as if it has been decimated by a missile and a second set which has been arranged to look like the plane crash.

"If this has been done by one of our agencies," said Jennifer, "Then it looks like there is a huge problem."

"We don't have any jurisdiction to go take a look at this," said Spencer, "But I'm not sure that we will get much from looking at this on the news feeds either. Someone is imposing a blackout on

# *Texan oilfields*

Clare was brewing some fresh morning coffee. The television was chattering in the background.

She could hear someone else moving about in the house, Chuck appeared.

"You know I'm wondering about all of this," said Clare, "You ask us over here to help you, and we've come along."

"But so far all that's happened is we are being chased around, found out a few things and are now in hiding. Not the greatest help."

"I know," said Chuck," Don't think I'm not grateful, though, Clare. It was better when I was still hidden away. Unfortunately, because some of the guys that invited me to Scottsdale were my long-term colleagues I trusted, then I felt this would be safer than it's turned out."

Clare pushed a mug of fresh coffee to Chuck and then put her hands around the edges of her own coffee mug.

"So, what shall we do?" she asked.

"We seem to know quite a lot now, and we have got some backup from Jennifer and her team.

"But everyone seems to be running scared and we're still none the wiser about who it is that has somehow ratted you out. What about you, do you have any ideas?"

"I've been wracking my brains," said Chuck, "I think we are on the edge of something enormous. There's a link between the terrorism and what the Senator has been doing with the energy discussions. I don't know how we will get more information unless perhaps Jennifer can help us.

"The thing is," said Clare, "I think Jennifer was also out of her depth when we drove back to Albuquerque, and they were chatting in the car. I was of the distinct impression that Jennifer works with simpler situations than the one we have at the moment. I think she's involved with airport security and things like that."

"But don't you also have a link to Jake, who's now at SI6, said Chuck, "They are a much bigger source of influence in these matters. If we can get them more in the loop over what is happening, perhaps we can resolve this."

At that moment there was some breaking news on the TV station. It was showing a live picture from an oil refinery near Houston, Texas. There had been an explosion and was now a local state emergency as the flames and smoke from the refinery curled upward.

"I don't think this is a coincidence," said Chuck. They listened to the voice-over from the TV station. It was describing an unknown explosion which had wrecked the facility. Chuck looked at the aerial pictures, which were from a plane circling some miles from the site.

"Look, it's another one where they're not giving us the full picture," he said, "This one is so big they can't just hide it as with the Senator but even so they are not telling us what happened."

Clare moved closer to the television set to see the picture in more detail, "Yes I see what you mean, you can't tell an awful lot from this except something big is on fire."

"I want to find out the reason for the fire," said Chuck.

"You think it's those missile devices?" asked Clare.

"Let's say I'm not ruling it out," said Chuck," and it is a striking coincidence just after that Senator was killed."

Clare said, "Look, should we contact Jennifer about this and maybe try to get a link up with the people in London."

"It's a good idea," said Chuck, "The problem is whether the CIA will allow the British security services anywhere near this."

"But I thought Jennifer said that the agencies were cooperating on this?" asked Clare.

"Yes," said Chuck, "What they say and what they do are not always the same thing. I guess that's why they sent Jennifer from airport security to handle this instead of bringing in a bigger team."

"You know," said Chuck, "I doubt whether they have even

linked what has been happening to us with what is going on with the Senator and the oil refinery."

At that moment, Bigsy appeared.

"Take a look at this Bigsy," said Clare and pointed towards the television. "An oil refinery has just blown up in Houston."

"You think it's linked with what happened to the Senator?" asked Bigsy.

"It didn't take you long to make that connection!" said Clare.

"We are going to need a bigger truck," said Bigsy.

"Ha," laughed Clare, then Chuck replied, "I'd think this was funny if it wasn't so serious."

"Look," said Chuck, "We can't work on this alone any longer. We need to link up with at least one of the other agencies."

"If that's the case, would they want to get rid of us," said Clare.

"Normally I would say yes," said Chuck, "but I think we are already in this up to our necks and I apologise for that. I'd hoped to get you to run some straightforward interference for me when I called the old gang back together. I didn't realise that I was being systematically hunted."

"But is there a chance that there are people on the inside working this?" asked Bigsy, "For example, there seems to be a couple of big cover-ups about the two recent events."

"I agree," said Chuck, "But I think this is something about

cause and effect. What we're seeing is the US government pulling in the strings around both the Senator's assassination and the explosion at the oil refinery. Something else we can deduce from this is that at the moment the operations seem to be centred in Texas. It makes me think that whoever is involved is still local. This may be something that can be nipped in the bud before it spreads."

"We should share the information with Jennifer about all of this," said Clare, "Although, I think Jennifer was already suspicious about telling too many people what was happening. SI6 in London are also involved anyway, and Jake is with that team."

"So, although we don't know what they are going after," said Chuck, "we should have some advantage in having three disparate groups involved. And that's before 'we the people' are making the cover-ups for the two big emergencies in Texas.

"You are right, Clare; we need to put a call through to Jennifer."

# *Two hours west*

Jennifer's phone rang. She could see it was Clare's special phone.

"Hello," said Jennifer.

"It's Clare, we need to talk. We put a few things together here," said Clare, "It would be best for us to meet together and again to pool our resources. Chuck's main motivation is to find out who is after him and make sure nothing can happen. We guess your motivation is on a much larger scale."

Jennifer considered for a moment,

"Okay," she said, "I'll meet you. We should not talk about this by telephone, not even using the phone I've provided for you. You are around 2 to 3 hours away now. I will find a place for us to meet, and I will text you the address on this phone. I'm assuming the two people you will bring are Chuck and Bigsy. I will also bring two others, that's Spencer who you met in the briefing room and another guy named Lucas who has some good hiking trail skills. He's ex-military."

"Are you going to tell your bosses about this?" asked Clare.

Jennifer replied," We have already told them an edited version of what is happening. We played it down. The link from the UK back to me is more likely to create ripples than anything."

Clare remembered she had told Jake to pass information to Jennifer when they had spoken by phone earlier.

"This is just to check," said Clare, "Have you received any of the information from Jake yet? That's the information I passed on earlier today?"

"No," said Jennifer," Not a word."

"Is this because the communication is slow or is someone checking what is happening before it is passed along?", asked Clare, exasperated that Jennifer had not been briefed by Jake.

"Honestly, I don't know," said Jennifer, "You have figured out I'm not particularly high up in the chain of command here? There's plenty of other people who could intercept and stop whatever is being passed through."

"But," said Jennifer, "On the other hand, I am part of the operations team here at the airport, and that does give me certain advantages. I'm going to suggest we meet at a covert location... It's an airfield about 2 hours west from you."

"Why is that?" asked Clare.

"I think I might go to get my hands on a plane which could

save us in time if we need to move around quickly," said Jennifer, "By taking it to Bluff, it won't trip any suspicions. No one will be looking there.

Clare smiled, "Splendid, we could be in Texas quicker than we thought,"

# The Mormons came through a hole in the rocks

"If we have plenty of stickie-ta-tudy, we cannot fail."

*-- Jens Nielson 1879*

# *Bluff, Utah*

Chuck looked around the house and across towards the red pickup truck they had swapped their belongings into.

They had parked the blue SUV in the wooden barn. Clare had told Jennifer its location, but Jennifer had said she would wait out a week before sending someone to collect it and to drive it back to Phoenix.

The airstrip they had been told to drive towards was about 2 hours away. It was on the Utah-Arizona border near to a place called Bluff.

"Why has Jennifer selected somewhere so far away?" asked Clare.

"Precautionary," said Chuck, "Two things - we'd see anyone following and we'll be able to see anyone waiting. It's a tiny airstrip."

Bigsy offered to drive for this section and once again they

were cutting across the desert, this time in a south-westerly direction. In the distance they could see various large red rock outcrops.

"We're driving along one of the routes that the Mormons took when they came down from the Chicago area," said Chuck, "Imagine having to drive across this terrain in a covered wagon. Imagine doing it when there weren't any roads. Literally through a hole in the rocks."

"It's easier to imagine than you might think!" said Bigsy. It's still desolate around here. Except when those massive trucks come honking over the horizon.

"I know what you mean when you say desolate," said Clare, "But I think I'd use another word like Majestic."

They reached the small town of Bluff and continued to head west to its outskirts where they found the small airstrip. It was little more than a shed and a runway.

"Well this is utilitarian," said Bigsy, "Do we need to drive along the runway to make sure there aren't any wild horses or cattle on it?" he asked.

Someone moved out from the nearby tin shed. Bigsy could see that there were two small aircraft inside.

"Hello, neighbours" said the man, "Can I help you?"

"Hi there, we are waiting for a plane to land here in the next few minutes," said Bigsy.

"Okay, But I don't think it's on my schedule," said the man, "Are you sure you aren't looking for somewhere else like

Cortez? That's a busier airstrip than here."

"No., we're sure we have the right one," said Beattie, "This is Bluff, isn't it?

Almost on cue, they could hear the distant growl from a small plane.

"Okay," said the man, "But I don't seem to have this in the log."

"I think the flight plan was only registered a short time ago," said Chuck, "This is an official plane, by the way."

"It's also quite a large plane for this airstrip," said the man, "We normally only handle single prop four seaters here. That looks like a twin turboprop. Beechcraft Super King 200, I'd guess."

Chuck looked impressed at the man's knowledge. The plane circled the entire air strip once and then made its way into a landing descent.

Bigsy noticed that it was a small twin propeller plane but had a row of windows along each side.

"I'd guess that it has flown down from Kirtland," said the man, "I think I recognise that plane. Ex-mil made to look civilian. See the loading hatch and the wingtip fuel tanks - dead giveaway."

Bigsy looked impressed, "Sure thing," he bluffed.

"Yes, we are about to hitch a lift from here," said Chuck. He realised that the man was ex-military himself.

# The Circle

"Okay, we'd better do the right paperwork first then," said the man, My name's Aaron, by the way, Aaron McKarty."

The plane had landed and was now taxiing towards them. It stopped on a large tarmac apron area and a small row of steps was released from towards the back of the plane.

Bigsy saw people climb out of the plane. He noticed as Clare recognised Jennifer amongst the group.

They waited for the group to cross the tarmac area, and then Clare spoke to Jennifer.

"That was quick and quite an impressive entrance," she said.
"I know," said Jennifer, "I know these guys who run this plane, and I have hitched us a lift to Texas. You met Spencer already, here's Lucas, and I also brought Davy who will drive the red pickup back to Durango. I guess you parked the SUV in the big barn?"

"Yes," said Chuck, "we decided it was best to hide it."

"Okay, we will lose the red one too," said Jennifer.

"We should leave our main discussion until we are inside the plane," said Jennifer, her eyes flicked towards the man in the hangar, "I shall go to explain our presence here today."

Chuck nodded. He knew that Jennifer would tell a believable fiction about what they were doing.

Bigsy walked across to the red pickup with Davy and they swapped the luggage across to the plane.

Bigsy gave the keys to the truck to Davy, who climbed into the cabin, gave a wave and drove off.

"We need to get the next leg of our flight itineraries logged so there's a small amount of paperwork before we can turn this around and leave here. The pilot reckons about 40 minutes before we can be on our way again."

"It's not like driving a car," said Bigsy.

They walked into the shelter from the sun. Even in the shadows, it didn't seem much cooler. Jennifer showed the man her various passes and security information. He seemed satisfied that everything was in order and then started to chat about some people that they both knew in common back at Kirtland.

# The Circle

# *Leaving, on a prop plane*

After a short while, the pilot beckoned for them to climb aboard. Bigsy noticed that the pilot had been around the outside of the plane, checking all the control surfaces. It intrigued him that the plane had only just flown in , but still everything was being checked before the next flight.

Chuck said, "Up in the air, a small glitch would be more problematic than on the road. No median, just a very hard ground."

It surprised Bigsy at the lack of formality for the luggage compared with his normal flights with all kinds of metal detectors and conveyor belts.

They climbed back into the plane through the rear door. Bigsy noticed that the fuselage roof curved, and that he had to stoop slightly as he walked towards the seat.

Unlike a commercial flight, they configured the seats in a small group of 4+4  with two seats in each group facing in opposite directions.  It made the seating like a restaurant booth with a small gangway between the seats. Bigsy noticed that there was a pilot and also a co-pilot in the front of the plane. The co-pilot had another job to check that everyone was seated, belted and secure ready for the flight.

Engines on the plane started and Bigsy noticed that he was seated quite close to their exhausts, which were quite noisy. The pilot prepared for take-off and then after only a few moments they had sped along the runway and were up into the air.

As the plane banked following take-off, Bigsy could see that they were over a large area of red desert with spectacular rock outcrops.

"We are taking off in the direction towards Monument Valley," said Chuck, "I don't know if you know it by that name, but it's the famous rocks used in many of the well-known westerns. You know John Wayne, that kind of thing."

Bigsy looked and could see both the red rocks and also a long valley which he worked out was the continental divide that Chuck described when they were on the road a couple of days ago.

The plane levelled out into a steady cruising altitude, and as it did so the noise seemed to subside in the cabin.

"So, what's the plan?" said Chuck, looking towards Jennifer.

"I could only get this plane for the flight to Dallas," she said, "Then we will be on our own again. I thought it would get us near enough to where the initial incidents have occurred. We can look at both sites to see if we can gather any more information."

"We also need to share our information, I've heard most things from Clare, but I understand that Bigsy also found out something from the geocache in the hotel."

"Yesterday it was straightforward. There was a message which linked the intended transponder sale to some kind of Chinese business deal. I think they were being sold to a Chinese holding company to provide the power of the technology and potential to sell it on.

"It ties in with what we have seen happening over the last few days," said Chuck.

"What - the two incidents with the senator and the refinery?" said Jennifer.

"Exactly, and both of them were related to energy futures in some way."

"The two incidents also happened less than 100 miles apart," said Jennifer, "It makes me think whoever is responsible for this is still working from somewhere in the vicinity. Not some kind masterminded global plot."

"That also ties up with the initial attacks at the hotel," said Chuck, "It looks to me as if there is someone who has been moving from Scottsdale towards Houston."

"That's a direct route," said Jennifer.

Spencer and Lucas were sitting in the second block of four seats. They effectively had two seats each. Allen called across, "Yes, that's about a thousand miles along the I-10, via El Paso and San Antonio.

# The Circle

"I get it, they are using these transponders to provide targeting," said Bigsy, "but I can't work out what they'd be using to create the explosions. A missile being launched would look too obvious. And you'd need something with that kind of firepower to work on that refinery.

Chuck look across towards Bigsy, "my guess is it something like drones that are being used."

Jennifer said, "No, I don't think so. I think they want to get to the drone technology and are using traditional weapons to simulate what a drone attack would look like. That's why everything is so localised. They are operating from a ground launcher."

Chuck looked impressed, "You seem to know a lot about this?"

"Yes, we run security drills over at Kirtland every so often. One of the scenarios is a ground launched rocket attack. We reckon with modern rockets; it can only be effective up to around 3 miles. That's for a precision hit, which is what seems to be happening with the Senator and the refinery."

Chuck replied, "It makes sense, and would also explain why the launch hasn't been spotted. A rocket attack rather than a missile, which would show up on radar and so on." Jennifer nodded, "That's until they get their hands on some of the drone technology available around the Kirtland military base," she said.

"I don't think people are aware of just how advanced a lot of this technology is nowadays."

Chuck nodded, "Yes when I was working on this program there were two types of assault drone in development."

"One kind was used for launching a payload, but the other kind was a kind of variation on the cruise missile and the actual drone was itself a weapon with its own built-in payload."

"If someone could launch a drone with a built-in payload, then it could be targeted and would have disappeared at the point of impact. Kind of Fire and Forget.

"Surely the people at the two sites will have figured this out?" asked Clare.

"Almost certainly," said Chuck, "Although they might not know the other part of this that we do. In other words, they may not know how these devices are being targeted so it will look like random shots in both cases."

"So, they may be looking for someone who can deploy a rocket launcher or something similar from close by whereas using a drone and the transponders the terrorists could be much further away?"

"That's right," said Chuck, "the US military uses these devices from a control centre in Nevada but can fly them into Iran. I don't think we are dealing with anything on quite that scale at the moment, but I do think the plans for the launch location could be many miles from where the targets have been bombed."

"Yes, and this is on US soil, too. US-launched against the US."

"But surely getting hold of USAF drones isn't going to be easy?" asked Clare.

"I agree," said Jennifer, and the way that bases like Kirtland are clamped down for such items is pretty impressive.

"So, there would be a supply of drones in Kirtland?" asked Clare.

"Yes," said Chuck, "Actually certain types of munitions are very closely monitored and only kept in a very small number of locations in the whole of the United States. The two main ones are in Nevada at Hawthorne and a much smaller one in Picatinny, New Jersey. There's also several chemical weapons storage locations, spread over the whole country."

"And forgive me for not understanding," said Bigsy. "Do these drones need to be launched by planes or are they something that can take off from the ground or all what?"

Chuck explained, "The one I worked with when I was on the base was something called the Predator. It was quite a large drone and could carry a couple of missiles."

"They are really UAVs which stands for unmanned aerial vehicles and the Predator is the most well-known.

Chuck described the predator and had a good working knowledge of it.

"Something you may be less aware of Chuck," said Jennifer, "Is that these Predators are used inside the US nowadays to control the Mexican border. So, within 5 to 100 miles of here all along the  border there are uses of these drones for surveillance patrols."

"I guess these devices are the ones just fitted with cameras and no other payloads," said Chuck.

"Yes, Jennifer, and their numbers have been increasing over the last few years - Ever since that so-called president pushed for the wall."

"But something that might not be apparent from description is that these devices are large. When I've seen them at the Air Force Base, they are at least as big as a small single propeller plane. That's not the thing you can hide, and you still need a runway for it to take off.

"But once they are in the air, they can fly higher than normal jet planes," said Chuck.

"So, let's put this together," said Clare, "we think that perhaps somebody is using the transponder technology with some kind of drone to create the strikes that have taken place so far?"

Spencer said, "When we are back on the ground, I can take a more detailed look at this and see if I can find out from the USAF records."

To everyone's surprise, the pilot was getting ready to make his descent into Dallas airport.

"That was so quick," said Bigsy, "we've hardly taken off."

The pilot smiled and continue to make his preparations for their final descent. "We will be on the ground in around 20 minutes," he said, "And the air strip we have chosen should mean that you have a similarly smooth exit."

Spencer added, "I have arranged for a couple of SUVs' to be available for us at the landing strip. I asked for drivers so that we can get around more quickly than trying to figure it out for ourselves."

Jennifer and Chuck both nodded, "Yes, I think we should try to get to the location where the Senator was killed first," said Jennifer.

"It should be easier for us with local drivers that have all the right badges and passes. Just remember when we are in the vehicles that we should not talk about the specific details of what we are doing,"

"Yes ma'am," said Chuck, smiling.

Bigsy watched in fascination as the plane landed. Just like the take-off, he had a great view forward through the pilot's cockpit and could see the approaching ground and the white stripes of the runway.

He noted that this runway looked much larger than the one he had taken off from in Bluff.

"Everything is bigger in Texas," he said dryly.

# *Regular Jeeps from the carpool*

"Hi," said Jennifer, "We need to be heading to the site of where Senator Williams was killed. You can see that I've got the right authority here. You also know that we are under strict radio silence on this, so I don't think I'd appreciate any of you tried radioing for confirmations."

The two drivers nodded and waited for everyone to get into the vehicles.

"It will take us about 45 minutes to get to the site where the aeroplane is supposed to have crashed," said Jennifer.

They drove along sedately with a long gap between the two vehicles. Chuck noticed that the drivers were following a kind of military pattern that he'd seen in the Middle East. The kind of pattern where they might be expecting things to happen from the roadside.

"Are these vehicles armoured?" he asked the driver.

"No, they are just regular Jeeps," said the driver, "We got them from the carpool."

They pulled onto another road. It was it a main route but there were diversion signs as they approached the area of the crash site. By now the crash site had been there for some time and the number of vehicles and the level of activity at the entrances was quite low key. The diversion around the area was extensive, and so most of the local traffic had decided either to avoid the journey or to take a different route.

As they arrived, the driver showed the guards at the checkpoint his pass and was waved through. The same thing happened with the second vehicle, so they were now on the inside of the cordon.

"Okay," said Jennifer, "I want us to look at the main crash site but also to continue past it. When I looked at it on the news cast everything looked somehow too neat."

Chuck nodded, "That was my impression too, like someone had sprinkled the wreckage after the event."

"Yes, it all looked very televisual," said Jennifer.

They were at the site of the wreckage now. It was harder to make out any patterns from the ground compared with the helicopter footage they had seen on the television news channel.

At the scene were more local police and a large flatbed trailer which was being loaded with the aircraft wreckage. A second vehicle had the remains of the car on it. Both had been parked inside a large tent.

Jennifer looked around the site and found the person in charge.

"Hi, I'm from the security services based out of Kirtland Air Force Base," said Jennifer, "They have asked me to come over here to take a quick look at the plane. She showed her pass and some other paperwork, which she pulled from a small bag.

"We were not expecting you," said the detective. "No matter," said Jennifer, "I only need a very brief look at the plane to see whether it is one of ours from the base." She could see the tail section and also the civilian N marking.

"It looks like a small light aircraft was in trouble and had crashed into the road," said the detective, "It's a one in a million chance that the Senator was driving along here at that time."

Clare busied herself with a camera and scribbled a few things into a notepad before walking back to Chuck.

"This doesn't look right," said Jennifer to them both, "It looks more like somebody has taken an old broken plane and sprinkled it around the area. I could go on to ask them about black boxes and other stuff, but I think we will be better off looking for other signs of what has happened."

She signalled to the detective. "Thanks, Detective. We will leave shortly but I'd like to just drive a little further along the road to check for anything else that may have dropped from the plane."

"You can't do that," said the detective. He stiffened. "I'm afraid that unless you have special clearance, we do not allow you go beyond the tape across the road over there.    He pointed to a further set of barriers, and Jennifer could see that beyond them was a collection of military vehicles.

 There didn't seem to be any activity at that point, but she was sure that it was a forward to station for something else.

# *Footsteps*

"Okay, she said, "We will be on our way."

They drove back along the road, past the roadblock that had been set up by the police cars. "We need to find somewhere to stop close to here," said Jennifer.

"This side lane looks promising," said Chuck.

There was a small turning to the left. Both vehicles drove in and stopped. Spencer was already on the computer and dialling up a map of the area.

"This lane leads through to a farmhouse which is back the way we have just driven," said Spencer, "If we follow the path from the farmhouse, it leads over those hills and past the military roadblock."

"Okay," said Jennifer, "which of us will go to check this out?"

Lucas stepped forward, "I think my hiking trails knowledge could be useful here."

# The Circle

"Good," said Jennifer, "Perhaps you, me and Chuck could make this journey. We still have several hours of daylight. We should travel light and only take the minimum with us. But that should include my camera," said Jennifer.

"What shall we do?" asked Bigsy. "I think we should take both cars to the farmhouse and use that as a temporary base."

"What if someone is there?" asked Clare.
"We should just explain that we will be on their property for a couple of hours whilst we are investigating something to do with the crash."

"Okay," said Chuck, that sounds like a good plan. They drove the two cars to the Farmhouse.

It appeared to be deserted.

"It looks as if they are out," said Chuck.

"Okay," said Jennifer, "Let's not waste time. Chuck you, me and Lucas should head off along that Trail. Bigsy - We should be back within three hours maximum."

Ed Adams

# *The Groove*

Jennifer, Lucas and Chuck walked fairly easily for the first
mile or so along the track. It appeared to be a well-used path,
but then at a gate the main path led off to the right. It looked
as if it would be heavy going from then on. A combination of
undergrowth and rocks. They would need to scramble across
this to get to the point beyond the military roadblock.

"I think this natural hazard will mean that the troops are not
being so fussy about blocking off this side of the access to the
site," said Jennifer.

"Yes," said Chuck, "although we will need to be careful
when we get closer; we don't want them to see us."

Lucas studied a small digital compass. "We are close now,"
he said, "I think we should drop down for the last part."
They were approaching a rocky outcrop elevated above the
road that they had driven along earlier. As they reached the

top, they could see that they had bypassed the military roadblock and were now within the area that had been cordoned.

Jennifer looked to the right, "Oh my god," she said, "That is the real site of the crash."

Chuck looked across as well and could see a 100-yard-long gouge in the road surface, it had a kind of 'V' shape to it and at the end there was an upturned crater.

"That's the shape of a high-powered air-to-ground missile with a hard warhead," said Chuck. "Something like a Hellfire. That's an anti-armour missile and would be the thing to use against a car."

"They were not messing around, and that's not from a surface launch. I'd say it was from a helicopter," said Jennifer, "Something like an Apache or a Cobra. Kirtland has both."
"Yes, and it's interesting that they have kept the road closed and preserved the situation instead of a complete cover-up," said Chuck.

"Agreed," said Jennifer, "If this was one of ours that had gone rogue, they would be rebuilding the road as fast as they could to support their cover-up statements. The fact they've left this means that they must still be trying to investigate what has happened.

"Yes," said Chuck, "It shows they don't know what happened, or who did it."

Jennifer took a few photographs using a telephoto lens.
"We should get out of here," said Chuck, "before we are noticed."

Lucas turned around and led them back towards the farm track. From there, it was a fairly easy downhill walk back to the cars.

# *On the radio*

The three hikers arrived back at the cars.

"What did you find out?" asked Bigsy.

"We saw the real sight of destruction," said Jennifer, "It was a missile hit. I have some pictures on my camera here. It looks like they fired it from a helicopter."

"Something else just happened," said Bigsy, "We've been listening to the radio and the conference that the senator was due to attend has been cancelled. They are saying it is because of the senator's death and that they are doing this out of respect. We are wondering if there is anything else behind it. For example, there were at least six other major speakers due to attend."

"Are you thinking the event itself could have been targeted?" asked Chuck.

"Yes, something like that," said Bigsy.

"That would be the third strike and all of them targeting this area," said Clare.

"Or someone's imagination getting the better of them?" added Bigsy.

"I know we are keeping this quiet," said Chuck, "but I think there must be some other people that know more about what is going on. Jennifer, do you think we should try to use your contacts to get more information?"

"It's a trade-off," said Jennifer, "At the moment we have freedom to act, and I think we have found out quite a lot of information. If we ask for formal help from the agencies, then they will take control of this. You can see that at the moment they don't appear to know what to do."

"We could try using the Jake angle," said Clare, "I'm sure the Brits can't help overtly but there may be some other channels through that?"

"That's a better idea," said Jennifer, "Although I am worried that nobody has contacted me to pass on the original messages from Jake."

Bigsy looked at Clare and then at Chuck, "You know something, we are now in this so deep that I think we are the best people to dig ourselves out. Jennifer, I know you've only just met all of us, but we have worked together successfully in the past. I think with your help we can get to the bottom of this."

Jennifer looked at Spencer and then Lucas.

"Okay, let's see whether this team can figure out the next steps."

# The Circle

# *Jake update*

It was Jake's third day in the hotel-like rooms opposite SI6 in Vauxhall Cross. The accommodation was comfortable, and he could access the Internet and use the telephone and the television.

He'd been monitoring events in Texas and had seen the news down rated by the media; it was the same for both of the main items he was interested in. In the case of the Senator's air crash, it was now all-but-gone from the news. The oil refinery fire was still on the news, but the attention had already shifted to the possibility of legal actions, litigation and huge pay-outs for local disruption.

Jake hoped that it would not be too long before Clare would be in contact again. He had been instructed not to call her for fear that Clare's phone was now being monitored by someone in the US.

Jake's phone rang, and he saw it was Clare calling him.

"Hi Clare, I was getting worried," said Jake

"You wouldn't believe some of our stories," said Clare, "but now is not the time. We think it would be useful if you could help us link up with SI6 for some of our investigations."

"Well, as I'm in their building that shouldn't be too difficult," replied Jake.

"I'll need to contact Amanda Miller who is the person who moved me here. Do want to ask me what it is that you think you need, or would you rather wait until you can have her in a direct phone call?"

"I think we should put it to her we need a secure line to have the discussion... Ask Amanda to do that and also tell her you need to be in the call. We will have Chuck, Bigsy, Jennifer and me. Actually, it's better if we don't tell Jennifer's name to Amanda at the moment."

"I think Jennifer is concerned that she might be being traced herself. We don't want another hunt like the one for Chuck to be started up by accident."

"Okay," said Jake, "I'll see what we can arrange. I think I'm in some protective custody at the moment. Actually, for a few days it's not all that bad."

"Jake I will call you again in a couple of hours."

Ed Adams

# *Predator*

Chuck had found a manual about the Predator for Bigsy. Bigsy was reading extracts from it on-line.

"The USAF describes the Predator as a Tier II MALE UAS (medium-altitude, long-endurance unmanned aircraft system). The UAS comprises four aircraft or air vehicles with sensors, a ground control station (GCS), and a primary satellite link communication suite. Powered by a Rotax engine and driven by a propeller, the air vehicle can fly up to 400 nautical miles (740 km) to a target, loiter overhead for 14 hours, then return to its base."

"So, the original use of a Predator was for reconnaissance?" asked Bigsy,

"Yes, but don't be put off by those peaceful sounding words like 'loiter'", said Chuck.

"Nah, 'Loitering with intent' has a whole other meaning our side of the pond," said Bigsy.

He continued reading:

"Following 2001, the RQ-1 Predator became the primary unmanned aircraft used for offensive operations by the USAF and the CIA in Afghanistan and the Pakistani tribal areas; it has also been deployed elsewhere.

"Because offensive uses of the Predator are classified, U.S. military officials have reported an appreciation for the intelligence and reconnaissance-gathering abilities of UAVs but declined to discuss their offensive use.

"Isn't it being used along the Trumpwall nowadays?" asked Bigsy, "I'm sure they are using some big drones as part of the policing."

Chuck added, "Yeah, the U.S. Customs and Border Protection (CBP) agency has flown Predator drones at an altitude of 15,000 feet for policing immigration, drug smugglers and terrorists along the U.S.-Mexico border. They rebrand the Predator B as the MQ-9 Reaper, which can remain in flight for 30 hours. It has a characteristic Big Brother white blimp on the bottom that monitors illegal activity on the 2,000-mile border.

"The CBP wants to have a cluster of 24 Predators/Reapers that can be deployed anywhere in the continental U.S. within three hours."

Chuck sniggered. "Yes, but they are keeping quiet about the missile aspect of it. The thought a drone with a missile payload was on patrol along the border adds a whole extra level to the creepiness of the administration."

Bigsy continued, "I suppose the ideas of the Predator can just be, well, miniaturised nowadays?"

Chuck replied, "You'll know more about this than me. I know how to set them up, deploy them and so on, but I'm not sure what I'd do if you gave me some modern tech instead."

Bigsy read some more:

"Command and sensor systems
During the campaign in the former Yugoslavia, a Predator's pilot would sit with several payload specialists in a van near the runway of the drone's operating base. Direct radio signals controlled the drone's take-off and initial ascent. Then communications shifted to military satellite networks linked to the pilot's van. Pilots experienced a delay of several seconds between moving their joysticks and the drone's response.

"I suppose the latency, er, delays to the control's responses were because it was using satellite link ups? Like when people are on telly being interviewed live in different countries?" asked Bigsy.

"Yes, and that's what we were trying to fix with the new homing beacons. Instead of controlling them like some remote-controlled plane, we could set them to home onto the gadget at the target end. An altogether smoother way to blow things up," answered Chuck.

Bigsy continued, "It reminds me of the differentiation within scientists Type A: Make things Type B: Destroy things. A bit like a scientist take on Boyle's law. $P1V1=P2V2$."

"Anyway, by 2000, improvements in communications systems perhaps by use of the USAF's JSTARS system made it possible, at least in theory, to fly the drone from great distances. It was no longer necessary to use close-up radio signals during the Predator's take-off and ascent.

"Satellite could control the entire flight from any command center with the right equipment. The CIA proposed to attempt over Afghanistan the first remote Predator flight operations, piloted from the agency's headquarters at Langley.

"To be honest, this is so old-fashioned compared with what you were testing," said Bigsy,

"I can see two ways that you'd have seen improvements. First, the whole control system could be streamlined and made less complicated by the use of homing beacons. Second, and perhaps after your time, the miniaturisation of this could occur. Think of computer technology. Nowadays an old tower PC is more than matched by a modern smartphone. Even domestic photo drones have been made smaller. You can buy a pocketable drone with 4 propellers that can achieve stable hovering flight, with a camera, for about US$350.

"Yes, but it has a limited battery life, not the kind of thing that could fly 400 miles or more," said Chuck.

"But think about it, you're answering the question. Make a cylindrical drone with its length based on its battery or deployment requirement. Add an explosive nosecone and give it homing pigeon targeting. I could almost draw the plan for one. A super Dyson," said Bigsy, "The Predator is, like so many committee things, vastly over-engineered. Look at all the specs and pieces that need to work together on the Predator,"

Bigsy picked up reading the manual again:

# The Circle

"The Predator air vehicle and sensors are controlled from the ground station via a C-band line-of-sight data link or a Ku-band satellite data link for beyond-line-of-sight operations. During flight operations, the crew in the ground control station is a pilot and two sensor operators. The aircraft is equipped with the AN/AAS-52 Multi-spectral Targeting System, a color nose camera (generally used by the pilot for flight control), a variable aperture day-TV camera, and a variable aperture infrared camera (for low light/night).

"Ku-Band, that's something the US Navy uses. On their ships you see those white small aperture VSAT blimps. I guess the engineers designing this thing were from the Navy. Designing with what they could get their hands on?" said Bigsy, aware that Chuck couldn't respond any further.

Chuck said, "Bigsy, I'm guessing that things have moved on since they designed these devices. When they were new, they were like something out of Star Wars. They even came disassembled in a Star Wars container."

"Ah yes, I'm coming to that," said Bigsy, "Each Predator air vehicle can be disassembled into six main components and loaded into a container nicknamed the coffin. This enables all system components and support equipment to be rapidly deployed worldwide."

"The largest component is the ground control station, and it is designed to roll into a C-130 Hercules. It sounds more like Stanley Kubrick than George Lucas. 'Open the Pod Bay doors, HAL'"

Bigsy giggled, "So you need one of America's biggest transport planes - a Hercules C130 - to get the Predator into position? But that's not all…"

"The Predator primary satellite link consists of a 6.1-meter (20 ft) satellite dish and associated support equipment. The satellite link provides communications between the ground station and the aircraft when it is beyond line-of-sight and is a link to networks that disseminate secondary intelligence. The RQ-1A system needs 1,500 by 40 meters (5,000 by 125 ft) of hard surface runway with clear line-of-sight to each end from the ground control station to the air vehicles. Initially, all components needed to be located on the same airfield. This sounds more like something the Russians would invent."

Bigsy said, "It's some vast Lego kit and probably why people are interested in what happened to your secret missile project."

"Yeah, but don't diss the Herk. It was a monster of a plane that could take off on a handkerchief and could fly level with three of its four engines out. They've got me out of trouble in the most outlandish places," said Chuck.

"Point well made, said Bigsy, "Designed in 1951. Kudos, Lockheed!"

Bigsy continued reading:

"Currently, the U.S. Air Force uses a concept called Remote-Split Operations where the satellite datalink is located in a different location and is connected to the GCS through fibre optic cabling.

"This allows Predators to be launched and recovered by a small Launch and Recovery Element and then handed off to a Mission Control Element for the rest of the flight. This allows a smaller number of troops to be deployed to a forward location and consolidates control of the different flights in one location."

"Aye, and there's the rub," said Bigsy," A single Predator costs $22m. That's a lot of wonga to have to recover from the desert."

"Yes, I agree, there's a money machine element to asymmetric warfare. It always sounds inexpensive to be using a drone, compared with, say, an F35, but we were always told it was 4 to 1 and then it went to 5 to 1. I think that was because the planes got more expensive, rather than the drones became better value," mused Chuck.

"So, we get up to the point where you were trialling these things," said Bigsy, "And nearly see the early demise of Osama bin Laden."

"Yeah, that was a covert period, indeed," said Chuck, " In the winter of 2000–2001, after seeing the results of Predator reconnaissance in Afghanistan, Cofer Black, head of the CIA's Counterterrorist Center (CTC), became a vocal advocate of arming the Predator with missiles to target Osama bin Laden.

"Black also believed that CIA pressure and practical interest was causing the USAF's Armed Predator program to be significantly accelerated. Black, and codename Richard, who was in charge of the CTC's Bin Laden Issue Station, continued to press during 2001 for a Predator armed with Hellfire missiles.

"Do you notice that turn of phrase too, 'Armed Predator' compared with the oxymoron of 'Unarmed Predator'?" asked

Bigsy.

"Then more weapons tests occurred between May 22 and June 7, 2001, with mixed results. While missile accuracy was excellent, there were some problems with missile detonation. No wonder! it was so blimming complicated," commented Bigsy.

"Then, in the first week of June, in the Nevada Desert, a Hellfire missile was successfully launched on a replica of bin Laden's Afghanistan Tarnak residence. A missile launched from a Predator exploded inside one of the replica's rooms; it was concluded that any people in the room would have been killed. However, the armed Predator did not go into action before the September 11 attacks. Instead, the CIA were batting around plans to capture ObL - Ouch!" said Bigsy.

"The USAF has also investigated using the Predator to drop battlefield ground sensors and to carry and deploy the Finder mini-UAV"

"Ahah," said Bigsy," so now we get to the Predator mini-me stage, where it can drop a miniaturised version of itself!"

Chuck commented, "When it's the War of the Worlds, that's exactly what will happen. Monster blimps spawning mini blimpette fighter units. We're all doomed!"

Clare had been quiet, sipping coffee in the corner of the room. "You've both had too much coffee and seen too many Will Smith movies."

# *ScanEagle*

Here we are," said Bigsy, "The ScanEagle - An altogether more pragmatically engineered machine. Officially, this one's for fishing."

He had been flicking around the internet. And now read a page from another big manufacturer - Boeing.

"ScanEagle is a small, low-cost, long-endurance unmanned aerial vehicle (UAV) built by a subsidiary of Boeing. The ScanEagle was designed based on a commercial UAV that helped fishermen look for fish. The ScanEagle continues to be upgraded with improved technology and reliability."

"Sometimes you have to look at the most improbable advances", said Bigsy, "Now fisherman will be pretty single-minded about their need to find fish. They'll want stuff that can work efficiently and effectively. Think about their fish finding sonar, as an example. Deeper Fish Finder Pro+ is so simple now that it works on an iPhone and displays shoals and their depth.

"It means the whole crew can be in on the hunt for the fish and can set the nets effectively or whatever it is they do.

"So, let's go back to the Scan Eagle. It is a descendant of another UAV. The SeaScan, which was conceived of as a remote sensor for collecting weather data as well as helping commercial fishermen locate and track schools of tuna.

"The resulting technology has been successful as a portable Unmanned Aerial System (UAS) for autonomous surveillance in the battlefield and has been deployed since August 2004 when it was used in the Iraq War.

"ScanEagle carries a stabilized electro-optical and/or infrared camera on a light-weight inertial stabilized turret system integrated with communications range over 100 km, and flight endurance of 20+ hours. ScanEagle has a 10-foot (3 m) wingspan and can fly up to 75 knots (139 km/h), with an average cruising speed of 60 knots (111 km/h).

"Some modifications featured a higher resolution camera, an improved transponder and a new video system.

"ScanEagle needs no airfield for deployment. Instead, it is launched using a pneumatic launcher patented as the SuperWedge (snigger) launcher. Think of it as a catapult."

"It is recovered using the SkyHook retrieval system, which uses a hook on the end of the wingtip to catch a rope hanging from a 30 to 50-foot (15 m) pole. Yay, Heath Robinson rules!"

"Wait for it... This is made possible by a high-quality

differential GPS unit mounted on the top of the pole and UAV. The rope is attached to a shock cord to reduce stress on the airframe imposed by the abrupt stop.

"There we have it - catapult launched and bungee cord retrieved. Bonkers? Or Genius?"

"I rest my case," said Bigsy, making his way towards the refrigerator

Chuck smiled, and Clare clapped.

"I think we are going stir crazy," said Clare.

# Part Three

# Don't Mess with Texas

"So dry the birds are building their nests out of barbed wire."

*-Texas Monthly*

# *Houston*

In Houston, it was only a few minutes after the phone call from Clare to Jake that the first news from Jake arrived with Jennifer, through official channels. She was contacted on her main cell phone and asked to take the call alone.

"Hello Ms Burns, they have asked us to contact you about certain topics related to a Jake Lambers, who is currently being held by the UK Security services.

"We'd like to ask you to come to our offices to discuss this."

"If you can tell us your current location, we will send around transport and will then ask you to accompany us to one of our main briefing center. I'm sure you understand this is a matter of National Security?'

"I do," said Jennifer, "but I'm also concerned for my own safety. I would rather tell you information from afar for the next few days and then return to base when things are a little clearer."

"Ms Burns we can't have you do that. We need you to come in now. Please tell us your address. We can be with you within the hour.

Jennifer walked back towards the cars and to Chuck and Bigsy.

"I can't do that right now," she said. She gestured to them they needed to start the cars and move on. "I will call you again later," she said.

"We need to get away from here," she said to Chuck. "They are tracing me at the moment. I think they have responded to Clare's call to Jake. I'm impressed that the Brits and the US would co-operate on something like this"

"I guess they must be rattled by what is happening," said Bigsy.

"Yes, and I wonder if they now think we are part of the problem, rather than part of the solution," added Jennifer.

"We need to move away from this area," said Jennifer.

"And I think we should also lose these two government vehicles," said Chuck, "And their drivers, nicely, of course'"

"We should go to somewhere with a reasonable-sized car rental and pick another two new vehicles that we can use ourselves. I still have cash. Can we get the drivers to take us to somewhere for this?"

"Sure," said Jennifer, "We are still about 20 miles southeast of the main Dallas Fort Worth complex. There's the large international airport in the centre. We would have a big choice there and still be difficult to find."

"We could stay in a hotel near to the airport and leave a gap before we pick up the new hire cars,"

"I like that plan," said Bigsy, "Gaps are good. We provide a small gap between losing these drivers and picking up the new cars. And if we use cash for the hotel, we have another gap in our visibility."

Jennifer asked the drivers to take them to Dallas Fort Worth airport and to drop them at the International departures area.

She made a point of saying several times they were travelling to Seattle, hoping that this would register with the drivers.

"Lucas, I think so far you are not caught up in this and it would make more sense for us to let you go now. That way you can have helped us, but not yet implicated in a way that anyone else knows about. Can you please head back to Albuquerque?"

"Even better," said Chuck, "Is if Lucas gets tickets for all of us back to Albuquerque."

"Or even better, we get tickets to somewhere else!" said Clare. "Somewhere that sends them in the wrong direction. What about New York?"

"If this was coming from the agency's money, I'm not sure we could do this," said Jennifer.

"Don't worry," said Chuck, "It's taken care of. I will buy the tickets to the random destination and Lucas should buy his ticket separately. It will break us up in case anyone is looking at the ticketing. We've arrived at the American airlines desk. I will use American Airlines to put us some flights to somewhere a long way away. "

"How about Seattle?" said Jennifer. "It is consistent with what I told the drivers."

"Good plan," said Chuck, "And there are also various military connections in Seattle. It would be a good place to make them think we are heading. Boeing and all that."

"Okay and Lucas can get a flight back to Albuquerque. See, there are direct flights from here to Albuquerque."

They made their way to the ticketing areas. Lucas booked his flight with American Airlines and remained separated from the rest of them.

"That's good," said Chuck to Jennifer, "He needs to be away from us now."

"You know something, I think I need to go to the cafe area and sit with the bags," said Chuck, "How can I put this; I don't want this bag to be too close to the airport security people?"

Jennifer smiled, "it's a bit heavy, is it?" she asked.

"It's a little unsuitable for flight," Chuck replied.

They located a small coffee bar and piled up their baggage.

Chuck said, "I will wait here. Bigsy, I think it's best that you buy the other tickets to our random destination. As long as its internal US we should not have too much trouble with getting the tickets. Look, here's some cash. We will give ourselves the best chance by not using credit cards. They will get our names, but they already know we are in the Dallas area. The best thing we can do is make them think we are leaving and give them somewhere to go to."

Bigsy smiled and picked up the pile of notes that Chuck had pushed across the table.

" Okay, we need to think about our next move," said Jennifer.

"First of all, I think we should stay here tonight," said Chuck, "Somewhere around the airport until we can figure out our next move. That still gives us the option to use planes or another car to move us along."

"Yes, and now there are five of us, it's easier for us to get a big single car, instead of two," said Lucas.

"Will your absence be noticed?" asked Chuck.

"I took care of that when we were last in the office," said Jennifer.

"I told them I was sick and that it could be two or three days before I was back."

# *Refundable*

Bigsy returned with the tickets.

"I got refundables," he said, "They were more expensive, but we can change them if we need to."

Chuck  laughed, "So we have now got some refundable decoy tickets?"

"I think we need to move from here now," said Chuck, "to find a base for the evening one of these airport hotels is best. At least it means we won't be where the drivers dropped us, and we have a trail of tickets that lead us to Seattle.  That should all give us a breathing space."

"Right," said Chuck, "Let's pick a hotel,"

He noticed that Clare had already picked up some airport brochures.
"Pretty much  all the main chains are here," she said.

"Marriot, Sheraton, Hyatt, Hilton, Holiday Inn, Embassy suites. You name it, they seem to be here."

"Okay, let's take one that's inside the perimeter if we can."

Clare smiled, "I like the Hyatt," she said, "It's got some cool facilities too."

"This isn't a holiday," said Bigsy.

"I know," said Clare, "but heck we should make the most of any downtime."

She looked again at the leaflet. "We are in Terminal C country," she said, "International Departures."

"Yes," said Bigsy, "I think that is Gate 26 over there."

"Then we are very well-positioned," said Clare," It says here that the entrance to the hotel is opposite gates 26 to 39."

Jennifer smiled, "You have no idea what it would be like to make this decision on agency money. We'd be staying somewhere across town in a motel."

"Excellent," said Chuck, "all the more reason to stay at the Hyatt. He patted the camouflage bag. I think the bank of Chuck will stand this, does anyone have some small change for one of those trolleys?"

"There's something else," said Clare, "we'd only expected to be here for two or three days to meet Chuck. I get the impression this will take a little longer. After we've checked into that hotel across the way, I will spend an hour going shopping. You have some clothes with you. I have almost nothing," she said.

Jennifer nodded, "Same with me,"

"Okay," said Chuck, "We should agree a time to meet somewhere in the hotel."

"How about the bar?" suggested Bigsy.

Chuck agreed, "Let's make it 7 o'clock this evening that we meet."

# *Cowboy boots from Sheplers*

Chuck had gone to the bar early; he had picked a corner table which had a commanding view of the room and was sipping on a Coca-Cola.

Clare was first to arrive, also early.

"Were you successful in your mission?" he asked

"What the shopping?" grinned Clare, "Oh, yes."

"And Jennifer too?"

"We sort of goaded each other on and it was quite fun using Bank of Chuck money. Thank you and I must repay you in simpler circumstances."

"No, it's my pleasure," said Chuck.

## The Circle

He noticed that Clare was wearing a new top and then noticed she was also wearing new skinny jeans.

Then he spotted the cowboy boots.

"Clare, it looks as if you've really gone to town with this."

"Yes, I found Sheplers. I also bought a couple of sunglasses would also be useful," she said, "A quick way to make a disguise. And the hats were unmissable. Quite a few people around here seem to be wearing them."

"Let's just hope we need to stay in Texas then," said Chuck.

"I've also got some news," said Clare, "I received a text from Jake about half an hour ago. He has asked for a meeting at 8 o'clock local time here. He says he will call my mobile phone number."

Jennifer arrived next; she was also wearing new clothes. Black trousers, black top and a grey jacket.

"Yeah," said Jennifer, "Don't mess with Texas."

"Very nice," said Chuck, "I see the two of you have been busy."

"At least we can both survive for a few more days on the road," said Jennifer. More than survive," said Chuck, "I think you will both do quite well."

"Something we need to get straight," said Jennifer, "I'm breaking all kinds of rules by using your money for this. I've kept the receipts and we should figure out how to rectify this later."

"Jennifer," said Chuck, "I think you will have worked out by now that our little group is fairly unconventional and trying to live off the radar. Let's say I have sufficient quotes supplies here for all of us and I don't want that to be an issue as we go forward."

"I'm very appreciative that you are helping me and, in your case, Jennifer, that you have taken some extra risks to break away from normal policies. I don't know how much you spent, and I don't care. Put it down to the cost of doing business."

At that moment Bigsy appeared with Spencer.

They were both carrying bags.

"That's a turn up," said Chuck. "The two ladies have bought their shopping, freshen up in their rooms, and come back on time. You looked as if you have only just returned from shopping!"

"I know," said Bigsy, "We were not as good at it. We were distracted. There was a great sports bar on the way into the shopping area. You know they had peanuts on the table to make us thirsty. We had to eat the peanuts and throw the shells on the floor."

"I've been into pubs in the UK with sawdust on the floor," said Chuck, "Over here its peanut shells."

Chuck waved a waitress over, and they ordered some drinks.

"Okay," said Jennifer," Let's talk. We need to figure out the next moves."

"Okay," said Clare, "Let's summarise."

"They invited us to Scottsdale via Chuck although we suspected that it would be more complicated once we got here."

"Chuck was invited for a mini-conference with a bunch of his old pals from the missile testing days."

"I guess that meant someone had broken Chuck's cover because he was missing after the last escapade."

"Yes, although, in fairness, we all thought Chuck had gone into hiding," added Bigsy.

"That is right," said Chuck, "and that's why I think it is one someone from the team I worked with that have called us together and is now systematically bumping us off.

"Right," said Clare, "**And** then as soon as we showed up you ran into Bigsy early and the pair of you got drugged."

"Yes," said Chuck, "But I think the only reason they drugged Bigsy was because he was with me. I think someone was trying to get me. I doubt that they even knew who Bigsy was."

"And then your friend Mike showed up and somehow extracted you both from your rooms and into the car. And then they chased you across the Arizona desert?"

"That's right," said Chuck.

"I don't really remember this," said Bigsy, "Whatever they

had done seemed to affect me more than Chuck. I remember being in some kind of rocky area with Mike and Chuck when we waited until the next day to be on our way again."

"That's right, we were waiting for the effects to wear off. And remember, Mike said that there had been two people breaking into my room before that happened," said Chuck.

"And Mike took you back towards Albuquerque?" asked Clare.

"That's right; that's when you, Clare, were still at the hotel and around the time that Jennifer contacted you."

"Yes, we met Clare at that diner in Albuquerque, but Mike dropped us at that shopping mall where we waited until the right time to get a taxi to meet Clare.

"And Mike headed off by himself?" Asked Clare.

"The next day we heard that news broadcast that Mike had crashed the car into the river."

"Which repeats the pattern we've seen with Ben and Klaus, that they are being bumped off one by one."

"We also found out that Tony Capaldi had left the Colorado University and was travelling somewhere. Our suspicions are that he was also heading towards Scottsdale, but we don't have any way to cross check that.

"I can help with that," said Jennifer, "Using my contacts in the airport security network."

"But let's wind back a little," said Pixie, "Something I

remember when we were being chased across the desert was that a plane pursued us. Maybe a helicopter. What was that about?"

Chuck replied, "No, I think you are probably suffering from the drugs. We were being chased, but it was a motorcycle. A hog. A mean looking Harley."

Clare giggled, "Ahah, so you were being chased by someone over 50?" she asked.

"What?" Asked Chuck.

"A middle-aged man who could afford a Harley-Davidson," she replied.

"I don't know who it was," said Chuck, "But we stopped the bike by me shooting out its tire."

"That would be the helicopter sound and explosion that I heard," said Bigsy.

"I think so," said Chuck, "That was the only thing following us."

"I'm already suspicious," said Clare.

"Some of this doesn't ring true. You go to the bar, get drugged and your long-lost buddy Mike conveniently finds you just before you are to be kidnapped?"

"Then he drives you away. Both of you actually. And someone chases you all on a motorcycle? Are you sure Mike couldn't have been involved in this?" asked Clare.

"I don't think so." said Chuck, "And anyway he's dead now."

"Not necessarily," said Jennifer, "Suppose the whole thing is a setup?"

"Maybe Mike is the one that has been hunting down the old team?" said Jennifer.

"And maybe he's also staged the car crash?"

"So, the guy on the bike could have been an accomplice of Mike?" said Clare.

"It is an interesting theory," said Chuck.

'It could also tie in with most of the action at the moment being between here and Albuquerque."

"I'm wondering if Mike was trying to find out something from one of you?" said Jennifer.

"This is something that one of you knew that would apply to the project?"

"Could it be where something was stored, on the base?" asked Jennifer.

"Some kind of secret or code or way something is hidden or something like that?" Asked Lucas.

"I think you might be right," said Chuck, "It was interesting when we were together in the desert that night. To start was I was waiting for the drug to wear off and at that point seem very sensible to stay hidden until the morning. As I came around, Mike started to chat about old times.

# The Circle

"Inevitably we talked about the work we've done together. But Mike knows that trying to talk to me wouldn't be a very good way to get information. I'm just wondering whether I said anything that he might have found useful related to the project.

Bigsy chipped in, "Yes, I was out of it pretty much all of this time."

"And Mike would have known that you couldn't have helped."

"But I seem to remember when I came to that you were somewhere away from Mike," said Bigsy.

"That's right, I'd gone for a walk. I'd told Mike I'd like to shake off the remaining effects of the drug. That was true but now you mention it I can remember thinking at the time, there was some kind of stabbing doubt in my head."

"I know that feeling," said Bigsy. It is the one you get when you've had enough to drink, and the next pint will send you over the edge.

"I'm not sure that's it," said Chuck, "but there's a kind of instinctive moment when I thought Mike was asking questions probably off-limits related to the project work."

"Can you remember what he was asking you about?" asked Jennifer.

"Launchers," said Chuck, "He was asking me about launchers."

I take it you mean that launchers for UAVs?" said Clare.

"Kind of," said Chuck, "but probably not the way you're thinking."

"He was asking me about catapult launchers. That's when I had the Bigsy drink effect moment."

"I started by saying I didn't know about this. There were two types of missile system we used to test. I guess you'd call them normal rockets the first type. And also, those Predator UAVs we talked about. There was another type - a smaller UAV. I didn't get involved but I knew they were being tested as well."

"So why if Mike has been bumping other people off would he have let you and Bigsy go?" asked Clare, "It makes little sense."

"Actually, I think it does," said Chuck. I knew that Tony Capaldi was the main person working with the smaller UAVs and that's what I said to Mike."

"It didn't occur to me that Mike was fishing for information and I gave him honest replies so he probably could see that I was not trying to hide anything."

"I still don't understand why he didn't finish you and Bigsy then?" said Jennifer.

"Mike is a pretty smart operator," said Chuck, "I think he worked out that it would be difficult to torture me to get the information if I knew it, but he could ask me gentle questions whilst we were waiting for Bigsy to recover. And if he left me alive, I could also help backup his disappearing trick when he drove the car off the bridge.

"I'd have been one of the last people to see him alive. I could pinpoint his location and also echo the story he was being chased like Ben and myself.

So is our guess that Mike is now trying to track down Tony Capaldi?" asked Jennifer.

"Yes," said Chuck, "I think that's highly likely. As is my suspicion that he is operating within this area."

"Although I very much doubt that he suspects we are on to him."

"So, are we running from shadows?" asked Clare.

"No, I don't think so, answered Chuck, but I think we can ask someone to take a look - Tom."

"Tom?" asked Jennifer,

"Yes, we let Tom go back to his homelands, which means he is well placed to look in the river, to follow any tracks left by Mike."

"How can we reach him?" asked Clare, "He's probably sitting in the middle of the desert somewhere. No phone signal...Please don't say smoke signals."

"No, Tom, is a very modern Navajo. I'll call him on his satellite phone."

"What?" asked Jennifer.

"We used to use them in the desert," said Chuck, "They were handy to have and so we just kept them, post inventory, I suppose you could call it."

"Tom has one, as do I, although if there's an ordinary cellular signal here then I can call his Iridium over cellular. Just add the 0088 prefix- then it's about five dollars a minute."

"Let's give to a go!"

Chuck looked up a number for Tom, "Here we go! - Hey Tom, I bet you didn't expect to hear from me this quickly? Say, you know that blue car that crashed off a bridge? What have you heard? Hmmm. Yeah. What did he look like? Who told you that? Did anyone else see? Where? What now? Who knows?
Tom, I owe you. Until the next time!"

"Wow," said Chuck, "That was interesting. Tom says that the police version is of a crash. Tom says differently. He says they rigged it. Someone paid two guys from his reservation to stage it. They work in a garage and took two thousand each to do it."

"The usual story, they couldn't resist spending some of their new cash and one of them ended up in jail. They were rounded up by the Navajo Police, and we cut a deal with them in return for information. The guy who paid them fits Mike's description. He's stashed away in a Motel. Right on the Ten."

Bigsy asked, "The Ten, I assume you mean the I-10?"

"There's still something that doesn't make sense," said Jennifer.

" I can understand being chased by bad guys, but why would the US Army be running a cover-up? The plane crash and possibly the refinery?"

"It doesn't tie together."

"But I think we know that the two sets of events are connected," said Chuck.

"All right," said Clare, "Let's see if we can work this out. Suppose that Mike or whoever it is has been able to sell the missile technology to some power or other. Suppose it's linked in some way with energy futures. Would the American government be trying to hide that there was some sort of terrorist offensive in play? And if so, why would they be doing this?"

"Perhaps they are being threatened directly and so far are powerless to figure out what to do?" said Chuck.

"So, they try to make the two events look like accidents? Surely that can only work for a little while. Maybe it's just enough time to buy time for them to figure out what is happening?" said Chuck.

"I'm not sure I'm buying it," said Clare.

Spencer had remained quiet through most of this he had been flicking through screens on his laptop computer.

"This may be relevant," he said. He had found a report that had been due to be discussed at the energy summit that had just been cancelled in Houston. The title of the paper was 'Energy Futures the Next 15 Years.'

There was a précis of the document. It described some of the situations that could occur and that in particular North America would need to find new sources for fuel and other types of energy.

It also discussed the emerging power of the Chinese economy and the additional pressures it was creating on the energy infrastructure.

It went on to say that China were much less fussy about the way that they would site the new power stations and that they were quite capable of creating a surplus within a few years.

The Americans were taking a strong-arm position on this. They did not want to be seen to be reliant upon yet another foreign power. Having had to deal with the Middle East for energy particularly oil over the last 20 years they were now far more determined to make themselves self-sufficient.

A large Chinese conglomerate called ChinaEnergy had been formed to try to influence American policy on energy futures. So far it had been unsuccessful and there had been a number of challenges placed in its path.

Spencer pulled up a different article. This was from the Huffington Post and was more of an opinion piece. It commented that the Chinese power brokerage could be sufficient to change the whole dynamics of the trading position between America and the rest of the world.

It could have a significant effect upon the US dollar and raise the power of the Chinese currency as well as the yen and the euro. In effect the US would no longer have the dollar as one of the world's global strongest currencies.

Clare chipped in, "But this is an opinion piece - the writer is grinding a political axe on this. It's one of those things that could take years to play out and I think that the American government are stalling all of this in any case."

"I think you're right," said Jennifer, "There's too many vested interests in the USA based around the energy business. Instead of doing deals, the Chinese were more likely to see a relaxation of our own standards to get to a similar position."

"What," said Bigsy, "the kind of thing where you find a piece of America to put power stations with no questions asked?"

"Kind of," said Jennifer, "if you think about it that's not so dissimilar from storing lots of nuclear warheads in the desert near to Albuquerque."

"So, are we dealing with terrorists or idealists or powerful corporations or what?" said Bigsy.

"I can see a picture beginning to emerge," said Clare. " There is some kind of big power interest in play and maybe they are using the terrorist angle to create a perfect storm. It could tip the negotiations towards the use of the Chinese power within the American economy."

"So, kill an energy aware senator up and blow up a refinery? And not forgetting that they have successfully stopped the conference in Houston," said Jennifer.

"And maybe the scale of this so-called terrorist attack is more limited than they imagine?" said Bigsy

Yes, and this is with just a few rockets sent," said Chuck.

"It's still enough to be pretty lethal and could be enough to tip the whole economics around," said Bigsy.

Spencer was still using the computer.

"Take a look at this," he said, "it's the recent share prices of some of the American oil companies. Since the explosion at the oil refinery and the cancellation of the conference there has been a significant write-down of share prices for the whole energy sector. In North America it's affecting the rest of the market too."

He looked across to the European stock markets.

"It doesn't seem to have had the same impact in London or Frankfurt and actually in China the prices are rising."

"A lot of what we're working on is supposition," said Clare, "We may just be tying two things together without any real hard evidence."

"I agree, it may not be the sort of thing you could prove in a court of law," said Chuck," but there's an awful lot of circumstances that seem to link these things together.

"And I'm guessing that if Mike is involved and the current damage is limited to a radius of maybe 100 miles or so that he is not using the UAVs yet?"

"I think that's why he's trying to find out about these launchers. The idea of using something like a Predator as part of a private initiative is little far-fetched. It needs a proper runway to take off and at a fairly advanced subsystem around it. The smaller UAVs that can be launched using the catapult launchers are a much better bet. The trick is to figure out how to add a payload to them. If the work that was being done by Tony Capaldi and the rest of the team managed to solve weapon carrying, then I think we have the basis of a much bigger threat from whoever is running Mike and whoever he is else is involved with."

"So, Jennifer, is there any other way we can get help from the people that are holding Jake?"

"You mean SI6," said Jennifer.

"Yes, but what I mean is whether we can use them directly without getting involved in the local agencies here?"

"I think the local agencies here are trying to cover up the previous explosions rather than figure out the bigger picture. "

"That's why they are trying to get me to come in," said Jennifer, "Before I know it be in Plano in one of the agency facilities and that will take me off the grid."

"I think we have most of the pieces now," said Bigsy. "We also have a pretty strong team here plus Jake and SI6 people as backup. There must be something we can do that will flush this out. Jennifer my worry is that this will become dangerous again for one or more of us."

"I think we need to find a way to make contact with Tony Capaldi, " said Chuck. "If Mike has called him to a meeting, I expect it's also back in Scottsdale where he met me. We really need some sort of confirmation of that before we start moving around again."

"I think this is where I will need to call in a few more

favours," says Lucas, "I can get information about flights and movements of passengers as part of my security role. This time it would be best if Spencer make the calls so that it dilutes attention. You have the full name of this person," said Jennifer, "We can call up to find out where and when he has travelled - he might even have declared his initial hotel in Arizona."

"This could be mechanical process, I don't like to say this," said Chuck, "but I think it might be too late to find Tony Capaldi now. If he travelled into Scottsdale, it could have been the day after me. When Mike left us, if he is still alive, I think he will have gone back to find this Capaldi before heading off to Texas."

"We should still check for flight information," said Jennifer, "Spencer could you get onto that?"

"I can't access this information from here," said Spencer, "it's all a secure link. I'll contact Lucas back at the office."

# *SI6*

Jake had been in a further discussion with Amanda Miller from the SI6 group. "The team in the US have asked for a meeting. They wanted to be secure and limited to a few people. It's difficult because how people think the Americans are trying to hide what is happening."

Amanda Miller grinned, "That would not be the first time. I assume Chuck is still in danger then?"

"It is getting more complex," said Jake, "We will need the others to help explain it. They will then want some help from you."

"It's a judgement call," said Amanda, "We have to decide whether there is any UK national security at risk. We would cooperate with the Americans as well, but you can understand that some of this is out of our jurisdiction."

"Yes," said Jake, "But please can we keep this to the Brits for the next session."

"That's fine," said Amanda, "and it's part of the reason that you were here, anyway."

"Can we set a time please, I'll text them," said Jake,

"Let's say two hours from now," said Amanda.

# *Liaison*

Chuck looked at his watch, it was almost 8 o'clock.

"It's time for our call from London," said Chuck, "they must be staying up late."

"Should we stay here?" said Clare "Or maybe it's better to go to one of our rooms."

"Let's use mine," said Chuck, "As I've paid for everyone else, they seem to have given me quite a decent-sized room."

They followed him to the elevator, and he pressed for the top floor. It said executive floor.

"Get you," said Bigsy.

"I know," said Chuck, "there are a few perks to having the payroll."

He led them to his room, which was a small suite. There was a separate room with a table, and six chairs separated from the bedroom.

"This will do nicely," said Bigsy.

They set up Clare's phone on the middle of the table.

At 8pm prompt, Amanda Miller called Clare's cell phone.

Clare introduced who was on the call and Amanda said 'hello' to everyone. She was with Jake and also Jim Cavendish.

"I think you should start by telling us what you know," said Amanda, "Jennifer, I know that both the CIA and the FBI are showing an interest in this, which seems to go beyond it being a matter affecting Colonel Manners and the inadvertent introduction of the three British Subjects.

Jennifer began, "Yes, I think the Agencies are also falling over one another," she said. "Let's start with a few of the things we've seen and the ways they link."

Jennifer explained:

"Colonel Manners and a few of his close colleagues from work at Los Alamos around seven years ago were all called to a hotel in Scottsdale. It is somewhere they all knew and had been a rest and recreation spot when they were on their mission.

"Some of their number died, in various unusual circumstances.

"Colonel Manners suspected something was amiss when he

broke cover to come to Scottsdale."

"What do you mean, broke cover?" asked Amanda.

"To most people, Chuck Manners was dead, killed on a mission around a year ago. The people he contacted, Clare and Bigsy, were not surprised to be approached by the alleged missing Chuck Manners and came out to Scottsdale at his request."

"We'd never really believed he was dead," said Bigsy, "So when he asked for us to contact him, we were happy to do so. We moved pretty much straight away to link with him."

"So, the three of you meet together?" asked Amanda.

"Well, Bigsy met Chuck first, someone drugged them and then an ex colleague of Chuck's called Mike rescued them. He drove them to a safe place in the desert,"

"But we think it has implicated Mike in the disappearance of the others," chipped in Chuck. "We think he was trying to find out something about the old project."

"So, he rescued you, then what happened?"

"This is about when you, SI6, picked up Jake," said Bigsy, "Clare was still separated from us, but you sent Jennifer to find her and someone else to locate Jake."

"That's right," said Amanda, "We were trying to keep you safe because we thought you had stumbled into something important and sensitive.

"OK," said Jennifer," So next we arranged for Clare to meet

with Chuck and Bigsy again. They located some information which we think is material to some recent events in Texas. The killing of the senator and the explosion at the oil refinery in Houston."

Chuck added, "It was a tortuous route to get that information but smacked of field skills of the kind that me and my colleagues would use. In other words, one of my buddies had left the messaging."

"The thing is, we don't know who sent the message to us, but it said that there is a conspiracy related to energy futures and the Chinese.

"So, the other piece we have," continued Jennifer, "is the weapon gadgets that Chuck was helping to support back seven years ago. It was a dead-end technology, but it sounds as if someone has resurrected it."

"Yes," said Chuck, "It provides a clandestine way to guide a missile into a target. The homing device is pretty much undetectable and can remain inert for up to, er, I'm guessing, five years."

"Okay," said Amanda, so you have put these events together..."

"Yes," said Chuck, "And we also think some of this is being covered up by the US Government. Both the death of Senator Williams and the Oil Refinery explosion are re-branded as 'accidents' by the media. We tried to get to the car crash spot and could see that there were two different locations. One shown to the press had a plane wreck sprinkled around it. A mile or so further along the same road there was a missile track that showed a major explosion from a missile had occurred."

"Yes, so our supposition is that they want to use transponders to send in missiles. The thing is, the range and radius of current operations isn't what you'd expect if they were targeting with a drone, which is the original design point of the transponder."

Jennifer added, " I think they are trying to simulate the effects of the transponder system now, but only have an airborne short-range missile rack at their disposal. They want the US to think they have something more, but they are still trying to acquire it."

Chuck said, "I think the original UAVs that we were trialling were fine for a military style operation. If you need to escape detection, you'd need something smaller I think the terrorists are using much smaller missiles - rockets even - which also have a much smaller range. I think this could get very messy if they got hold the small-scale UAVs. That would give a massive range and create a terror weapon that could operate over thousands of miles.

"I also think the reason Mike has been chasing people is to find the launchers for the smaller weapons. The most likely type is the Scan Eagle sized weapons, which launch from a small catapult. It's my guess that one of the team knew how to make this work and just as importantly, where to find these launchers."

"Okay," said Amanda, "but I can't understand why the US Government would keep this so quiet and why they would hide the aftermath of the various attacks."

"That is what we want you to help us find out," said Jennifer,

"It looks to me as if the FBI have already been involved in both the Senator scene and the Oil Refinery," said Jennifer, "As it's become a cover-up, I doubt whether it is being treated as domestic terrorism."

"So, the CIA would also be involved?" Asked Amanda.

"Definitely," said Chuck, "This will be multiple agency. Some kind of Joint Terrorism Task Force."

"We need to find out if there is a new JTTF based around this situation," said Chuck, "I guess you already know that the original project seven years ago was Project Esther?"

"OK," said Amanda, "It's time I explained a little about what we know. Yes, we knew about Project Esther, but only recently. Someone from a JTTF called Alabaster called our team. They were looking into an old programme called Esther and were asking us a few routine questions. Like you say, they told us enough about the project such that we understood it was to do with guidance systems, but they also played down its significance and told us it was now defunct."

"They explained they were trying to track down the original members of the team because there were some missing components they wanted to track. They didn't say what or why, though."

"We treated it as routine and along the way they gave us a few names: Chuck, Mike, Ben and a few others. They said they were looking for these people and they could transit through the UK."

"A later update told us that two of them, Klaus and Ben, had recently died. They emphasised that if we could locate any of the others, then we should let them know.

Within 24 hours it escalated because of a random call from Colonel Manners to the offices of 'The Triangle' which is the company run by Jake Lambers.

The call was to three of the principles of the company and, if genuine, it would show that Chuck Manners was still alive and not killed in an explosion as it said in his record.

The reason for the interest from the JTTF was that it could show that Chuck was acting subversively against the interests of the USA. Getting access to his contacts was one way to bring him in.

That's when we pulled Jake from the offices and across to SI6. We'd told the Americans we had Jake and that he might try to contact Chuck.

"That's also when I took a careful look at what was happening," said Amanda. "After the exchange between Clare and Jake, it became apparent that Chuck was being chased, but not so clear who was doing it."

Amanda added, "It made me wonder if there was a different agenda at play - one to neutralise the whole team that Chuck was a part of."

"I'm still acting with the CIA on this," said Amanda, "but I decided to take this call separately. I want to ascertain if there is a double agenda at play. "

Chuck commented, "There is something going on. The JTTF would tell you more than they have on this occasion. Also, you wouldn't get a JTTF if it is mainly a situation about the bumping off of half a dozen ex-military community."

"I have to agree," said Jennifer, "there must be a bigger situation in play."

Amanda paused. Jake could see he was thinking what to do.

"Hello, Hello," asked Jennifer, "Is the line still working?"

"Yes." said Amanda, "I'm thinking. I'm trying to work out other angles."

# *Joint Terrorism Task Force*

"The most obvious to me is a cover-up," said Chuck, "That could be because the US Government are up to something themselves."

"A more likely situation is that they don't know what to do," said Clare, "That would suggest they are trying to buy time by not letting too much information out."

"I like it," said Bigsy, "It's a fairly obvious explanation and fits the situation well. The JTTF has been charged to solve something big; the time is ticking, and they are already facing some early examples of a problem. They are trying to hide the current situation while they figure out how to solve the bigger problem."

"Yes," said Chuck, "I think it fits too. I'm guessing that the US Government have received a threat and are trying to decide their countermeasures. That's the role of the JTTF. In the meantime, they are being faced with the escalation of the threat that they are handling."

"Yes," said Jennifer, "and it is first one Senator, then a refinery and then something bigger. - But not the cancelled conference of energy executives."

"Is there a way we can find out about this?" asked Chuck, looking at Jennifer.

"I wonder if this is where SI6 can help us?" asked Jennifer, "If you could gain some kind of access to the JTTF, we might get more information."

"I can try," said Amanda, "but I wonder if it will have the right effect, or whether everything will just become more secure."

"That's what we need to find out," said Chuck, "But I wonder if we can also bait the question?"

"What do you mean?" asked Amanda.

"Well, if we can give them something that will intrigue them to let us know the background, it could help a lot."

"Do you have something in mind?" said Amanda.

"Yes," said Chuck, "I think we should tell them we think we know who is looking for the Project Esther components and that we think we know why."

"And who and what is that?" asked Amanda.

Chuck said, "You must trust me on this one, but I can answer both questions."

"He's right," said Jennifer, "I think he knows."

"But do you know too, Amanda?" asked Jennifer.

"I don't have the information that Chuck has about most of this," said Jennifer, "So No, I don't know."
She looked across to Chuck. She could see that Chuck recognised she had just lied to Amanda, but Amanda was only listening to the call and wouldn't be able to pick up on Jennifer's visual cue to Chuck.

"Okay," said Amanda, "I will make enquiries about this JTTF. As they gave me a code name for the JTTF at the beginning of their enquiries about Colonel Manners, I will use that as my route to get further information."

"When should we expect to hear something?" asked Jennifer.

"You must give me 24 hours," said Amanda, "On second thoughts, let's try to set the next call for a more civilised time for both of us. How about 10 am your time?, that will be 5 pm for me. That's about 32 hours away."

Chuck and Jennifer looked at one another. "Things here are moving fast," said Jennifer. I realise you'll need some time to get to people, well go with your plan; if anything untoward happens, we will use Clare's cell phone to communicate."

"Okay," said Amanda, "We'll use that as a plan. In the meantime, we will also be scanning our comms for any other signs of activity."

The line clicked off in the office where Amanda, Jake and Jim Cavendish sat.

"It's all sounding intense," said Jake. "Do you think you'll be able to get anything from the JTTF?"

Amanda spoke, "Our best chance is to do as Chuck suggests, to let them know that Chuck has some other information. The downside is that they will probably be picked up with half an hour of the call. I can't imagine that the CIA will leave Chuck and the others to run loose once they know they have information or may be implicated in some way."

"Will you be able to deal directly with the JTTF?" Asked Jake, "or do you think you must bring some other bosses into the situation?"

"I was wondering about this myself," said Amanda, "I should make an immediate report of all of this, but truthfully I'm concerned that if I do that, then we'll see everyone rounded up."

Frankly, we are better off leaving them in the field. They seem to get on and finding are finding out plenty, even if some of it is circumstantial.

"Welcome to our world," said Jake, "You'd be surprised how often the circumstantial stuff plays out as accurate."

"What will you do with me while this is going on? I can only watch so many box-sets." asked Jake.

"I will need to keep you here longer," said Amanda. "It's mainly for your own safety, no one can get to you here. If I'm truthful, it also means I'm certain that the comms to Clare and

Bigsy will stay open."

"I trust that these temporary facilities are not too bad?"

Jake nodded. He would be comfortable enough here for another few days.

Amanda asked Jim to take Jake to the secure facility and to check if Jake needed anything. Amanda walked out of the room and into a corridor.

She decided she would approach the operations centre first about access to the JTTF. She already had the name of her contact and would use that to report to them as if on an operational matter.

Amanda returned to her office and composed a note to the JTTF leader. It was simple enough.

"My contact in Arizona has information about component placement from Project Esther. Wants to talk. Can we arrange?"

To Amanda's surprise, the reply came back in a matter of a few minutes. It was suitably terse, like her original email.

"We should meet," it said, "Come to the Duchess, at 11:00"

Amanda smiled, then groaned. The Duchess Belle was a known off-site venue. The CIA Station for London had a main office in the US Embassy buildings in South London. Before that, it had been in Grosvenor Square, where the Barley Mow had served a similar purpose.

Using the Duchess Belle was a way to signal Amanda that the

meeting would be brief and informal. The pub was less than 10 minutes' walk from the American embassy, but for a visitor to the embassy, it was a welcome relief to go to the pub and miss all of the lovely US security.

Amanda knew that the pub was like another agency office, albeit with an easier access.

Amanda looked at her watch. She would need to leave soon to be there on time. The person she was meeting would not wait more than a few minutes past the appointed time.

In the pub, Amanda ordered a cafe latte and studied the room. It was still early, and there were only a few people in the bar. Two tourists in one corner. Two suited consultant types studying a laptop in another and a man at the bar sipping a pint of bitter.

It was five minutes to the due time, and she saw who she expected to be her contact walk in.

The man walked to the bar and ordered a coffee. He nodded towards Amanda, "let's get a seat," he said.

He acted as if he already knew Amanda, although she still didn't know exactly who she was meeting,

"I'm the person who received your request. My name is Spencer Brown." He shook hands with Amanda.

"Hello and I'm Amanda," she replied.

"So, what do you think you have?" asked Spencer.

"We have a strong lead from Colonel Manners," said

Amanda, "He thinks he knows what they are looking for."

Amanda summarised the main facts to Spencer.

They both sipped quietly on their coffees. Amanda kept the explanations correct but sparse. The main point was to explain that Chuck had some further information which could be useful. But in return, the JTTF would have to give a little information too.

"Do you have your passport with you?" asked Spencer.

"Er, yes," said Amanda. She knew that to get in and out of some embassies she needed to carry her passport and security passes.

"Okay," said Spencer, "I suggest we take a short walk onto American soil."

He gestured towards the direction of the door. They would be going to the Embassy buildings situated in Nine Elms, just along the river from the pub.

"Okay, let's go," said Amanda, "You know I will need to be back to make a call to Manners in a few hours."

"That's fine," said Spencer, "we'll make sure you are back in time."

They strolled the ten minutes back to the Embassy and on this occasion, Amanda could use a fast path route to gain access, sped on her way by Spencer's passes and authority.

"We'll be going to an underground part of the building," said Spencer, "I will need to ask you to leave phones and so forth behind in a secure locker."

Amanda knew the drill, which was very similar to the one at SI6. She wondered if they used the same contractors, although the US version of everything looked somehow more American.

They were soon in a secure area. "You have to be escorted here at all times," said Spencer, "I'll introduce you to someone else in a minute who will be your host for the time you are here."

They entered a room which was a mess of coffee cups and scraps of papers. Various laptops were switched on and a big screen at the end of the room said simply 'Thistle'.

"Okay everyone," said Spencer, "This is Amanda from our friends at SI6, she can help us locate Colonel Manners, one of The Six. The team we are trying to locate. I've brought her here for a cross briefing on what we know.

Another person in the room stood. It was a heavily tanned Colonel with the American Army, in a dress Uniform.

"I'll take it from here," said the Colonel. My name is Edgar Foster, I'm your local liaison point for this program which is being run from Washington."

"We think there's a significant threat to US Domestic security in play. That's why we have been watching the people we are referring to as 'The Six'. We think someone in this group has devised a weapon capable of creating extreme damage to the fabric of the US. Not by use as a massive weapon of mass destruction like a nuclear bomb or a chemical attack, but rather by structured precision hits on selected targets."

"That's what we think has happened with the Senator and the Refinery, but we have several other threats in current play. These have all been notified to us before they happened, but unfortunately, they don't give a sequence or anything to help us take full countermeasures.

"When the first block came in, we didn't know whether to believe them. We have many spurious warnings, but with these, after the senator and the refinery, we knew that they were quoting the same code words . That's why we stopped the energy conference actually, we realised that it could be an obvious next target.

"The first few were all in Texas?" asked Amanda, "is that the same for the rest? In the current list there's a couple more within a 100-mile radius, but after that they start to become further afield."

"We'll tell you that in a moment," answered Colonel Foster.

"You said there was a code, does that mean there's other information too?" asked Amanda.

"Initially there wasn't anything else to go on," said the Colonel, "To be honest, initially we thought everything we had heard was a hoax. Students or something similar. The reason was that there were so many targets nominated all at once. We now find that the targets selected were not the first two on the list but randomly selected from the longer list."

"So that after they blew up the Senator, I assume you treated the rest of the list seriously?" asked Amanda.

"We had discovered the list again before the second event

took place at the refinery but there wasn't time to move on all the different locations."

"At the moment we have another six targets within the United States. There are another six listed in other parts of the world."

"Why haven't you made a formal announcement about this on television, or the media? asked Amanda.

"For predictable reasons," said Colonel Foster, "We don't want the effect of the terrorist targeting to create the fear that they are hoping for."

"Is this being done in the name of something or for ideological reasons?" asked Amanda, "or is it connected with a demand?"

Amanda knew that the information she had received from Chuck and the others was that this was linked in some way to energy trading.

"We link this threat to something related to a deal with the Chinese", said Foster, "I haven't details of that here. The problem I see is that if we concede this based upon the threats, there's no reason the people doing this won't then ask for something else. We have to stop them at source, so it ends this whole thing."

"Our best lead on this is The Six. We think one of them is behind the terrorist threat and that they are trying to extend its effectiveness."

"When we looked at the two initial explosion sites both of them seem to use hot fix missiles. These are stand-alone missiles that can be targeted usually by laser beam. Based on what we have heard, it is possible that someone has changed the guidance systems for these missiles."

"If we are right, then these missiles have a fairly short range. They used on a battlefield and fired from a truck or similar. They are the weapons used by mercenary soldiers in places like Afghanistan."

"I don't think they have the sophistication to launch the attacks being described in the rest of the list."

"Can you tell me the other targets?" asked Amanda.

"I'm afraid it is highly classified," said the colonel, "I have not been told; I can only assume it is at the level that would affect national security."

"This smacks of an act of war," said Amanda, "For example is this the Chinese declaring war on the United States?"

"I think you are understanding why we are treating this so carefully," said the Foster. "That is also why we have two special units providing coverage of the sites of the initial explosions. We wanted to make them look like accidents so we could spin the news whilst we try to work out what is going on."

Amanda nodded. She could see that the suppositions from Chuck, Jennifer, and the rest of the team on the ground had been fairly close to what was happening. They just hadn't worked out the scale of what was going on."

Amanda spoke to the Colonel," You can't expect to keep hiding this for much longer. I'm amazed that the press is not already picking up on this."

"We have given the press a good story about the Senator, which doesn't impact what's been happening with the security aspects of this. It also makes the Senator look very good and I think at the moment everyone is focusing on that aspect."

"With the explosion at the refinery it's much more about the environment and pollution than those kinds of things we kept the story away from the true source of the explosion."

"But if one more of these things were to happen, then surely the media would piece it together?" said Amanda.

"What about the Chinese angle," asked Amanda, "Can't you bring that out into the open? I'm afraid that the politicians are all over that one," said the Foster, "At the moment there is a risk of economic downturn based upon the increasing power of the Chinese. What we're trying to do is avoid a situation where Chinese market entrants took over the American economy."

"I think it aims this terrorism at trying to chip the balance of power towards more Chinese takeovers. That would severely interfere with what we think of as the Western world and Western economies."

"Okay," said Amanda, "I appreciate your frankness on all of this. What I'd like to suggest is that we arrange another meeting which includes Colonel Manners, Jennifer and the rest of the team still based over in the USA."

I prefer that we do this at SI6 though and I'd like to reciprocate your kind offer to bring me here and instead that I would ask for you to bring maybe two people along with yourself, Colonel and Spencer. I should have a way to make a direct link to Colonel Manners and can also have one of his UK team here in my offices at SI6."

Colonel Foster seemed impressed that Amanda had access to Manners and his team and even had one of them in SI6.

The colonel nodded , "Yes all right then, we will make the arrangements. What time do we need to be at Vauxhall Bridge?"

# You can't touch this

"When you reach the end of what you should know,
you will be at the beginning of what you should sense."

*–Kahlil Gibran*

# *Trap*

Spencer looked at the map.

"I think the most likely area for any kind of attack would be from the East," he said, "It's past the outskirts of Plano and turns back into deserts and mountainous areas. Can we think of some logic why we could explain Capaldi in this area."

"Yes, I think he needs to be visiting somebody to the west of Plano, may be across into Arkansas." said Spencer, "That would mean somewhere like Little Rock. I know it's amusing," said Spencer. "But if we pick Little Rock, then there's a direct route that runs from planar across to the east and then up into Arkansas state."

"Second, we find a location or a potential meeting."
Spencer studied the map, "There is an interesting place called Sulphur Springs on the way. The main advantage is that it has a range of motels on the main route."

Chuck had a look at the map that Spencer had pulled up, "Yes, this looks a good area. Now we need to track down Tony Capaldi and get him over to this part of Texas. We can be in Sulphur Springs in about three hours"

"Right now we do not know where Mike is, nor do we have any idea who is running him, "said Chuck.

"Look," said Colonel Foster, "The Chinese company in the trading arrangement is called EnergyChina. There are two possibilities; one would be that it is EnergyChina and another is that it would be a major shareholder. We have already run some investigations of this back in Langley.

Chuck asked, "Is there any way we can get more insight into what EnergyChina have been doing?"

"The US government has been watching energy China for some time. They have an interesting track record in their country. Because of their tight links with the militia and politicians and the freedom with which it pays backhanders, EnergyChina are doing what they like. The problem we've always seen with this company and others in China is their ability to upset the global economy for energy pricing."

"From the United States we've had a strong relationship with some middle eastern countries and have been able to keep a balance of pricing and futures for energy. Now that China has created such a new and powerful industrial drag on fuel reserves, there is a new force in play. Because China also has its own natural reserves and an endless ability to dig new pipelines and create new pieces of industrial infrastructure, it means that there is every chance that energy prices may get manipulated."

"We should also recognise that EnergyChina has seen a massive increase in its share price because of the injection of funding from the ChinaFin. ChinaFin is not a state-run organisation but has a major shareholding via Cheung Chau.

"I think we are on to something," said Chuck. "In some form or other, EnergyChina and ChinaFin are financing the plot that is running here in Texas."

Ed Adams

# *Conference Call*

The team had assembled back in Chuck's room for the call the next day. Clare had her iPhone set up, plugged in and ready to go. They sat around the table, waiting to hear any further news from Amanda.

At the appointed hour Clare's phone rang, and she picked up.

"Hello Clare, it's Amanda again. Things have moved on here since we spoke last. We are still in our SI6 headquarters and Jake is with us. There are some other people here this time. They are from the US government and our people based in London."

"Please, could you introduce yourselves," asked Jennifer.

Amanda asked the Colonel to introduce himself and his colleagues.

"Okay," said Chuck, "Before I say anything further, what else can you tell us about what is happening?"

# The Circle

The Colonel explained the same story that he had already described to Amanda. When he got to the part about there being several other targets, Chuck was very interested.

"Do we know where those other targets are?" asked Chuck. "Are there any further targets close to the ones we have already seen?"

Colonel Foster said, "I am under instructions that this is classified information."

"That may be so," said Chuck, "But at the moment we are the people closest to solving this and I need to know whether there are any targets in this vicinity?"

"Why is that?" asked the Colonel, "I think it is becoming evident that at the moment the person conducting these outrages is still using short-range missiles. I think the reason he has called upon all of us that were in the original team is to find out from one of us what happened when we use the drones with the much longer ranges."

"This is my new information," said Chuck, "We were testing two kinds of drone: The very large ones - The Predators which have massive wing spans and are not something you could carry in hand luggage. But Barbara Somerville and Tony Capaldi were also testing the smaller drones the kind that I used for naval reconnaissance. They are about the size of a large toy plane with a 4-foot wingspan. They don't need long runways to take off; we can launch them using special catapult launchers.

"That's what Mike was trying to find out from me when we were in the desert. Did I know where the catapult launches took place? I didn't but I think Somerville and Capaldi both knew about this. My guess is that Mike has called them to Scottsdale and is trying to link up with them and get the information about the catapult launchers. Then he could take a small van with a launcher and several of those UAVs and he would be a mobile arsenal.

"But where would he get the armaments?" said Amanda, "The UAVs are passive devices."

"That's the point," said Chuck, " I don't know, but I think Barbara Somerville or Tony Capaldi will know because of the work we all did. I think the equipment was stored somewhere in the desert, close to the Kirtland base. However, the area is so large, if you don't know where to look, you won't be able to find the equipment."

"So, here's my scenario," said Chuck, "If there's another target close to the current ones I think they will try to take a shot at it with one of their rockets. That keeps the pressure on whilst they figure out how to get the UAVs and the launchers from wherever they are being held."

"In terms of threat it would work because it will become a point where the US government won't be able to contain the number of stories any longer. I think if there are three separate incidents within a single US state let alone anything further afield then the free press will make noises of its own about what is going on."

Amanda replied, "I think you are right, Colonel Manners. It is an ultimate form of leverage using a tiny unit to create such havoc. Of course, if they get access the homing control system and the real UAVs then it escalates this to another whole level."

Chuck replied, " Yes, that's why I need to know whether there are any other sites in the general area that could be targeted."

There was a long pause.

Bigsy and the others could hear murmuring from the London office. "I should get agreement to release the classified information," said Colonel Foster. "But I will tell you one thing. One of the other targets is, frankly, a lower priority target than the major ones on their list. It is the downtown area of Plano, around the Dart terminal."

"What's Dart?" asked Clare,

"That's like the main transit hub," said Jennifer. It's right in the middle of downtown Plano.

"I can see some logic to this," said Chuck, "If I only had access to rockets then something like that would be an interesting target. The reason is simple. I can choose an arc from that location where I fire upon the target. I only need to be 20 or 30 miles away, drive close enough, target and wham, preferably from an area that is isolated. Do you see what I mean?

"Okay," asked Bigsy," And the difference between rockets and missiles?"

Jennifer answered, "rockets just fire, missiles can be guided,"
"Ahhh," said Bigsy, "That makes sense."

"If I want disrupt everything, but I don't have the UAVs, I can simulate their effect within a small area, so long as I have some rockets."

If I am still trying to get access to the UAVs then firing a short-range rocket from a secluded site with very accurate targeting can keep the pressure on the US government until I can get the real weaponry from wherever it's currently stored."

"I concur," said Colonel Foster, "The question is whether we can work out where this would be fired from."

Spencer was sitting with the team in Chuck's room and was already looking on his computer. "There's a couple of areas that would fit that description," he said, "They are both some way out from Plano."

Chuck glanced at the map that Spencer had produced. "It's still problematic," he said, "This is too big an area."

"Or it's too big an area if we can't think of a way to attract the terrorists. I think we need to come up with a plan to make it easy for them to decide where they should take their missile."

"And how can we do that?" asked Clare.

"I think we need to use our other members of the team as incentive," said Chuck, "I still don't know whether we have found Tony Capaldi. If we can find him we could use him to help limit the area that Mike or whoever it is is operating within. We use Capaldi to attract Mike to a particular zone. And once we have him pinned down then we stand a better chance to stop him."

## The Circle

Jennifer asked Chuck, " It sounds good in theory but surely he is as professional as you are. Won't he work out you are trying to do something like this. He'll know it is a trap?"

"Not if we can get Capaldi directly involved in this process. At the moment Capaldi won't know that Mike has officially crashed his car into a river. We need to get Capaldi to call Mike direct, but ideally to have a cover story about why he is not in Scottsdale.

"You know we tracked down Capaldi," said Spencer. "He flew from Columbus to Phoenix, via Chicago."

"He arrived in Phoenix two days ago."

"I expect he has done the same as me," said Chuck, " and headed for that hotel in Scottsdale. Will he be there under his own name asked Spencer or will he have something else?"

"The difference between him and me seems to be that he's happy to use his real identity," said Chuck, "He was showing up as a university tutor in Columbus."

"Great," said Spencer, "That will make it much easier to find him."

Spencer got the name of the hotel from Chuck and was quickly onto the case to find the information.

"Right," said Chuck, "I think we have the basis of the plan. If we can contact Capaldi, we can ask him to meet Mike in a certain part of Texas. We should work out the areas from which he is most able to have a range on Plano and try in effect to force Mike's hand with where he is more likely to launch his attack on Plano.

"I think that means we need to make sure it is further out from Plano so that it stretches the line between Mike and Plano."

"I've worked out a plan," said Spencer.

"Capaldi likes golf. There's about a dozen courses to the north of the Dallas Fort Worth area, in a place called Fresno. It is less than 30 miles from Plano, has plenty of hotels and a secluded wildlife area. I'll just check the hotels and book Capaldi into one of the expensive ones around there. It looks as if the Omni Frisco Hotel is a good one. It's fancy, close to the golf, close to the Dallas Cowboys, you get my drift."

"It's also got controllable exits, if things cut up rough," said Chuck, looking at the hotel's location on the map.

"Yes, and if I wanted to fire a rocket, I could go over to the LLELA Nature Preserve, which is a few minutes away from the hotel. Line of sight to Plano or Fort Worth from there." added Chuck.

"Do you think Mike works alone?" said Bigsy,

Chuck replied, "No, he had the extra heavies that chased us. He will have some further help, but it is interesting how a tiny unit can create such a large amount of devastation."

"Guess that's what we were trained for," said Chuck.

"So if we can pin down Mike's unit, it would remove his leverage from the discussion about energy futures."

"We still need to find out who is driving the whole plan,"

said Jennifer.

"I agree," said Amanda from the speakerphone, "We will still need more help from you Colonel Foster,"

"This puts me in a difficult situation," said Colonel Foster, "I should communicate most of this back to my team in Langley."

"The problem is that Mike gets information from somewhere," said Jennifer, "There seems to be a leak and also there seem to be people trying to stop us from tracking this down," said Jennifer.

"That's a big problem for me also," said Colonel Foster, "I think most of you seem to know one another but I'm afraid I have to continue to treat most of this with suspicion. For example, Colonel Manners you have been with most of The Six and know all of them. As we now think one of them is the suspect in all of this, it keeps you as someone under suspicion."

"I think we only have one shot at this," said Chuck, "At the moment we know that Capaldi has been called by Mike. We also know that Mike is likely to find out information from Capaldi about these launchers and possibly these UAVs. I'm guessing there is a mothballed stash of them somewhere in Kirtland. Right now, it is needle in a haystack, but with the right information, they could be gone in a few minutes.

Chuck said, "We can create a trap. If we don't do it then Mike will be through our fingers with access to a more extensive form of firepower."

# *Tony Capaldi*

Spencer had tracked down another one of the invited guests. Tony Capaldi. Sure enough, he was in the Scottsdale hotel and staying under his own name.

"Okay, we need to contact Tony direct now," said Chuck, "I should do it, he will know who I am, and we can easily talk together about old times."

Bigsy commented, "You know, you may need to figure out whether he is working with Mike."

"I agree," said Chuck, "I shall need to listen out for any signs."

Chuck used the hotel telephone to call the number for Tony's hotel room. He dialled the switchboard number at the hotel, and he asked for Tony Capaldi. There was a few moments pause and then a ring tone.

"Hello," said a voice.

## The Circle

"Tony?" Asked Chuck

"Yes, this is Tony, who is it?" asked the voice.

"Tony, it will surprise you to hear that this is Chuck Manners," said Chuck, "I think they called me just like you to visit Scottsdale."

"My God, Chuck Manners! It's been a long time. I assume you are still in scrapes? I've taken a more business-oriented route nowadays. To be honest, I thought it was you that was making the calls and sending the invitations. I'm told that Mike and Barbara will also be here. I'm guessing it wasn't you making the invitations, then."

"No, Tony, I think it's something to do with the work we did previously.

Tony continued, "I'm thinking it was Mike who called. He called me earlier and said that he would be in town in a couple of days. I guess you got the same message as me that this was important and that we need to be at all costs."

"Yes," said Chuck, "but Tony, I need you to do something for me now."

"Buddy, what is it?" asked Tony.

"There is something not right about all of this," said Chuck, "and I think you can help us to understand it. Did you know that Ben and Klaus have both been killed in the last two weeks?

"Wow. I'm shocked. I had no idea," said Tony, "to be honest I'm out of the community nowadays."

"Right," said Chuck, "But this is very important. We think it somehow involves Mike. He invited me to the same meeting, and I was in Scottsdale two days ago. I got chased by some bad guys and I'm lucky to still be alive."

"We think Mike is trying to get some information that only a couple of us will know. It's relates to the project, and it's the stuff that I think you and Barbara were working on. We shouldn't really talk about it by phone.

"Let's just say it is connected with the little things in the desert… "

"Okay," said Tony, "I understand - yes that was me that used to work with Barbara. But all of that was a long time ago."

"Yes," said Chuck, "However, we think Mike has gone renegade and is now working for another power. We think he is trying to find out about these small things and maybe where some of them are kept."

"I understand," said Tony, "And to be honest I'm not sure that I want to be mixed up in any of this. I came along because someone used the code. You know the emergency protocol."

"That's the same with me," said Chuck, "I had actually gone invisible before this and broke cover to be involved."

"So where is Mike now?" asked Tony.

"We think he's in Texas?" said Chuck, "actually we want you to come over here to help us track him down. We think he needs to be removed from play now."

"Removed from play... sounds a bit drastic... Are you working this alone?" asked Tony.

"No," said Chuck," and this whole thing has, let's say, escalated. "

"Chuck, what if I just turned around and went back to Ohio?"

"I think you could do that," said Chuck, "but I'd be fearful that Mike or someone he's working with will be after you. I think you probably hold the key to this. To what it is that Mike wants."

" I thought the whole point with that program was that they deemed it redundant," said Tony.

"Yes, it is to the military but not to someone involved in terrorism."

"Okay," said Tony, "I guess that Mike is doing this for money? And are you sure it's Mike and not somebody else?"

"If I am honest, we are still working on theories for most of this," said Chuck.

"Look, Tony, do you think you could get over here to us to meet us and we can give you more information? I think I can help us track down what is happening with Mike."

"Where are you?" said Tony.

"We are  close to Dallas," said Chuck, "in a fancy hotel, actually.  Do you think you could get a flight across to us from Phoenix first thing tomorrow?"

 "Sure,"  said  Tony.  "I will check with the airport and try to be out on the first flight.

# *AVGAS 110LL (blue)*

The next morning Chuck was awake early. He had packed all his belongings back into the camouflage bag and was ready to leave the hotel. He had instructed the others to be ready early and had said 7 o'clock was their departure time.

It was currently around 630AM in the morning and he was idly watching the television and looking out of the window of the hotel across towards the vista of the airport.

The daybreak news programme on the television switched to a story from a road in Arizona. There had been a major early morning crash. A truck carrying aviation fuel had crashed into a taxi and a fireball had ensued. The occupants of the taxi had been killed outright, although the truck driver was nowhere to be seen.

Chuck looked at the broadcast. It showed an aerial view of the tanker and large billowing clouds of smoke. There was still much traffic blocking both directions around the crash scene. Chuck was immediately suspicious of the coincidence of this situation. Also, that the avgas truck had so readily caught fire. Normally there would be sufficient emergency safeguards to prevent this from happening. Although this hadn't used any rockets it looked suspiciously like another incident created by Mike.

Chuck called Clare on the hotel phone. "Has Tony checked in by text as we agreed," he asked, "There's nothing," said Clare, " One message saying he left the hotel at about 05:30 this morning but nothing from the airport."

"Check out the news," said Chuck," Channel 9."

"I've already seen it," said Clare, "I thought momentarily it could be connected but decided it would be too much of a coincidence."

"I don't think so," said Chuck, "These many accidents following us around are almost certainly connected. Colonel Foster referred to The Six. There's Mike, me and Barbara left now."

# *All together now*

Chuck move downstairs to the lobby of the hotel Clare and Bigsy were already waiting. Jennifer and Spencer arrived a few minutes later.

"Did everyone see that news broadcast?" asked Chuck, Spencer nodded but Jennifer shook her head.

"I didn't have the television on this morning at all," she said.

"There's been a massive road traffic accident in the Phoenix area," said Spencer, "A tanker carrying Avgas crashed into a taxi. There was a fireball and the taxi occupants were killed."

"No," said Jennifer, "are you saying you think it's Tony."

"We don't know," said Chuck, "he has left the hotel by now. Clare has a text from him, but he should have texted us again when he reached the airport - so far nothing."

"Are you saying you think they have killed him?" asked Jennifer., "If so then he will have also taken his knowledge about where those launchers and UAVs were stored with him?"

"If Mike has got access to the launchers then it could work to our advantage," said Clare, "I think I have an idea."

She turned to chat with Jennifer, "If my plan works, we will need more help from those guys in the UK."

Chuck nodded. "I know, that's what I thought, it makes me think Mike found out the information from Tony or that he has got the information by some other means. I can't imagine that he would lose his last link to the information about the UAVs and the launchers."

# *International call*

Clare's phone rang.

"It's an international call," she said, "I'd better take it."

"Hello, this is Amanda Miller,"

"Amanda, I thought we'd only use this phone in an emergency?"

"That's right," said Amanda, "We have one right now."

Clare waved to the others and quickly said, "It's Amanda Miller and she says it's an emergency!"

Amanda heard Clare and then continued, "Since our last call, we have alerted our own systems and, via GCHQ, they have passed a wiretap requirement along to the NSA - that's the American Security services."

"Wiretap? of whom?" asked Clare.

"Of Mike Lee," answered Amanda, "We had to fib a little and say we thought he was smuggling drugs,"

Clare repeated, "They've been wiretapping Mike."

Amanda continued, "It turns out he called someone from MOFCOM - That's the Chinese Ministry of Trade and Commerce. He told them he thought someone was on to him and gave Chuck's name and last known location - which was the hotel in Scottsdale. I can only think the worst."

Clare replied, "That's all we need, I'll warn Chuck."

"Yes," said Amanda, "I thought Chuck might be even more in danger now, which is why I called."

Clare said, "Amanda, thank you, and now this phone line has been used, I may just keep you up-to-date on any further developments."

"Okay," said Amanda, "but be careful - signing off," The line chirruped, and Clare realised that Amanda had probably called her securely.

"Chuck, Bad news, I'm afraid, Mike has told the Chinese about you. Amanda thinks they may send out a search party for you."

"You should go to ground," said Jennifer, "Would you like me to help you with somewhere on the base?"

Chuck shook his head, "Normally I'd shrug off this kind of thing, but Mike is good. Look at his hit rate. He's knocked out nearly the entire team and improvised local facilities to make them look more like accidents. Jennifer, thank you, but No,

## The Circle

I'll be better off alone. It will keep the nasties away from all of you, too. I will lose my cell phone and get a different car. I'll leave Clare with some of my carry-money too, it's in a separate small go-bag. This time I won't disappear long-term, just until we've seen the back of Mike. I'll text Clare with my revised cell phone number."

Chuck looked quickly around the circle of them all. "It's been a pleasure," he said.

They looked back at him and Clare stepped forward to give him a hug.

"Right, time to hit it," he said as he strode towards the air terminal.

# *EnergyChina*

Bigsy read from his laptop,

"EnergyChina is best described as a giant corporation of China, a big oil company with an aggressive corporate swagger, tight political and military connections and a couldn't-care-less attitude about the views of others." Clare nodded, "A monster Corp!"

Bigsy continued, "Although EnergyChina is the most profitable company in Asia, this success may result from corporate management, but can also be attributed to the near duopoly on the wholesale and retail business of oil products it shares with EnergyChina in China."

Clare commented, "It's amazing that these mega corporations exist, yet we have hardly even heard of them!" Bigsy continued, "Or, in my case never heard of them...

Because of the EnergyChina link to Sudan through the parent company China Petroleum Products, several institutional investors such as Harvard and Yale decided, in 2008, to divest from EnergyChina. Sudan divestment efforts have continued to be concentrated on EnergyChina since then.

Fidelity Investments, after pressure from activist groups, also announced in a filing in the US, because it had sold 87 per cent of its American Depositary Receipts in EnergyChina in the first quarter of 2009."

"Wow, so some of the western smart-money has already pulled out," said Clare.

Bigsy read from his screen again,

"Another major controversial issue is EnergyChina's development in gas reserves in Tarim Basins, Xinjiang. It is now constructing a pipeline across Tibet to Gansu province in China, eventually leading to Shanghai.

"Some argue such a project might pose a threat to the environment, because the construction of the pipeline might affect wildlife in the regions where it runs. Also, the exiled Tibetan government argued that such a project is part of China's strategy to merge political control of the Western Region in China, including Tibet. However, no known environmental or social impact assessments have been conducted, as the environmental record of Tarim Basins is very poor."

Clare looked at Bigsy, "Wow, so they are a mega corporation, shunned by western smart money and building new politically sensitive pipelines, oblivious to eco-concerns. Big business, aye?"

Bigsy smiled back, "The trade-offs of modern civilisation?"

# Pressing the wrong buttons

A blackout is when you force all lights to go out, creating a
completely black look.
There are multiple ways to achieve a blackout.
The two most common are via a cue and a Grandmaster/Blackout
fader.

*ETC High End Systems*

# *Bunker*

Barbara Somerville was surprised to receive instructions to go from the hotel in Scottsdale, to a smaller one in Gallup, on the route to Albuquerque. She had followed the instructions, drawn on by the code included with the messages. It was a special code only known to the members of Project Esther.

The Gallup hotel wasn't as pleasant as the ritzy one in Scottsdale.

There was a knock on her door; she looked through the viewer.

"Mike," she said, "Are we ready to go?"

"We are the only two left now," said Mike, "And the way I have set things up Colonel Chuck Manners is the one that will appear as prime suspect."

They walked towards the blue F150 pickup truck that Mike had hired. He started it up and they moved off to join the traffic on the I-40.

"I'm already dead officially," said Mike. "And you and I are the only people from Project Esther who know about the location of the UAVs."

"Yes," said Barbara, "And we can only be within a few miles of the storage bunker now."

"It's amazing how much stuff they store under the desert in this area," said Mike.

"I know," said Barbara, "although most of it is off-limits because it's classified as military ground."

"Or we have given it to the Navajo nation," added Mike.

They were still outside the perimeter fencing but could now see a range of corrugated huts and several bulges in the desert floor.

"There we are," said Barbara. "Those are the storage facilities. They don't look very well-fortified, but it's almost impossible to get from here to those bunkers."

"Normally I'd agree with you," said Mike, "But it's different if you've got one of these." He pointed to the skyline. They could see a black dot in the distance. It was moving rapidly towards them.

Barbara recognised the outline of an Apache attack helicopter. It approached their car close hugging the ground. It swung past the fence and turned ponderously towards the bunkers. There was a hiss and Barbara saw a small rocket fired into the bunker, which burst open in a hail of metal fragments and dust.

There was a huge amount of noise and dust as the helicopter settled down onto the ground and four men entirely in black ran forward towards the bunker.

# The Circle

Within a minute they were loading large square boxes into the helicopter and within three minutes returning to the helicopter which was ready to lift off again.

In the distance Barbara could see a dust trail as several armoured vehicles were moving towards the scene.

"Thank you for helping with this," said Mike to Barbara, "your part in this won't go unrecognised." He turned towards her, and there was a single shot. Barbara fell backward.

Mike carefully placed something on the floor next to Barbara's body.

Mike waved towards the helicopter which was circling overhead. A single man on a zip wire descended and clipped Mike onto a harness. The two of them swung away from the fence and as the helicopter started its ascent it winched them back on board.

"How many did we get?" asked Mike," as he looked to the people in the helicopter.

"A dozen," said the man who had just hauled him in on the winch. "Twelve NA-12 systems. Twelve Nathans."

"Hot-digitty-dog, that's more than enough," said Mike.

# *DEFCON*

The news of the attack on the Kirtland airfield reached Jennifer quickly. There was a security blanket placed over what happened, but because it had taken place at Jennifer's own base, she was able to get inside information from Lucas, initially via Spencer.

Lucas had called Spencer and told him what had happened.

"It looks as if someone has broken into one of the storage bunkers at the back of Kirtland, out in the desert. It was a secured area but was unused nowadays. They used a helicopter to get in and took some containers."

"There was a truck outside the fence which I think was calling the helicopter in. Another one of the old team, The Six, was found in the truck but also there was a payphone which appears to belong to Chuck Manners. We only know this because the phone that the dead woman had included a number for Chuck which rang the phone in the car. The forensics guys have fast tracked the fingerprints on that phone, and they match with Chuck."

# The Circle

Jennifer had revealed this information to Bigsy and Clare.

"We still don't believe that Chuck is involved in this in any way other than as someone who is being hunted and framed," said Clare, "I think all this is being used to divert attention from the people who are really responsible."

"Will the security blanket continue on what is effectively the third attack?" asked Bigsy.

"Yes, it is," said Jennifer, "this has raised the whole DEFCON alert status of the US."

"I've heard of DEFCON" said Clare," but I don't really understand the different levels."

"We are normally functioning at DEFCON 5," said Jennifer, "This sequence of events has taken us all the way to DEFCON 3. That's the one where the Air Force has to be ready to mobilise in 15 minutes. You can see that the terrorists kept the helicopter attack very brief. By the time any land forces could reach the bunker they were long gone."

"With a faster mobilisation we stand a much better chance to intercept whatever's happening."

"Will those planes be able to stop the missiles now in the hands of the terrorists?" asked Bigsy.

"It kind of depends," said Jennifer. "If that Colonel Foster implies that they have a list of the planned targets then that would give military the best chance to deploy countermeasures."

"Isn't it kind of weird that they would raise the DEFCON level but still keep a secure blanket over what has been happening?" Asked Bigsy.

"Less unusual than you might think," replied Jennifer, "We sometimes get heightened security at the Air Force Base. Usually it only goes to DEFCON 4. When that happens, we are usually expecting it to be part of an exercise. However, everyone always takes it seriously."

"I guess a lot more of the senior people know what is happening, now," said Clare, "They can't keep a lid on this indefinitely."

"I think with the violence of the attacks now they will try to end this with extreme prejudice," said Jennifer.

"That puts Chuck in a very dangerous position too," said Jennifer, "As Mike has managed to make it look as if Chuck is involved then he will also be on the hit list."

# *Amber Alert*

The DEFCON alert had also rippled through to London and Colonel Foster and the rest of his team were aware that things were escalating.

Jennifer had asked Clare to arrange for a follow-up call with the team in London. "We need to know those alternative targets now," asked Jennifer.

Colonel Foster paused to consider. "Amanda, this is the second visit I have made to your building. We are operating outside of protocol. Now that we are at US DEFCON 3, we should not really be giving you this kind of information."

"But I suppose you could have provided it at DEFCON 5?" asked Amanda.

"Let me just go to check that with the control room." said Foster, "it will only take me, say, five minutes," Foster pointedly looked towards his desk before exiting the room.

"Okay, I think that was a hint," said Amanda, "Lets copy that list," she flipped the sheet around on his desk and snapped a copy into her second cell phone.

Bigsy explained to Amanda," Now that they have taken those guidance systems and missiles, they are fully equipped to target any of those locations on Foster's list"

"I understand from Chuck that the basis of the targeting was to know the address of a particular transponder unit and use that to dial into the missile guidance system."

"My guess is that they will now take the captured equipment to somewhere remote and set up a base from which they can launch their next attack. We must move fast. I reckon they will go for a shorter distance target the first time to gain confidence in their approach."

"Yes, maybe Plano would be the next target, unless they have taken their helicopter on a very long flight."

"I think that's unlikely, said Jennifer, "the further they fly in the helicopter the more likely they are to be picked up by US defence radar."

"Exactly," said Bigsy, "So they probably drop somewhere in one of the desert areas in the general Albuquerque and Phoenix area."

"That's a large area anyway," said Jennifer, "It is," said Clare, "but there's also quite a lot of movement around some of those parts what with all the tourists and similar access."

"It is also the access that the Native Americans have two large tracts of this land. It's the Navajo Nation. Quite a lot of it is still formally Indian Reservation territory. It's very unlikely that if they landed in one of those areas that they will go undetected for too long."

"This is useful, said Clare, "because it narrows down the areas."

"When we left Tom, he gave us his contact number. We've already called him once. I thought it was funny. Here was a native American Navajo, in the middle of the desert giving us his sat. phone number.

"Now is the second time that it becomes useful," said Bigsy. "I think it can help us in two ways. We can ask Tom about the helicopter, but also check whether he knows the whereabouts of Chuck.

# *Tom*

Clare made the call to Tom.

"Hello," said Tom.

"Hello," said Clare, "It's Clare, who you met with your friend Chuck Manners a few days ago."

"But Clare, you are my friend now, also," said Tom, "I have been expecting your group to call."

"Tom, we have some difficult things happening here and our good friend Chuck is again in danger because of some of it."

"I know more about this than you think. Our friend has been with me since last night. He is safe until we can work out what to do."

"There was a helicopter attack in the desert yesterday," said Clare.

"They have taken some very dangerous weapons from a

hidden bunker near Kirtland. We think they have taken the helicopter into a base somewhere in the desert. It is likely to be somewhere isolated but that will have road access. I hoped that you and your friends can help us find where they would make their base."

"The desert talks to us," said Tom, "If someone is disrupting it, we, the Navajo, will know."

"We have some other people looking into this," said Clare. "They are trying to do something clever with electronic surveillance to see whether they can find the base."

"Maybe this will be an example where we all work together to find them," said Tom, "We can use this phone to communicate. If I go deep into the desert, I will plan for someone else to call you. They will say they are a friend of Tom and want to speak to you."

"Tom, we have noticed that Red's prophecy about the animal skills has been coming true as we have been on this quest," said Clare.

"And I think there will be still one more to play out before the end of this," said Tom.

Clare looked towards Jennifer and Bigsy. "I think we have the right people involved now. If anyone can find that place in the desert it will be Tom and his people."

# *Monumental*

Chuck could see Tom coming towards him. He had been staying in a small miner's shack deep in the desert to the south of the area known as Monument Valley.

Chuck knew the landscape from other visits, but still couldn't help but be blown away by it as one of the most majestic points on earth. This valley monuments were sandstone masterpieces towering at heights of 400 to 1,000 feet, framed by scenic clouds casting shadows that roamed the desert floor. Famous for many westerns, Chuck was rather sensitive to the thought he could be in a shoot-out from within it.

Instead, he marvelled at the angle of the sun accenting the graceful formations and  providing spellbinding scenery. The landscape overwhelmed him, not just by its beauty but also by its size. Miles of mesas and buttes, shrubs and trees, and windblown sand surrounded the fragile pinnacles of rock comprising the magnificent colours of the valley.

Chuck also realised it was like being on the inside of a natural fortress. The Navajo charged tourists admission and insisted that they drove on a set route around the spectacle.

The Navajo, and Chuck had an altogether freer licence. Tom had approached the last part of the journey on horseback. He had also used a horse to get Chuck to the location the first time.

"The advantage of here is that it is inaccessible by road and hidden from air," Tom had explained, "You are now in a sacred area and have protection of the gods."

"You also have good water and a plentiful supply of tinned food," Tom pointed towards the miner's shack.

"This will keep you off of the radar until we can work out the next moves. A shrew can catch a cobra."

"I have already put out word of what we seek," said Tom, "There is no way that a noisy helicopter can be in these lands without us knowing its whereabouts. I expect I will hear within another hour."

"Meantime I think we should sit and enjoy this special place." He sat atop a boulder and looked at the scene. Chuck became aware too of the smallest movements.

Tom was true to his word, and within the hour his walkie talkie radio crackled. The news was good. They had located a base in between the rocks. There was a small camp with several men, a military helicopter, two trucks and activity which seemed to be building something.

"It's got to be them," said Chuck. Tom nodded, "I know the place they describe. We should go there to check - it is about 15 miles from here."

"We will also need to let Clare know," said Chuck.

Tom led outside to the two horses he had brought. The one he had ridden and another one. They climbed onto the horses and Tom led Chuck carefully towards the track where he had parked his Jeep.

"I will make the calls to Clare from here." he said, "and another one to my friends to tell where we think these people are based."

"He spent a few minutes talking first to his friends and describing the area. Then he called Clare and gave a more basic description of the area. It is hard to find if you do not know the desert," he said. "We will be there in about one hour. I can send you GPS co-ordinates when we get there."

He signed off and they started their bumpy drive towards the helicopter base.

# *A quicker scramble*

Jennifer had heard the call to Clare, and they decided that they needed to inform the people in London. Jennifer also said, "We should be careful that we don't start a major search mission across the desert."

"If the people hiding are wired in with radar, they will spot that we are sending reconnaissance waves around the area and either go to ground or move out.

"At the moment, with some stealth we should be able to catch them.

"It is ironic that the type of weapons we are hunting would usually be used for this search," said Bigsy.

"Yes, well, the not so big secret about those devices is that they are also offensive and not just for surveillance. You'll have worked that out by now," said Jennifer.

"So it's best for us to wait until Chuck and Tom get close to the location then, said Clare.

"Yes," said Jennifer," then we will have a fix that we can use quickly. DEFCON 3 should help us scramble quickly."

# Know a pistol shot's effective range

Desperado, why don't you come to your senses?
You been out ridin' fences for so long now
Oh, you're a hard one
I know that you got your reasons
These things that are pleasin' you
Can hurt you somehow

*- Donald Hugh Henley, Glenn Lewis Frey*

# *UAV*

Chuck and Tom made their way towards the location in the Jeep. For the last part of the journey, they had to leave the vehicle behind and move to foot. They both carried a small backpack and trod softly as they approached a scene with lights and several voices.

They worked out that it wasn't the main team, but the perimeter guards for the area where the helicopter was stored.

Tom called in a reference using his radio walkie talkie. "This isn't exactly GPS," he said, "but my friends will convert it and call Clare."

At that moment there was a noise behind them. A small crack from a twig.

"We need to move," said Tom. He pointed to the side walls of the canyon they had entered. "We need to be a little higher to gain some advantage."

A shot hissed through the rocks. Then a burr sound from an automatic pistol. "They are close," said Chuck, "should we stand our ground?"

"No," said Tom, "we need to get higher. And they are at least 60 yards away. Their shooting is so wide."

He led Chuck through a small gully by the edge of the canyon walls. It led upwards. They crossed a small bowl of rock some 100 yards higher than the valley floor. The other side, the gully continued.

There was another crack. A sniper was getting a range on them.
Then a rattle sound from a handheld machine gun.

They are gaining on us, said Chuck.

"Just a little higher," said Tom.

"Look we both have weapons, we could finish them," said Chuck.

"Keep going," said Tom, "my way is more certain."

With that, he looked back, and then so did Chuck. The well-armed team following them were gaining ground and had just entered the small bowl thorough which Chuck and Tom had passed a minute earlier.

Then Chuck saw the surrounding rocks move. There were at least a dozen Native Americans camouflaged in the rocks. They pounced upon the men following. There was a blur of metal through the air. And silence.

The entire team of pursuers had been dispatched by the group of Navajo.

"I know," said Tom, "That was the old way. But it is

sometime still necessary."

They looked back further. Their elevation meant that they could now see across to the rest of the camp.

It was a small area and contained the helicopter, two ruggedized Jeeps and in the centre was a small catapult launcher. The men were placing the UAV into the launch system.

Chuck looked at how small it seemed, compared with the Predators he has seen during the tests seven years ago. Miniaturised warfare, he thought. Deadly Toys.

The people in the base were hurriedly preparing the launch. They had heard the gunshots and probably knew they were being followed.

A few minutes later there was a loud bang as the catapult launcher fired the small missile into the air. It surprised Chuck at how fast it accelerated when it was free of the launcher. It also gained altitude quickly as it headed away from them towards the east.

Then there was another explosion. Another two just behind. Chuck was aware that a dark shadow had just passed over his head. He looked towards Tom and realised that both he and Tom were now laying on the ground. He could feel a heat blast.

Then another bang and the sound of jet engines. He realised that a plane or a couple of planes had borne down on the site and destroyed pretty much everything in the area. He realised that he was shaking and could hardly move. The shock waves from the explosion had winded him badly and maybe broken some bones.

He gingerly felt his body and decided that all the main parts were still there. He looked towards Tom who was similarly in a kind of post explosion shock. He realised his hearing was damaged from the shock waves. Below him he could see that the Navajo people surrounding the bowl of the recent massacre were all similarly winded.

Then he saw more shadows. Dark profiles of men with guns. Desert-camo. They had appeared from the sky.

There had been a two-pronged attack on the area. Both bombers and then Para troops. He assumed they would be seals or similarly expert people. He moved his hands to above his head and gestured for Tom to do the same.

They waited and in a couple of minutes had been scooped into nets, like some deep-sea fish catch.

# *DFW*

They were back at Dallas airport, sitting around a table in the hotel across the way from the International terminal.

"I hadn't expected to be in America for so long," said Clare. "Me neither," said Bigsy.

"It's been a blast," said Chuck.

"Yes," said Jennifer, "Literally a blast."

"And I can honestly say it's the first time I've been scooped like a fish," said Chuck.

"Just be pleased it was fishing nets rather than harpoons," said Jennifer.

"Yea, you can tell when it's the Navy on manoeuvres," said Bigsy, alluding to Chuck's rescuers, "Navy, in the middle of the desert."

"Technically we were not operating on US soil, either," said Jennifer, "It was the Navajo Nation's patch where we carried out the operation."

Well the DEVCON status is back to Five," said Jennifer, "and I don't think most of the general public even know that this has occurred."

"The news bulletins about ChinaEnergy were pretty mysterious," said Clare, "Seeing the board overthrown within 24 hours of the desert mission was a very suspicious coincidence."
I think you'll find Foster had something to do with that," said Jennifer, "And the subsequent disappearance of those three board members . What is it you Brits say? 'I couldn't possibly comment.'"

"So, are you heading back to London now?" asked Jennifer.

"And Chuck, I guess you are about to disappear again?"

"That's right," he said, "Did I ever mention my dual nationality?"

"No," said Jennifer," and please wait until I've caught my plane out of here before you start waving alternative passports around."

"Look guys," said Chuck, "I know I got you all - including Jennifer and Tom - mixed up in more than you expected, and I don't think any of you will be able to brag about preventing 'the end of the world as we know it.'"

"But hey, thank you all." He shook hands and slapped the backs of each of them. He reserved a small kiss to the cheek for Jennifer and Clare.

"And Chuck," grinned Clare, "what's the other expression - 'don't call us, we'll call you?'"

# *Free to go*

"As for those suspicions about EnergyChina being behind some of this, well the core three members of the board all stood down the next day and have been replaced."

"The new board is, how shall I say, kindly disposed towards the West.

"I don't know anything about that," answered Amanda, "Although I think maybe Colonel Foster would have some knowledge of what happened. He'll deny it; some baloney about being based here in the UK and too far away from the action."

"And there's something else. It's a small package that arrived here, addressed to you. It was couriered over from Arizona, actually. You'll understand that we've had to scan it before we could let it into the building."
He passed it over to Jake.

"I think you should open it when you are with the others back at your offices, but don't worry, I promise it is nothing unpleasant."

Back in London, Jake was back in one of the conference

rooms in SI6.

"You'll be pleased to know you are free to go now," said Amanda. 'They have rounded up the miscreants and accounted for the missing UAVs. Unfortunately, the plans for the design was also destroyed in the fireball in the desert when the American planes bombed the terrorist camp.

"I saw something about the old board members not being seen since their last board meeting," said Jake.

"Free to Go."

"…And safe?"

"…And very safe. Good luck to you and the others."

Outside. Jake could taste the November air. Sharp and cold.

"Free to go?" he asked.

They shook hands, Jake picked up the small parcel.
"It's not the rolling credits music, is it?" he quipped.
"Here, let me show you out," said Amanda, as if they were in her home rather than a top-security establishment.

The leaves had fallen, yet it was a blue-sky day. He'd walk across Vauxhall Bridge and maybe stroll back towards Parliament before deciding how to get back to Hoxton.

Clare and Bigsy would be back the next morning, when they would open the parcel from Arizona.

# The Circle

# More Ed Adams Novels

| Triangle Trilogy | | About | Link |
|---|---|---|---|
| T1 | The Triangle | Dirty money? Here's how to clean it. Money laundering | https://amzn.to/3ç6zRMu |
| T2 | The Square | Weapons of Mass Destruction – don't let them get on your nerves. A viral nerve agent being shipped by terrorists and WMDs | https://amzn.to/3sEiKYx |
| T3 | The Circle | The desert is no place to get lost. In the Arizona deserts, with the Navajo; about missiles stolen from storage. | https://amzn.to/3qLavYZ |
| T4 | Cosy | Cosy Crime in Devon | https://amzn.to/3wQVNED |
| **Archangel Collection** | | | |
| A1 | Archangel | Sometimes I am necessary. Icelandic-born, Russian trained agent Christina Nott, learns her craft. | https://amzn.to/2Y9nB5K |
| A2 | Raven | An eye that sees all between darkness and light. Big business gone bad and being a freemason won't absolve you. | https://amzn.to/2MiGVe6 |
| A3 | Card Game | The power of Tarot whilst throwing oil on a troubled market | https://amzn.to/2Y8HLgs |
| A5 | Play On, Christina Nott | Money, Mayhem, Manipulation. Christina Nott, on Tour for the FSB | https://amzn.to/2MbkuHI |
| A6 | Corrupt | Parliamentary corruption. Trouble at the House | https://amzn.to/2M0HnOw |
| A7 | Sleaze | Autos, Politics, Gstaad | https://amzn.to/3sE3UDt |

# The Circle

Printed in Great Britain
by Amazon